John Maszka is a terrorism scholar and professor of international relations. Born in America, Professor Maszka earned his PhD in the UK and has lived and taught all over the world. John has encountered many first-hand experiences with extremist violence and has interviewed and befriended dozens of individuals and families from around the world who have lived through extremist violence of various kinds.

For Anais.

John Maszka

The Locket

AUSTIN MACAULEY PUBLISHERS™
LONDON • CAMBRIDGE • NEW YORK • SHARJAH

Copyright © John Maszka (2020)

The right of John Maszka to be identified as author of this work has been asserted by him in accordance with section 77 and 78 of the Copyright, Designs and Patents Act 1988.

All rights reserved. No part of this publication may be reproduced, stored in a retrieval system, or transmitted in any form or by any means, electronic, mechanical, photocopying, recording, or otherwise, without the prior permission of the publishers.

Any person who commits any unauthorised act in relation to this publication may be liable to criminal prosecution and civil claims for damages.

This is a work of fiction. Names, characters, businesses, places, events, locales, and incidents are either the products of the author's imagination or used in a fictitious manner. Any resemblance to actual persons, living or dead, or actual events is purely coincidental.

A CIP catalogue record for this title is available from the British Library.

ISBN 9781528980784 (Paperback)
ISBN 9781528980807 (ePub e-book)

www.austinmacauley.com

First Published (2020)
Austin Macauley Publishers Ltd
25 Canada Square
Canary Wharf
London
E14 5LQ

Table of Contents

Chapter One   11
    The Visitor

Chapter Two   13
    Seriously Though

Chapter Three   15
    The Story

Chapter Four   17
    Engaging Conversation

Chapter Five   21
    Graziella's Secret

Chapter Six   24
    The Locket

Chapter Seven   26
    A Gift from Caesar

Chapter Eight   28
    Antony and Cleopatra

Chapter Nine   30
    Thea Musa

Chapter Ten   32
    Y2k

Chapter Eleven   35
    The Deal Breaker

Chapter Twelve   37
The Long Night

Chapter Thirteen   39
The Awakening

Chapter Fourteen   43
Frankenstein

Chapter Fifteen   48
Taranto

Chapter Sixteen   49
Escape

Chapter Seventeen   52
Schriver

Chapter Eighteen   54
Fugitives

Chapter Nineteen   56
The Power of Love

Chapter Twenty   58
Humble Beginnings

Chapter Twenty-One   60
Suspicion

Chapter Twenty-Two   62
Where Am I?

Chapter Twenty-Three   65
A Name for the Authorities

Chapter Twenty-Four   67
A Sad Goodbye

Chapter Twenty-Five   69
Four Years Later

Chapter Twenty-Six   71
    The First Memory

Chapter Twenty-Seven   73
    The Secret Link

Chapter Twenty-Eight   76
    War in Heaven

Chapter Twenty   79
    Nine Fallen

Chapter Thirty   81
    The Place of Remembrance

Chapter Thirty-One   84
    Gabriel's Mission

Chapter Thirty-Two   87
    Jack and the Beanstalk

Chapter Thirty-Three   89
    Worm Holes

Chapter Thirty-Four   93
    The Offer

Chapter Thirty-Five   96
    Prague

Chapter Thirty-Six   107
    The Castle

Chapter Thirty-Seven   119
    Seth's Father

Chapter Thirty-Eight   126
    Seth's Mother

Chapter Thirty-Nine   132
    The Proposition

Chapter Forty   **137**
    Celestial DNA

Chapter Forty-One   **142**
    Faith

Chapter Forty-Two   **144**
    Night Is Coming

Chapter Forty-Three   **149**
    Glass Doors

Chapter Forty-Four   **151**
    Alone in Novosibirsk

Chapter Forty-Five   **155**
    Krzegosz

Chapter Forty-Six   **159**
    Getting Acquainted

Chapter Forty-Seven   **164**
    A Bad Idea

Chapter Forty-Eight   **166**
    Krzegosz's Secret

Chapter Forty-Nine   **173**
    Tolmachevo Airport

Chapter Fifty   **177**
    Mochishche

Chapter Fifty-One   **181**
    The Stockpile

Chapter Fifty-Two   **184**
    A New Beginning

Chapter One
The Visitor

Death was nothing like I imagined it would be. We have these ideas of seeing a bright light or having our entire life flash before our eyes—I didn't experience any of those things. For me, when the darkness fell, it plummeted. All around me, emptiness enshrouded what used to be my life: my plans, my thoughts, my identity—everything vanished.

Time is inconsequential here. Days, weeks, maybe even ages passed until miraculously—far away in the distance—I spied a speck of light. One single dot of clarity emerged in a universe cloaked in obsidian. It grew brighter and brighter until it erupted into a massive explosion, engulfing the barren void in a brilliance ten thousand times brighter than the sun.

The light became more blinding than the darkness and I threw my arms up to shield my eyes. From between my trembling limbs, I could barely detect something moving towards me. Imperceptible at first, a form slowly began to take shape. At first, I felt only terror. But then, a mysterious calm eased my apprehension and instinctively I knew that I had nothing to fear.

With eyes of fire and skin that glowed like polished bronze, the celestial envoy waxed illustrious beyond description. I couldn't even begin to describe the thoughts that raced through my mind. Actually, 'thoughts' isn't the right word. They were more like feelings or sensations: fear, anxiety, excitement—'instincts' is a better term. Steeped in insecurity, I became painfully aware of my own insignificance: a tiny speck of worthless dust cowering beneath a mighty redwood. But that's not really a very good way to put it either.

"Greetings friend!" the emissary announced. His words washed over me like a warm, vivid memory—both soothing and electrifying at once.

"Welcome!" he added, sounding more like a host than a guest.

"Welcome?" I cleared my throat as the words got caught in my oesophagus. "Welcome to *where*? Where am I?"

"That depends on you," the stranger quipped with a reassuring smile.

"I don't understand."

"You will. That's why I'm here."

My visitor's calm, casual assurance made me feel even more at ease. "Well, who are *you*?" I petitioned reluctantly—my broken spirit daring to embrace the promise of a new beginning.

"I've been known by many names," he answered unassumingly. "You might know me as Gabriel the archangel."

I know what you're probably thinking right now. You're imagining me running down the middle of a busy street with one of those hospital gowns on. You know, the ones that never quite cover your behind no matter how cleverly you think you've tied them.

On Earth, most people of celebrity status are kind of arrogant. You can't really blame them, I guess. I mean, we kiss their ass so much—how can we expect them to be otherwise? I half expected Gabriel to pull out an autographed 8x10 glossy of himself, but he was nothing like that. Gabriel's smile displayed a confident humility. It was as though he knew what an amazing creature he was, but he took no credit for it himself. Someone once said that true greatness defies arrogance. They must have met Gabriel.

At this point I was feeling more than a little overwhelmed, and 'stupid' doesn't even come close to capturing how I must have looked. I guess it didn't hurt that I played the role so well.

"You're Gabriel?" I marvelled.

"In the flesh," he beckoned in a voice that rumbled like a gentle waterfall. The very sound of it reminisced of summers past spent fighting pirates and swimming with mermaids. "But that's of little consequence. I've come to congratulate you on your great victory and to ease your pain by revealing to you the wonderful purpose your life has served."

"What great victory?"

"What great victory? You've conquered the most insidious evil of all: the selfishness inside your own heart. And so, the King has sent me to reward you and to tell you the story."

"A story?" I mimicked daftly.

"No, *the* story. Now, what is it that you desire most?"

Cherishing the last vision, I saw before I died: soft, almond eyes filled with tears of true love, pure joy, and deep impenetrable sadness—I didn't hesitate for a second, "I want to keep my promise."

"And so, you shall," Gabriel assured me with a heartfelt look of genuine approval. "And so, you shall."

Chapter Two
Seriously Though

I'd give you my name but I don't know what it is. Everything about my existence is gone. I can remember the colour of a rose, but not the colour of my own eyes. I can recall the cities of the world, but I have no idea which one I called home. My place in the generic family of man is lucid—it's my individual identity that escapes me. Like a sojourner lost in the desert, I see the glowing orb in the sky but my footprints have disappeared behind me.

Ironically, the one remaining memory I still possess of my life is the moment of my death. The years of care and worry weighed heavy on my brow when the cheat stole in and shorted me of the little time, I thought I had left. Deep furrows and leathery crags ravaged my skin while my pulse still raced at the scent of her perfume. The source of my grey hair also racked my body with excruciating pain, but none of that mattered to me then. Don't get me wrong, I don't claim to be different or special in any way. I'm sure I was just as vain as everyone else throughout my life, worrying about my looks and what other people thought about me. Racing the clock and chasing the wind.

On Earth, time is linear and everyone is so obsessed with it. We spend our entire lives trying to get to point B, only to wish we could go back to point A again. No matter how much money or fame we achieve, and regardless of what we accomplish in life, time is the one thing that we can never get enough of. And yet, like mice on a treadmill or a dog pursuing its own tail, we waste our lives by chasing the hands on a clock. Everyone is trapped in a prison of time. Ironically, most don't even want to be free. In fact, I'm pretty sure that they used to torture people by depriving them of any sense of the time. We humans are such strange creatures.

Facing that last moment changes you though, even though it's hopelessly too late. For once you see with the utmost clarity what really matters. It's life's ultimate sucker punch. Still, you can't help but be grateful. That's how I felt anyway. I would have never figured it out on my own. I'm pretty stupid when it comes to things like that…important things that is.

In those final seconds when every last breath hangs in the great merchant's balance and the scales of time are tipping against you, you'll give anything just to feel the heartbeat of the one you love one last time. That was me. Clinging to life, but not my own, I fought the darkness for one last glimpse of my heart's desire. And as the last few precious rays of light slipped away; I swore an oath to the one I love before the torrent swept me away.

So, there you have it. Stripped of self, I'm a blank slate. The faces, the names and the people I once knew are all forgotten now with one exception: the vivid memory of my love lives on. Even here in this forsaken place, her perpetual presence warms my heart. She's both an intense hunger and my only source of sustenance. Like an ember, she burns within me—a faceless, nameless reflection of the man I wanted to be. That I can remember, but nothing else.

When my body died and the darkness came, whistling a faintly familiar tune, I thought it signified the end of everything. Maybe it *was* the end of my life as I knew it, but for some unexplainable reason the bitter emptiness that snuck up on me also spared me the loss of my most precious possession. Be it sleight of hand or a strange twist of fate—it's a gift nonetheless. And somehow, even when everything else about me died, the memory of my love lived on.

As I stood there in the light of Gabriel's magnificence, I was at a complete loss for what to say or do next. Searching inward, I noticed that my skin looked somehow younger, more invigorated and less decrepit.

"Am I getting younger?" I marvelled, examining my arms with delight.

Gabriel smiled at me through his eyes. "Does that seem so peculiar to you?"

"Well, *yeah!*" I exclaimed with glee. "Doesn't it seem peculiar to you? This is the most remarkable thing that's ever happened to me! How is it even possible?"

Gabriel observed my intense elation with curious wonder as I ran my fingertips across my skin, marvelling over its fresh elasticity.

"There's nothing so very remarkable about it. Your body is simply reflecting what's been in your heart all along."

"But I'm getting younger! I mean, I'm actually getting younger! Who's ever heard of such a thing?"

"The effects of time don't last. You'll see. Better things are yet to come, I assure you."

Gabriel's confident assertion sparked hope in my soul. A sanguine longing winked at me like a shooting star, blazing its path through nocturnal skies of eternal doubt. Although silent and breathless at first, those unmistakable rays of morning peaked out over the horizon and warmed my soul after a long, sleepless night. Miraculously, the prospects of a new day awaited me once again. Suddenly my desolate existence teemed with meaning, and a newfound purpose filled the languishing void. So, with a child's trust, this old man believed. Emerging from the shadows of doubt and pain, like a toddler, I took my first step in faith.

First step to where, you ask?

At the time, I was wondering the very same thing.

Chapter Three
The Story

"So, what's this story all about, Gabriel?"

Smiling obligingly, Gabriel cleared his throat. It's odd, you don't ever really think of angels clearing their throats, but I guess they do. You also can't even begin to imagine what an angel's voice sounds like until you've actually heard it for yourself. It's everywhere at once: all around you and inside your head at the same time. Inescapable as a foghorn yet as intimate as my own thoughts.

"The story begins before the dawn of time," he opened. Closing his eyes as if to conjure up a distant memory. "But a summer day in 1998 will do just fine, for now."

On an August afternoon, white marshmallow clouds floated across a periwinkle sky like massive dollops of whipped cream, casting their havens of shade on the contented lunchers below. It was unseasonably cool in Palo Alto for that time of year and the air had already turned from the stolid humidity of summer to the crisp, lively newness of autumn. Rather than the usual complaints about the August heat, everywhere people chattered away in voices filled with the fresh expectation of change.

On this particular Sunday afternoon, two friends relaxed outside on the terrace at Bon Appétit—a French café they loved to frequent—where they would laugh and converse with each other and pretty much anyone else who happened to wander in. Craig flirted with the waitresses and struck up conversations with people at other tables. It was the most natural thing in the world for him.

Mathieu, on the other hand, was nowhere near as outgoing. Still, he loved to be in his friend's company as there was never a dull moment with Craig around. The man was an absolute magnet when it came to people.

Mathieu and Craig had studied together at Stanford for the past five years. Craig was finishing his doctoral research in biotechnology, and Mathieu had one year left in medical school. During that time, they'd become more than colleagues—the two were like brothers.

Craig grew up in Quebec, and Mathieu was from Benin, so the two often spoke French when they were together. In fact, it was their common language that cemented the friendship in the first place. They first met at a midnight showing of *Jean De Florette,* and the two quickly became good friends. Neither realised that the events of this day would change their lives forever.

A young woman meandered into the café and sat by herself at a table near the door. This being her first weekend in Palo Alto, she didn't know a soul. Other than to place her order, she never even glanced up. Graziella simply stared down at the table as though she were in her own little world. Captivated, Craig instantly became hopelessly infatuated and he didn't hesitate for a second.

Winking at Mathieu, Craig raised his eyebrows and punned, "*Coup de main!*"

Most men were intimidated by Graziella's looks. Not Craig. He strolled right over to her table, sat down and struck up a conversation.

"*Bonjour, Mademoiselle!*"

Graziella barely even made eye contact. "Hi," she mumbled quietly, nodding as she spoke.

"*Entre nous,*" Craig's eyes beamed flirtatiously, "*J'adore.*"

Graziella sipped her espresso. Raising her shoulders slightly, she admitted, "I don't speak French. Sorry." Then she let them drop.

"*Come stai?*" Craig inquired without the slightest hesitation.

"*Bene, grazie!*" Graziella smiled and even let out a little chuckle. "*E tu?*"

"I'm very well. Thank you," he proffered in a very goofy British accent.

Graziella peeped out from behind her invisible barrier, "I'm Graziella."

Craig was in love from that very instant. He found Graziella enchanting and her accent exotic and intoxicating. Craig couldn't decide what attracted him more: those adorable dimples that winked at him when she smiled or that enthralling voice. Even her name fascinated him—*Graziella*.

"You have such a lovely accent. Where are you from, Graziella?"

"I grew up in Italy, but I spent the last five years studying in Budapest."

"Budapest? How riveting! What were you studying?"

"Egyptology."

Chapter Four
Engaging Conversation

In contrast to Craig, Graziella was a complete wallflower—and an exquisite one at that. Her wonderfully proportioned body, wrapped in flawless, olive skin, glowed like Venus in the summer sky. Graziella's teeth gleamed perfectly straight and white, and her silky henna locks tumbled down her back like rose petals awaiting a lover's caress on creamy satin sheets. Everywhere she went, people were drawn to her. But Graziella's physical rapture was exceeded only by her extreme introversion. She never really made any friends.

Perhaps this is the reason that Craig gained the boon over every other guy on campus, he could bandy with her about literally anything and everything. And he did. Craig also made Graziella laugh—often hysterically. Sometimes, Graziella would laugh so hard that she couldn't stop. Tears would stream down her face as she tried desperately to catch her breath.

Craig soon discovered that the best way to get Graziella to open up was to ask her about anything pertaining to Egyptology—particularly the rivalry between Seth and Horus.

"My absolute favourite Egyptian myth is the legend of Seth and Horus. There are so many variations," Graziella explicated, "and the details can get really confusing, but the story itself is pretty basic. The most common version pits Horus against his brother Seth."

Graziella turned her espresso cup back and forth in the saucer while she contemplated her next sentence. "Seth is the son of Osiris and Isis. He kills his father Osiris in a jealous rage and chops him into fourteen pieces."

"*What?*" Craig winced squeamishly.

"I know, it's pretty gruesome. But Isis puts the pieces back together, and she brings Osiris back to life."

"How does she manage that?"

"True love." Graziella's face lit up. "Isis is the goddess of love. She breathed life back into Osiris, and the two made love so passionately that day that Isis bore another son—Horus. So, Horus is actually Osiris' posthumous son." Graziella leaned in as she expounded, "That means he was born *after* Osiris died."

Craig bit his lip to keep from laughing out loud. "Yes. I know what the word means," he really wanted to say—but didn't.

Graziella returned to her monologue. "In a sense, Isis reincarnates her dead husband in the body of her son. Horus becomes the literal embodiment of Osiris—kind of his clone."

The word 'clone' caught Craig's attention. He'd been working diligently on a dissertation topic for the last three months, and he'd recently settled upon an examination of the likelihood of cloning adult humans. Experiments with cloning were routine as of the last few years, but no one had successfully replicated an adult human. No one ever even tried—at least, not that Craig knew of. But Craig believed it could be done, even though the extant body of literature predicted that only embryos were replicable. The prevailing theory based this conclusion on research involving fewer complex organisms. Craig hoped to prove that the cloning process, in the case of more multifarious organisms such as humans, could in fact produce a full-grown adult rather than just an embryo.

Conventional wisdom also argued it unlikely that an exact replica would result even if a complex clone were successfully produced. Of course, this argument remained entirely theoretical as no empirical evidence existed either way. But Craig disagreed with this argument as well. Craig's research led him to believe that the complex DNA strains that make up each of the trillions of cells in the human body are mapped out in such a way as to allow mass replication. He reasoned that if the billions of DNA strands in each cell could be cloned to produce an exact replica, then organs and complete bodies could be replicated as well. In fact, Craig theorised that multiple replicas could be produced simultaneously.

But what was soon to become the truly inspiring breakthrough of Craig's work still eluded him. Craig believed it would one day be possible to actually transmit digital data from a computer file to a living organism, and vice-versa. This technology would allow for digital mapping and storage of perfect DNA sequences in computer models. The application could then be used to clone perfect humans completely free of defects and diseases. But Craig was still developing his theory.

Craig had become so engrossed in his daydream about becoming a great bio theorist and ushering in a new paradigm in scientific thought that he hadn't been paying attention to Graziella at all.

But Graziella jabbered on about Seth and Horus, apparently unmindful that Craig had momentarily left the conversation. She expatiated with her hands, moving them here and there to enlarge upon her words. Her face, and indeed her entire upper body, became almost animated as she continued her soliloquy.

"What I've always found fascinating is that in Egyptian mythology, Horus is considered the god of light while Seth is considered the god of darkness and chaos. But that isn't the way I see it at all. The more you learn about Seth and Horus the more alike the two become."

Graziella's eyes were alight with fascination, "Do you know why the Egyptians associated Seth with things that were red and considered him to be the lord of all the redheads?" Raising an eyebrow and nodding her head knowingly, she answered her own question. "It's because the word for red in hieroglyphics is almost identical to the word for desert. Isn't that fascinating?" Graziella took another sip of her espresso, holding the tiny cup daintily between her fingers.

"Fascinating," Craig agreed. Graziella's question caught him off guard. He'd let his thoughts drift off again. But this time he wasn't thinking about his dissertation, he was daydreaming about Graziella's lips.

Staring at the sugar packet dangling between her fingers, Graziella also appeared to be lost in thought. Then she mused, "I don't necessarily view Horus as good and Seth as evil. No two sides of any story are ever that black and white. In my mind, Seth and Horus represent two sides of the same person."

Making direct eye contact with Craig for the first time, Graziella interjected thoughtfully, "I think Seth is the lord of the outcasts. He's the lord of all the people who don't belong anywhere: the different people…like redheads."

Graziella had made a joke. It was cute but not all that funny. Craig, being the stand-up comic genius that he was, laughed to be polite. But he was actually more amused by how funny Graziella wasn't.

Graziella completely lost herself in conversation—if you could call it that—she did all the talking. "Look at me!" Graziella blushed. "I *never* talk this much. Not even to myself!"

She curled a strand of her hair around her index finger and contemplated, "I think we all have a Horus inside of us, and we all have a Seth inside of us as well. Eventually, one or the other takes over. I don't think it necessarily has to be Horus though. In fact, even Horus himself represents the two different people in all of us. He's depicted as a man with the head of a falcon and long grey feathers. His right eye represented the sun, daytime, and intellect. But his left eye represented the moon, night-time, and passion. The ancient Egyptians believed that just as the sun and the moon reign in the sky at separate times, our intellect and our passion reign in us separately as well."

Craig pretended to be asleep.

Graziella shook him. "Stop it!" she giggled.

Craig had only just met Graziella, but already she'd completely opened up to him. Meanwhile, Mathieu patiently held vigil from his table across the terrace. In his intoxication with Graziella, Craig had completely forgotten about his friend.

"Oh, Graziella!" Craig suddenly remembered. "I want you to meet my friend, Mathieu." Slipping his hand under her arm, Craig led her over to the table.

"I'm so sorry!" Craig apologised. "I didn't mean to leave you over here by yourself."

One glance at Graziella and Mathieu forgave him. "Who could blame you?"

The three of them spent the next four hours sitting at the table, talking, and laughing. Craig introduced Graziella to everyone that came into the café whether he knew them or not. At one point, Craig actually led the entire café in a rendition of *Gens du pays*—the unofficial national anthem of Quebec. And he came pretty close to convincing Graziella to teach him the Italian national anthem—*Inno di Mameli*. Craig got her to hum a bar or two, but she could never finish an entire phrase without blushing and bursting into laughter.

The fun and light-hearted moments in the café coalesced into the most wonderful day Graziella could remember. In the months that followed, the three friends met together often. By May, both Craig and Mathieu were nearly finished with their doctoral work. Mathieu planned to return to his home in Cotonou to run the main hospital and marry his betrothed, Bangoura. Mathieu's heart broke with compassion for his people. He often spoke of Benin's high infant mortality rate, and he deeply wanted to use his medical training to make a difference in his country.

"Eighty-nine out of every one thousand infants perish in my country. Adult life expectancy is just as bleak—only fifty-five years!"

Graziella listened with tear-filled eyes as Mathieu recounted the hardships faced by the Beninese people, particularly the children. She had a special love for children, and it was her dream to one day become an obstetrician.

Graziella had also begun to fall in love with Craig, but her feelings terrified her. Unable to deal with her affinity for Craig, Graziella tried to ignore it. She tried to deny the desire she harboured for him, but ultimately, she couldn't. Instead, Graziella's fear increased and she became really, really sad. She'd finally made two very good friends. In fact, Craig and Mathieu were the *only* friends she'd ever made, and she didn't want to lose them—she'd been emotionally isolated and lonely for so long.

Graziella resolved not to let her silly crush on Craig interfere with the amity between her and her two friends. But the more time she spent with Craig, the more intense her feelings became. She couldn't get the scent of his cologne out of her mind. She'd had a sense of Deja vu from the very first moment she met him—although it was barely perceptible in the beginning—it propelled her back to a place in her life that she couldn't remember. It made her feel safe.

Graziella couldn't help but notice how Craig's eyes crinkled when he smiled, or how the touch of grey sprinkled along his temples made him look so distinguished. Slowly, she began to give in to her amorous feelings and allow her imagination to wander from time to time. It wasn't long before Graziella was spending all of her time daydreaming about Craig.

The two started spending more and more time alone together, but Graziella struggled with intimacy of any kind. As patient as Craig was, he was beginning to show signs of frustration. He wasn't sure what to make of the invisible barrier that always seemed to come between them whenever he got too close. Fearing the inevitable, Graziella knew she'd eventually have to reveal her secret.

Chapter Five
Graziella's Secret

One morning before classes, Graziella called Craig and invited him to dinner.

"Craig?"

"Hey, baby! I was just thinking about you."

"I wanted to make us dinner tonight. I reserved the kitchen in the dorm. Can you come over around seven? There's something I need to talk to you about."

"Is everything alright?" he poked pensively.

A terrible sadness began to well up in Graziella's heart. She didn't know why, but Graziella felt certain that Craig would break it off with her once she told him her secret. She truly loved Craig and the thought of losing him hurt unbearably. But Graziella had decided that the time had come. Come what may, she would tell Craig her secret tonight.

"Can you make it?" she insisted.

"I-I have a lab at five-thirty," Craig stammered, somewhat surprised by Graziella's sudden change in tone. "But I can come right after that—between seven-thirty and eight?"

"Sounds perfect." Graziella exhaled and regained her composure. "See you then?"

"Okay," Craig agreed insecurely. "I love you," he added, sounding more like a question than anything.

"I love you too, Craig."

As Craig hung up the phone, he felt apprehensive. Graziella had never controlled the conversation like that before, and he couldn't remember the last time she called him Craig. What could she need to discuss?

Later that evening, Graziella began to lose her nerve. She avoided the subject all through dinner. After a long silence, Craig opened nervously, "So what did you want to talk to me about?"

Mustering her courage, Graziella broke into tears. "I was molested!" she blurted out, trying to hold back the words, but they just wouldn't stay in any longer. "A long time ago…"

Graziella paused. Her eyes barely made contact with Craig's. She hoped the fact that it had happened a long time ago would mean something to Craig—that the passage of time would somehow make a difference. Graziella felt like damaged goods, and she searched for some affirmation from Craig that he still wanted her.

"It was a long time ago," she repeated, sniffling and calming down a little. Graziella wiped her eyes and let out an exasperated sigh. "I barely even remember what happened anymore. I was pretty young." Then she just stared at the floor.

Craig held her hand and gently kissed her forehead. "Who would do that to you?"

Fumbling with her shirt, Graziella retreated within herself and began to shake. Her eyes instantly overflowed with tears all over again. She pushed Craig away and quickly bolted towards the door.

Craig scrambled after her. "Don't go, Graziella. Please don't leave." Craig caught her just before she reached the door. Wrapping his arms around her, he held Graziella from behind.

Leaning against the wall and weeping violently, Graziella spun around and shouted angrily, "I know you're never going to want me, so just forget it! Okay? Just forget about me!" She grabbed the doorknob and yanked on it.

Craig started to cry as well. "I love you, Graziella! *Please* don't leave me."

Craig had always been so playful—kind but playful. Graziella detected a sincerity in his voice now that she didn't recognise. She didn't know whether she could trust it. But she loved Craig too, more than anything, so Graziella slowly let go of the doorknob and stood there for a while staring at the ground.

"When my father died..." her words were interrupted by a gush of emotion. "When my father died, his brother started coming around the house a lot."

Craig listened attentively—just thankful that Graziella was still there.

Sounding as though she were testifying before a grand jury, Graziella recounted the details, trying desperately to convince Craig of her innocence. "We'd never met him before. Apparently, he'd moved to the United States after high school. When my father died, he came back for the funeral. Then he stayed and offered to help out for a while. My mom was grief-stricken and my grandmother was getting old. Since my father didn't have any other family, it seemed like a blessing at the time. I was only fourteen." Closing her eyes and choking down a spate of tears, Graziella struggled to continue. "I didn't know I couldn't trust him."

"One afternoon, I came home from school and he was there. He told me that my mother and grandmother were out shopping and that they'd be home any minute. But he lied. My grandmother suffered a stroke that day, and my mother stayed with her at the hospital. She asked my uncle to stay and watch after me. They were gone all night."

Graziella's countenance changed from desperation to outrage. She clenched her fists and pounded them against the wall. "He raped me!" she screamed and shook frantically. "He raped me over and over! He wouldn't stop! He hurt me so badly!"

This was unlike anything Craig ever witnessed before. Graziella's face was contorted—both half-crazed and half in shock at the same time. Craig stood helplessly behind her. His arms wanted to comfort her, but he was afraid. He didn't want her to escalate further if he touched her. So, he just stood there.

After what seemed like hours, Craig lifted one arm and gently brushed his fingers against Graziella's back. She soaked it in. Graziella had been waiting for him to touch her. She needed Craig to hold her, but she was too ashamed to ask. Craig turned her gently toward him. His stare was pure, and Graziella believed at that moment that she could see right into his soul.

"Please don't leave me," was all he could get out. A vast array of emotions vexed his spirit, but Craig's primary concern was losing Graziella. He earnestly implored her, "Please, Graziella. Please don't leave me."

Craig's shameless begging touched Graziella's heart. She eventually confided that intimacy of any kind, even platonic friendships, became nearly impossible for her.

"I withdrew from everyone, and I never told a soul what happened. I became convinced that everyone would think I was dirty. I know it sounds terrible, but I believed that even my own mother and grandmother would stop loving me. I especially feared that *they* would find out, so I kept silent."

Craig didn't know what to say. "How can I help you, Graziella?"

"I don't know. I wish I did." Graziella wiped her nose and sniffed as she continued her story. "My interest in Egyptology sprang out of my trauma. After my uncle raped me, I was so afraid and ashamed that I withdrew into a world of my own. I completely immersed myself in books—any kind of books. I read everything and anything I could get my hands on to escape the reality of my intense loneliness. Eventually, I became fascinated with Egyptian gods and goddesses. They were gallant and powerful, yet I could relate to them because they felt pain just like me."

Craig shook his head consolingly.

"After I graduated from high school, I left for Budapest. I tried desperately to leave the past behind and start completely over. For five years, I believed I'd been successful. Whenever I began to feel afraid, I distracted myself with a book or a trip to the museum. I finished my bachelor's degree and earned a master's in Egyptology. Eventually, the past stopped haunting me. Or so it seemed. When I received my acceptance letter from Stanford, I thought I could leave the past behind once and for all—far away on another continent. What I didn't realise is that subconsciously I was still running. And my past—anyone's past—is never more than a memory away. When I fell in love with you, I realised that I hadn't made any progress at all. I'd just been ignoring my pain by refusing to think about it."

The two moved back to the small kitchenette table and sat down. Clearly very fragile and insecure, Graziella attempted to be strong. "I don't know if I can ever make love to anyone. What kind of a life would you have with me?"

Graziella was willing to let Craig go. And if that was the case, she wanted to know then. But Craig didn't break it off with her. Instead, he got down on one knee and slid his hand under hers. "Will you marry me?"

Chapter Six
The Locket

Craig and Graziella planned to marry in June just before Mathieu assumed his new position in Cotonou.

"Mathieu, will you be my best man?" Craig didn't need to ask, and he knew it. But he also knew that Mathieu would never presume such an honour on his own—he was very traditional.

"Of course," Mathieu accepted proudly. "I wouldn't miss it for the world."

Even though the wedding would be simple with only a few guests, Graziella's days were spent in a flurry of activity in the weeks leading up to the big day. The two planned to marry in Graziella's hometown of Taranto, and so much still needed to be done.

On the day of the wedding, Graziella glowed radiantly. Her simple yet elegant dress mirrored her personality in every way. She held a bouquet of roses in her hands, and dozens of tiny, confetti flowers bloomed in her hair. Tears welled up in Craig's eyes as he memorised every detail of his bride to be. Since there were no living male relatives to give Graziella away, Mathieu walked her down the aisle. After presenting her to Craig, he assumed his place beside the groom and handed Craig the ring. Craig slipped the ring on Graziella's finger and the two recited their vows.

"Graziella, I promise to love you until the day I die and beyond. Nothing will stop me from spending eternity with you—no matter what."

Torrents of joy streamed from Graziella's eyes as she stated her vows. "Craig, I promise to be faithful, and to give my heart to you alone—forever."

The two repeated their vows in Italian for Graziella's mother and grandmother, and then the minister pronounced them husband and wife.

After the wedding, Craig and Graziella—that is, Dr and Mrs Ryan—shared a truly wonderful summer together. They honeymooned in Italy, shared long walks on the beach, washed each other's back in the shower and promised their undying love to one another. But even in the shower, Graziella always wore the locket that her grandmother gave her as a wedding present. She kept a small wedding photo of her and Craig inside one of the locket's adjoining frames, and she cherished it with all her heart—Graziella never took it off. For Craig, the locket symbolised Graziella's timeless wonder. She was a garden of delights—a true treasure trove of surprises. And Craig marvelled over each new discovery.

Her grandmother had received the keepsake as a gift at her wedding, as did her grandmother before her. The heirloom had been handed down in this way for hundreds of years. It was rumoured to have originally belonged to Thea Musa, the Roman queen of Parthia. Graziella's grandmother told her that the locket once contained a small portrait of the queen, but the family sold it during the great drought of the 1890s in order to survive. Legend has it that, even after centuries of oxidation, Thea Musa's red hair still captivated all who saw her, and her almond eyes mesmerised men from beyond the grave.

Chapter Seven
A Gift from Caesar

"The locket was rumoured to have been a peace offering from Caesar Augustus to King Phraates IV. It contained an inscription in an unknown tongue, and it was esteemed to be invaluable due to its great age."

Gabriel paused for a moment. He appeared to be gathering his thoughts. Then he leaned in close and confided, "What Augustus didn't know was that the locket had once belonged to Lucifer himself. It had been passed down for thousands of years until the last native Egyptian pharaoh, Nectanebo II, sat on the throne."

"And this is the same locket that Graziella received from her grandmother?" I marvelled.

"The very one," Gabriel nodded. "The locket's secret was never disclosed to anyone. And so, when Egypt fell under the power of the Roman yoke, Ptolemy Auletes offered it to Caesar in tribute along with many other items from the royal treasury."

"Did it really once belong to *Lucifer*?" The inflection in my voice spiked in proportion to my scepticism.

"Actually, the locket never *rightfully* belonged to Lucifer. The truth is he stole it."

"Stole it? Stole it from whom?"

"All I can tell you is that I was there when the King presented it to Lucifer a long, long time ago—before the Great War. He was granted the honour of bestowing it upon the true recipient."

"And Lucifer knew who that was?" I injected, attempting to retrieve the missing pieces of the puzzle.

"He pretended to," Gabriel alleged.

"I'm sorry, Gabriel, but I'm totally lost here. How was Lucifer supposed to give the locket to the rightful owner if he didn't know who it was?"

"When the King presented the locket to Lucifer, he announced that the rightful owner would be able to read the inscription."

"Well, what did the inscription say?"

"That's never been revealed to anyone," Gabriel disclosed in a steely tone. "The inscription can only be understood by the one for whom the message is intended."

"So, Lucifer couldn't read the inscription either?" I sleuthed.

"No, Lucifer couldn't read the inscription. But he pretended that he could, which is why so many of the angels were willing to follow him in rebellion."

"What rebellion?"

"Oh, certainly you've heard of the war in heaven? A third of the angels cast down?"

"Sure, I have," I snorted with sarcasm… "In Sunday school! But you don't expect me to believe that…"

"Believe what you like," Gabriel interrupted. "Your lack of acceptance makes it no less real."

"Okay…" I conceded with a bit of a smirk. "But if Lucifer wasn't the rightful owner of the locket, he must have known that the rebellion would ultimately fail, right?"

"You have to understand—at that time none of us had any idea that there would even be a rebellion, much less how it might turn out. The only thing Lucifer knew was that he couldn't read the inscription. But he pretended he could because he coveted the honour for himself—whatever that honour entailed. This was Lucifer's great sin."

"Selfishness?"

"No, it wasn't really selfishness, it was more like ambitious pride. In a sense, you could say that Lucifer gave up everything he had for this all-consuming need to be first. And once unleashed, it became clear the he would never settle for being second to anyone—not even the King."

"But what about after the rebellion?" I gestured with karate chops to indicate the temporal distance between before and after. "Surely Lucifer realised the hopelessness of his situation *after* the rebellion, didn't he?"

"The best that I can tell from his actions, Lucifer believed in his heart that the rebellion *would* succeed. After which he planned to force the King to reveal the meaning of the inscription. But of course," Gabriel smiled graciously, "he couldn't afford for anyone else to know that."

"And it's been kept a secret all these years?"

"You're the only human ever to learn the truth."

Chapter Eight
Antony and Cleopatra

In the early hours of the morning on September 2, 31 BC, Antony and Cleopatra found themselves aboard separate ships in the gulf of Actium. Just as they were about to face the forces of Octavian in battle, Cleopatra sent word to Marc Antony, "My love, the gods have given us a perfect baby girl! Please come to us as soon as you can."

Sometime earlier, while awaiting the arrival of Octavian's fleet, horror struck the hearts of Anthony's men when malaria swept through the ranks.

"This is an evil omen," cursed Quintus Dellius, one of Antony's top generals. "Everywhere, men are seized by convulsions, and they suffocate to death in the open air. Just look at them writhing in pain until their heart explodes in their chest—blood pours out of them like piss! This is Marcus Antony's doing! He and his whore Cleopatra, and their bid to place that bastard child, Caesarion, on the throne...*they* have brought this upon us."

"What will we do?" a subordinate wailed.

"This plague won't stop until every last one of Antony's men is left wallowing in a puddle of their own piss and blood. I will *not* bear the guilt of their death on my hands. Run up the white flag—we defect to Octavian at once!"

Gaius Sosius, who commanded the left wing of Antony's fleet, tried to stop Dellius but he was too late. Relating the news to Marc Antony, "My lord, Antony," Sosius exclaimed, "General Dellius has defected to Octavian—and he's taken our battle plans with him!"

When Octavian's fleet finally arrived, the destiny of the Roman Empire hung in the balance. By midday, Octavian's fleet had assumed the upper hand.

"Commander Publicola," Antony instructed with doubt in his eyes, "I want Sosius to sail south. This should cause Octavian's ships to fan out and create an opening in their formation. Meanwhile, we'll escape to the open sea with Cleopatra's ships and flee to Alexandria where we'll meet up with the rest of the fleet."

But the rest of the fleet never made it out of the gulf. Octavian's forces decimated the ships that stayed behind. Afterward, Octavian pursued Antony to Alexandria where his remaining troops deserted in such enormous numbers that rather than face Octavian, Antony retreated. Upon the mistaken report that Cleopatra and the child were captured and killed, Marc Antony committed suicide.

Hearing of Antony's death, Cleopatra entrusted the child to the care of a servant.

Heartbroken and disconsolate, she instructed the old woman, "Take the child as far from Alexandria as possible. She isn't safe here."

Cleopatra let her resplendent clothing fall silently to the floor—her soft, caress-able skin now stinging with remorse. She pulled back the blanket and crawled into her lonely tomb where the bittersweet, aromatic petals of relief waited in the fangs of an asp. Cleopatra longed with breathless anticipation for its lethal passion, and she welcomed the acrid venom coursing through her veins.

The servant arrived in Parthia in the dead of night. Gravely ill from the long journey, she knew that she could no longer look after the child. So, she carried the infant to the gates of the Parthian royal palace.

"This is where a princess belongs," she cooed to the sleeping baby, "and you're as true a princess as ever there was."

The servant watched over her precious charge all night and died just as the sun peaked over the horizon. A few hours later, an imperial procession approached the palace bearing a peace offering from Caesar Augustus to King Phraates IV. The gift was an ancient locket that contained an inscription in an unknown tongue. Augustus himself had placed the locket around the neck of a young Italian slave girl named Thea musa.

"Why did Augustus send the locket with a slave girl? Wasn't he concerned about its safety?"

"Augustus sent it with Thea musa precisely because he was concerned for its safekeeping. It was common practice to send priceless gifts in such a way so that if the imperial convoy were ambushed, they'd be unlikely to be discovered. No one among the imperial company knew about the locket but Thea musa. This was according to Augustus' express instructions."

Chapter Nine
Thea Musa

When the young Thea musa stepped down from the chariot, she saw the dead servant stretched out beside the screaming infant. Filled with compassion and missing her own mother, she picked up the baby and rocked it in her arms.

"Sshh...sshh," she whispered, bouncing the infant gently to pacify her.

Thea musa noticed that the child became mesmerised by the locket hanging around her neck. "Do you like this?" she asked as she made it sparkle by turning it in the late morning sun. "Yes, I think you do. Would you like to have it?"

The baby smiled in reaction to the soft, friendly tone of Thea musa's voice, so she gently placed it around her neck.

"Here you go," she swooned. "It looks better on you than it does on me, anyway."

The locket matched the baby's luxurious garments and blankets much more than it did the old rags that Thea musa was dressed in.

When the king gave audience to the imperial envoy, there before the throne knelt Thea musa with the baby.

"Slave girl," the king's attendant addressed Thea musa in Latin, "you may approach the throne with the emperor's gift."

Seeing the baby's curly, red locks, Phraates assumed that she was one of Augustus' own children sent as a peace offering and that Thea musa had been sent along as a servant for the princess. Phraates accepted the gift and raised the child as his own daughter, naming her Thea Musa.

Even as a young girl, Thea commanded the hearts of those around her. When she was old enough, Phraates married Thea and the two had a son together which they named Phraataces. Thea poisoned Phraates and then married her own son. The two reigned as king and queen until they were forced to flee to Syria in 4 AD.

"I'll serve you wherever you go, my queen," Thea musa promised. Like so many others, she'd also fallen in love with Thea. And she'd spent her entire life enamoured by her magnetism.

"No, Thea musa. It's time for you to serve yourself. Take this," Thea offered, placing the locket around Thea musa's neck. "Something to remember me by."

Thea musa opened the locket. It was the only gift she'd ever received in her entire life. Thea had placed a small portrait of herself inside. With tears in her eyes, Thea musa hugged her mistress good-bye.

"It's beautiful!" she whispered. "Thank you. I'll never take it off."

"Go now," Thea insisted as she cupped her face. "Orodes' soldiers are coming!"

"Did Thea realise that Thea musa was the one who'd given her the locket in the first place?"

"No," Gabriel shrugged, "to her it was just another locket, one of dozens that she possessed."

"It's quite a coincidence that Thea picked that particular locket to give to Thea musa. Don't you think?"

"'Coincidence' is your word."

"So how did the locket end up in Graziella's family?"

"Thea musa returned to Rome where she fell in love and got married. The locket was handed down from generation to generation until it finally made its way to Graziella."

Chapter Ten
Y2k

The newlywed's magical summer equinoxes early when Craig received a very handsome offer from the Pentagon in the beginning of August. With the Y2K scare full on, Craig's recent dissertation in biotechnology arrested Washington's attention. Dr Craig Ryan's star was now on the rise, and he was viewed as one of the brightest young luminaries in his field.

Back in the states, Dr Zahradnik, an official from the Pentagon, consulted with Craig.

"Your dissertation is most impressive, Dr Ryan. Those of us at the Pentagon are especially interested in your theory about storing digital information in living organisms. I'll cut right to the chase," Zahradnik levelled, his over-starched shirt lining his neck like a whitewashed fence. "The Pentagon is concerned that Y2K will crash its networks and it doesn't trust its most highly classified secrets to a technician who can simply fix its system's internal clock. No, the Pentagon is contemplating a much more serpentine solution. Presupposing you're correct and it's possible to copy the data in the Pentagon's mainframe onto the brain of a living organism, the Pentagon would like to extend the contract to you."

"What exactly would this contract entail?" Craig lifted the two thumbs from his folded fingers into the shape of a field goal.

"The proposition is simple enough: we require a backup copy of all our data. Only we're not looking for a computer-based solution."

Squeezing his upper lip between his thumb and forefinger, Craig stared at the table. Then he looked up at Dr Zahradnik. "Theoretically, what you're suggesting is possible. But there's no known technology as of yet that can accomplish it."

"I realise this. That's why we're recruiting you. We want you to design the technology."

"In four months?" With an uneasy laugh, Craig flatly rejected the plausibility of the idea. "I've tinkered with some hardware and I have a basic idea where I'm headed with it but," Craig shook his head, "even if I were able to perfect the hardware in such a short window, the bridge between theory and application is hypothetical. There's no certainty it would even work. Not to mention security."

"Security?" Zahradnik inquired, resting his elbows on the table and tapping his fingertips together.

"Well, of course," Craig asserted. "From where I'm sitting right now, I couldn't guarantee the security of your data. I'm in no position to offer *any* guarantees at this stage of R&D. Prudence dictates establishing a consistent track record over the next few years with considerably smaller amounts of data before attempting to replicate anything nearly as large and sensitive as the Pentagon's files."

"There's no time for that," Zahradnik insisted as he folded his arms.

"But even if I were able to meet your deadline, the ethical review process alone would take longer than four months."

"Let me handle the bureaucracy," the doctor countered. "From where I'm sitting, I *can* offer a few guarantees. If you deliver on your end, I'll get everything else approved. What do you say? Money is no obstacle. The Pentagon is prepared to offer you a very competitive compensation package."

Dr Zahradnik reached inside his suit coat and pulled out an envelope from his breast pocket. As he handed the offer to Craig, he added, "We'll cover all of your expenses while you're here, of course, and you'll have every resource the American government has to offer at your disposal."

"You want me to work here in D.C.?" The crack in Craig's voice revealed his surprise.

"I'm afraid there's no other way." Extending his hand, Dr Zahradnik rose to his feet. "Think it over and get back to me. My card is in the envelope."

Craig left the interview deep in thought. He savoured the opportunity and definitely felt up to the challenge. But tragically, it would mean either asking Graziella to take some time off from school or the two of them spending time away from one another.

I don't want to ask Graziella to put her schooling on hold, and I definitely can't bear the thought of being separated from her—not for any sum of money.

The drive back to the hotel was filled with contemplation. Craig reluctantly decided to turn down the position without even looking at the offer. Absorbed in his thoughts, Craig hardly noticed the scene unfolding in the back of his mind: a pale hand pulling back a veil, revealing...

The sound of a car horn blaring snapped Craig out of his stupor.

His mind had wandered off and he'd begun to drift into another lane. The heavy D.C. traffic was unforgiving, especially at this time of the evening. Gripping the wheel with both hands, Craig focused on the traffic the rest of the way to the hotel.

When he discussed the offer with Graziella, she absolutely insisted that he take it.

"This represents a huge opportunity for you, baby, and I won't stand in your way. I'll put school on hold for a few years, and you can accept the assignment. So how much money are we talking about here anyway?" Her voice turned deep and raspy, almost like a chain smoker's when she mentioned the money.

"I don't know," Craig admitted indifferently as he rubbed his thumb along the curve of Graziella's eye. "Once I'd decided not to take the position, I never even thought to open the envelope."

"Well, open it!" Graziella demanded excitedly. She grabbed his hand and yanked on it like it was the handle of a slot machine.

Craig opened the envelope and covertly unfolded the letter. He teased Graziella by trying to look disappointed. "Oh," he grumbled in a monotone voice, sounding like Eeyore from Winnie the Pooh.

"How much?" Graziella was about to burst with curiosity.

Craig had to fight to hold back his elation.

"How much?" Graziella exacted, trying to snatch the letter from his hands.

Craig buried the offer under his shirt and ran towards the bed. Graziella followed hot on his heels, grabbing at the back of his shirt.

"Give it to me! Give me the letter!" she laughed hysterically.

Craig dove onto the bed and hid his face under a pillow while Graziella climbed on his back and tickled him, trying to reach under his belly to retrieve the letter.

"Stop tickling me," Craig giggled as he squirmed, his rigid arms stretched out protectively at his sides. "Please! You know I hate to be tickled!"

"Only if you tell me," Graziella extorted. Raising her hands above her head, she extended her thumbs and index fingers. "Tell me," she threatened playfully with her six-guns ready. "I'll do it, I swear."

Craig peaked out from beneath the pillow. Graziella looked like a voluptuous she-clown waiting to bludgeon her straight man with her bony props. He braced himself apprehensively—face down on the bed and giggling.

"Alright, you asked for it." Graziella dropped her arms down and bore her fingers into Craig's sides. "How much? How much?"

"Alright," Craig pleaded. "Alright, I'll tell you...I'll tell you! Stop it! Please!"

Graziella stopped and climbed off of Craig's back. She curled up beside him on the rumpled blankets and brushed her hair out of her face. Craig rolled over and pulled the now hopelessly wrinkled paper out of his shirt. Staring at it, he comically pretended to be contemplating whether to reveal the figure or not. Graziella scowled with her eyes and raised her arm again with index finger extended.

"Okay," Craig surrendered, intercepting her finger with his open palm and calling a truce. Sombrely, he looked at the letter again and then mumbled, "$3.9 million."

Graziella jump in his arms and screamed at the top of her lungs! "AHHHHHHH!"

She beat him with the pillow and smothered him with hugs and kisses. Then, clamouring to her feet, Graziella pulled Craig up as well and the two of them jumped up and down on the bed.

"Neither of us ever even *imagined* having money like that! This is a dream come true!"

Panting and sweaty, the two collapsed on the bed and soaked in their tremendous good fortune. They stared at the ceiling in total shock. After about ten minutes of reflection, Graziella jumped to her feet.

"We need to celebrate," she beamed. "Let's go shopping!"

Chapter Eleven
The Deal Breaker

In the weeks that followed, everything seemed so perfect! The two newlyweds moved into a spacious apartment near the Pentagon which Graziella decorated while Craig settled into his new appointment.

Thinking through the entire sequence as he paced the floor, Craig tried to anticipate any contingencies that might arise. "The transfer process basically operates along the same concept as copying data from one hard drive to another," he mumbled to himself, gesturing with his hands as the data figuratively transferred from one imaginary hard drive to the other.

"However, there's no way to know how successfully the data will be stored in a living organism. More importantly, I doubt whether it could ever be retrieved again."

Sitting at his desk, Craig doodled a flowchart diagram on a legal pad. A series of arrows represented data transferring out from the Pentagon's mainframe computer (PMC) to various question marks which he circled.

"Theoretically, storage is less problematic than retrieval," he reasoned as he traced over the unidirectional arrows. "This will require an organism with the capacity to store a large volume of data such as the brain of a primate or possibly even a human."

Craig erased the question marks and replaced them with the letter (R) to represent the various recipients. He tapped his No. 2 pencil against the legal pad, and like a master chess player, he contemplated the next several moves.

"The greater obstacle involves the fact that writing data to an existing brain will most likely permanently delete any and all information that's already there. In all likelihood, the process will completely incapacitate the host—memory, motor function and coordination will all be lost. This could make it extremely challenging, if not completely impossible, to recapture the data."

Craig added arrows to his flowchart to indicate the data traveling back out of the living hosts. Then he scribbled X's through the arrows. He tore the piece of paper off the legal pad and crumpled it up in frustration. Jumping up out of his chair, Craig paced the floor some more—thinking out loud how he might overcome this problem.

"The only way around this dilemma would be to transfer the data to an empty receptacle."

In other words, Craig needed a clone.

"I wouldn't be erasing any information because the brain of a clone would be a blank slate from the beginning. Yes, that's it!"

Sliding back into his chair, Craig quickly drew another flowchart. This time, one arrow flowed out of the Pentagon mainframe (PMC) and another out of an unknown source (D) which represented the donor. Both arrows flowed into a clone (C).

"The challenge in this scenario is transferring both the DNA from the donor and the data from the Pentagon mainframe at the same time. It has to be done simultaneously or one will overwrite the other—at least in theory. The truth is I have no idea what would happen."

Given this particular unknown variable, Craig decided that the safest alternative would be to pursue simultaneous transfer and hope for the best. Finally, this left the task of choosing which living organism he would clone. This turned out to be the deal-breaker.

"It would be unethical to clone a human being. But if I cloned an animal, even if the transfer were a success, how would I ever reclaim the data?"

Craig tossed his pen down on the table. He'd hit a brick wall—none of his research turned up a viable option. He brainstormed the problem for another twenty minutes or so while he played the bongos on his desk calendar. Finally, he gave up and accepted the inevitable.

"I'll have to tell the Pentagon it can't be done. But before I do that, I'm going to try one last thing."

Craig decided to experiment with a program he'd written that would essentially bypass the system's internal clock and write the data to a hard drive without actually date-stamping the file.

"If it works, I can make as many files as necessary to copy all of their data," "Plus, I won't have to go back to the Pentagon empty handed."

The idea seemed viable enough, but still, Craig meticulously considered every potential outcome.

"I'll need to run a trial burn before I try to sell the idea to Zahradnik."

So, Craig made arrangements to enter the main frame in two days. Circling the date on the large, flat calendar, Craig grabbed his car keys and went home.

Chapter Twelve
The Long Night

Two days later when Craig entered the secure area just outside the mainframe, he marvelled over how little security there actually appeared to be. Once inside the mainframe, Craig opened his briefcase and pulled out a CD. Popping it into the drive, he loaded his software and performed the trial burn.

"So far so good," he triumphed conservatively. "Now I need verification that the data will upload again without syncing to an internal clock. Once that hurdle is cleared, I'll need to check the data for accuracy."

The first test went smoothly: the data uploaded fine. The second test, checking the data for accuracy, would take hours and hours to complete. So, Craig decided to finish it up at home. He packed up his things, including the uploaded data files he'd copied, and left. The drive home was a blur—Craig was completely preoccupied with his work. When he arrived, he found Graziella waiting in their cosy apartment. She'd prepared a special candlelight dinner and her face literally glowed, but Craig was distracted—his thoughts were somewhere else.

"What's wrong?" Graziella cajoled him as she massaged his neck and shoulders.

Craig didn't want to ruin their evening, so he tried to pretend that everything was fine. But Graziella could tell that he wasn't himself.

"There's nothing that you can't tell me, baby. You know that, don't you?"

Craig kissed her on the lips and smiled, "How'd I ever deserve someone so wonderful?"

Over dinner, he told her about his decision not to back up the Pentagon's data using a bio-organism. "I can't do it, Graziella. I don't want to let you down, but it's just not ethical." Craig stared at his plate and poked at the stir-fried vegetables with his fork.

Graziella touched his arm reassuringly. "You'd be letting me down if you *did* something unethical." Her kind, caring, expression relayed that she'd happily sleep under a bridge and eat out of a can before she'd ever let him do anything that went against his conscience. He felt relieved.

Then Craig explained to Graziella in great detail, as if he were trying to convince himself, all the merits of his alternative plan. Tapping the prongs of his fork against the floral print place mat, he vented his concern, "The problem is, I don't know whether my software will work. And even if it does, there's no guarantee that the Pentagon will go for it."

Graziella played the devil's advocate. "Well what's the worst that could happen?"

"For one thing, I could lose my job," Craig speculated.

"That wouldn't be *so* bad, would it?" Graziella tried to cheer him up. Straddling him in his chair, she bit her bottom lip seductively. "You could spend more time with me."

"You make unemployment sound pretty tempting, Mrs Ryan." Craig nuzzled Graziella and caressed her hips. "I would definitely love to spend *a lot* more time with you."

After the two cuddled and kissed for a few moments, Craig put his hands on Graziella's face and looked her straight in the eyes.

"I love you so much. Whatever happens, I swear I'm going to take care of you. I don't ever want you to worry."

"I'm not worried," Graziella aired confidently. "I'm married to the most brilliant man in the world."

Chapter Thirteen
The Awakening

Later that evening, Craig uploaded the Pentagon data on his PC and began to pour through it. He skimmed through hundreds of pages of intelligence and searched for signs of inconsistencies or missing characters—anything that looked askew.

Graziella sat next to him and drew little circles on the back of his neck. "Come to bed with me, baby," she tantalised with a naughty smile. "I miss you."

"I'm sorry," Craig groaned, "there's just so much to sift through! And this is just a tiny fraction of what's in the main frame. I need to make absolutely certain the program copied the data accurately." With an apologetic frown, he speculated, "I'm probably gonna be here all night."

"All the more reason to give yourself a break," she baited him. "Come on, what do you say? Just a *little* break?" Graziella gestured with her thumb and index finger. "You know you want to," she whispered while she slid her hands up under his shirt.

Craig closed his eyes and let his head fall back while Graziella scratched his back and kissed his neck. "Mmm...I *really* want to. That feels so good." Graziella was just about to close the deal when Craig broke free from her spell. "I can't. I'm sorry."

Clearly Craig's work was important, so she eventually gave up and went to bed alone. Craig read through the night, searching for chopped sentences or abrupt transitions. Everything appeared to be in order until just before sunrise, when he came across a file that detailed how men, women and children were being held in camps around the world.

"These poor people," Craig despaired, shaking his head in disbelief.

Craig thought he'd misunderstood at first, so he scrolled back and read it again. But he hadn't read it wrong; the file detailed an elaborate ring of concentration camps completely owned and operated by the government. What absolutely horrified Craig were the detailed descriptions of a variety of bizarre medical experiments that the Pentagon surreptitiously sponsored.

"What *is* this? These look like lab notes."

The dated entries were actual laboratory notes with copious logs specifying each cruel and horrendous treatment. Intricate observations of the subjects' emotional and physical reactions were also documented. Craig's skin crawled as he contemplated the unimaginable suffering—coldly chronicled in unbelievably detached and indifferent detail. The sun rose on a very different Craig Ryan that morning.

"What should I do?" he pondered alone. But in his heart, Craig already knew what to do. "What else *can* I do? I need to expose this data—*all* of it."

But then Craig considered the reality of the proposition. "Even with the evidence I've already retrieved, with no date-stamp or proof of where it came from, I can't prove anything. For all anyone can tell, I might have typed it up right here at home."

Running his fingers through his hair and yawning, Craig realised that he needed some caffeine. As he rinsed out the coffee pot and ground the beans, Craig muttered through the problem. "I need a copy that I can produce as evidence at some point to someone—but who? Who do you turn the U.S. government over to?"

Then in a classic Cybil moment, Craig answered himself. "The obvious answer is 'nobody'. You can't trust anyone with this data. You should just destroy it."

Craig scooped the fresh-ground coffee into the filter. At that very moment, as if the aroma from the coffee opened his eyes, it became crystal clear what he would do.

"That's it! I don't have to expose them," he sneered. "I can just shut 'em down. I could upload a virus and wipe out all of the Pentagon's data."

Taking the plan to its natural outcome, he concluded, "Oh yeah, that's a great idea. If you do that, they won't even bother to arrest you, they'll just shoot you on site."

Craig decided to think his strategy through a little more thoroughly.

"I need to be able to justify my actions. I need evidence."

Craig didn't want to be guilty of an unnecessary crime. "The Pentagon must also have tons of other information that's not incriminating—information that can save lives. I don't want to permanently destroy all *that* data. If I'm going to upload a virus, I need to make a copy first. I'm going to need to copy all of it."

Craig poured the water, flipped the switch, and paced the kitchen floor, waiting for the coffee to brew.

"That's problematic." He exhaled heavily. "The only storage unit large enough to contain that much data, besides another mainframe system, is the brain of a primate."

Thinking back to his crumpled flow chart, Craig revisited the main obstacle. "But I need to be able to retrieve the data as evidence. How would I ever retrieve the data from the brain of an ape? There's only one thing I can do," Craig resolved, "I need to clone a human and simultaneously upload the Pentagon data into its brain."

Since Craig knew of no other individual that he could ethically clone beside himself, he prepared to do just that. He poured himself a cup of coffee and began to pack all of his hardware into two large cases.

"This is crazy. I don't even know if this stuff works."

Drinking his coffee, Craig tiptoed into the bedroom. He didn't want to wake Graziella, but he was so tempted to crawl into bed with her. He slipped under the covers next to her and she instinctively curled up in his arms.

"I'm so happy you finally came to bed. I can't sleep without you."

Craig kissed her on the forehead and held her close. The scent of her perfume still lingered faintly in her hair. Craig loved that smell—it was *her* smell, and it conjured up wonderful memories of their honeymoon in Italy. The thought of all those experiments juxtaposed against that magical summer filled Craig with such insecurity. He realised for the first time just how much they stood to lose.

What am I doing? Craig doubted his instincts, and he doubted his ability to protect Graziella should something go wrong. *What did I drag her into?*

When Graziella woke up, the first thing she did was press Craig to stay home with her.

"Stay home with me today, okay? I'll make us a nice breakfast and we can stay in bed all day," she started to giggle. "Please stay home with me? Please, please, please, please, please?" she begged.

"It's *so* tempting," Craig caressed her gently, "but I have to go to work today. I'm already late."

"You suck!" Graziella pouted with an overly expressive frown.

"I what?" Craig interrogated her as he attacked her with his fingers and tickled her nearly to death. "I what?"

"You suck, Dr Ryan," Graziella giggled. "You're a sucky doctor...Ahh!" She screamed and kicked her feet trying desperately to guard her ribs from his intruding appendages.

As Craig got dressed for work, he decided not to tell Graziella what he planned to do. He didn't want her involved, and he definitely didn't want her to try and talk him out of it. He knew she'd probably succeed.

"Graziella," he broached the subject carefully, "I have a solid week of work ahead of me. If I want to make my pitch to Zahradnik convincing, I'd better have all my facts straight. I'm not going to be very good company, so I was thinking—why don't you go home to Taranto for a week and spend some time with your family?"

"No!" Graziella refused. "Absolutely not! A week is too long for us to be apart. Besides, we were just in Italy."

"Sure, we were, but think of how little time you actually spent with your mother and grandmother during our honeymoon."

Thinking of her loved ones, Graziella felt bad. She hadn't been home more than twice in over six years. Her eyes became sullen as the guilt worked its way to her heart. "Maybe you're right."

"You know I'm right." Craig put his arms around Graziella's waist. "I don't want you to go either," he whispered in her ear. "I'm going to miss you terribly, but I honestly do think it's a good idea."

With the resilience of a child, Graziella perked right back up. "Okay, I'll go," She announced, turning around and giving Craig a big hug.

"Let's look online and see if we can book you a flight out this morning."

"This morning?" Graziella objected, refusing to let go of him. Her feelings were hurt. "Are you trying to get rid of me? Is there someone else?"

"No, silly!" Craig chuckled. "There will *never* be anyone else."

"Promise?" Graziella petitioned insecurely.

"I promise," Craig assured her.

As Graziella packed, she began to acclimate to the idea of going to Italy. "Now that I think about it, I don't really need to pack that many clothes."

"Yeah, you'll only be gone a week."

"No. That's not why. Now that we're rich, I can take Mommy and Nana shopping in Rome!"

"Don't go spending all our money too soon," Craig joked with just a hint of seriousness in his voice, "I haven't earned it yet."

At the airport, Craig saw Graziella to the gate. When the flight boarded, their good-bye was unbearable.

"I changed my mind, baby. I don't want to go."

Putting Graziella's safety above his own feelings, Craig wouldn't hear of it. He took Graziella's hands and held them close to his lips. "I insist." He could only imagine the things that could go awry. Trying to console his bride, he kissed her hands and added, "It's only for a week. We'll be together again before you know it."

Graziella stomped her foot like a two-year-old, "That's too long!"

"Hey," Craig bubbled, "I have an idea! How about I come and join you just as soon as I'm finished?"

"Really?" Graziella's joy beamed through her tears. "When?"

"Well," Craig calculated, "today is Thursday. Hopefully I can wrap things up over the weekend and be in Taranto by Monday. We can all go shopping in Rome together. How does that sound?"

"That sounds wonderful!" Graziella hugged him tightly and clung as if for dear life.

"Last call for passengers boarding flight 779 servicing Rome, Nice, and..."

"That's you," Craig noted sadly, easing out of her death grip. "I love you and I'll see you soon, okay?"

"I love you too!" Graziella asserted passionately as she turned away. "Come soon!" she called back just before disappearing into the tunnel.

As Craig left the airport, he felt conflicted over what he planned to do. Nonetheless, he consoled himself with the thought that if anything erratic did occur, at least Graziella would be safe and sound outside the country. Hopefully, nothing would go wrong and soon Craig would be joining her in Italy.

Chapter Fourteen
Frankenstein

Craig entered the Pentagon with the two large cases containing the equipment and resources he would need. After gaining access to the mainframe, he unpacked everything and quickly began to prepare the software and set up the transfer mechanisms.

"The entire cloning process shouldn't take more than an hour," Craig calculated, "but I can't even begin to guess how long it'll take to copy all this information."

A flurry of questions pestered Craig's mind: *How long can I stay in here before they start to get suspicious? How long will it take to copy the data? One hour? Twenty hours? Will it all copy? Will I run out of time?*

It was impossible to determine how long it would take to transfer all of the data without knowing how much there was—and Craig didn't have a clue. "I don't dare stay in here more than twelve hours. After that I'll have to stop. They're sure to become suspicious if I stay any longer."

While Craig could have probably justified staying longer, he certainly didn't want the wrong people poking around. Once he finished writing the data, he planned to upload a virus to induce a millennium crash.

Craig mumbled a prayer, typed his visitor's log-in code, and pressed enter. As the software uploaded into the mainframe, he passed the time by anxiously talking to himself.

"Okay Craig, you should run a final drill to make sure you haven't forgotten anything. Let's see, this software operates much like an analogue to digital converter in reverse. It translates digital data into a format that can be stored in living tissue…"

Talking to himself made Craig feel a little less apprehensive, but as he started to think of all the many indeterminate factors that could complicate the procedure throughout the various stages, his anxiety level spiked right back up again. It didn't help that the software was taking so long to upload into the mainframe.

"Come on, already."

The green light on the LED display slowly filled more and more of the empty bar on the screen. While he waited, Craig fidgeted and perspired from nervous tension. After another twenty minutes or so, the LED finally read full.

"Looks like you've cleared your first hurdle," Craig congratulated himself.

Avoiding a security breach while uploading unauthorised software into the Pentagon mainframe was a major coup. Craig fully expected to need an override authorisation code. This would have required a detailed explanation of what he was doing and why. Craig came prepared to offer one, but still, it could have definitely raised suspicion or caused delay.

"No clue how that happened," he mumbled to himself. "But at this point, I'll take whatever breaks I can get."

"Okay," Craig walked himself through the next few steps, sounding like he was reading from a set of instructions. "First, I set up the overhead scanner."

Looking around, Craig decided to use two rectangular tables to serve as gurneys.

"Next, I assemble the tripod stand and connect the boom. To this, I attach the retractable arm, and clamp on the scanner."

Craig lifted the scanning device out of the box. He thought about how he'd modified it to photograph both the exterior surface and the interior cavity of the donor. Kind of an x-ray and scanner combined, it now generated a three-dimensional image against which Craig hoped the transferred DNA sequence would map and model itself.

"That's the part that remains to be seen," he remarked pensively.

Noticing that the lens was missing, Craig called out in his best Dr Frankenstein, "Where's the eye, Igor?" He often employed humour when he felt upset, sad, or nervous. At that particular moment, Craig was feeling an odd mixture of all three.

"I don't know, Master. It was here before!" he answered as he rummaged through one of the cases.

"Well hurry, Igor—it's the most crucial piece!"

"I'm hurrying, Master! I'm hurrying," he placated playfully as he scurried to the second case with a noticeable limp. "Aha! Here it is!"

Having triumphed in his little treasure hunt, Craig attached the lens to the scanner.

"Alright," he paused to assess his progress, "after a quick double-check to make sure all is in order…"

Craig switched characters mid-sentence to the serial killer in *Silence of the Lambs*. "…it assembles the bio replica on one of the tables," he ordered himself in a freakish tone. "It assembles the bio replica on one of the tables," he repeated—this time with a little more intensity.

When he finished assembling the bio replica, it resembled a large wax manikin. Craig quickly undressed and, clutching the remote control, he stretched out on the empty table to ensure the scanner full access to his body. With a deep breath, Craig closed his eyes and pushed the button. The scanner started with a whir, and the retractable arm moved it slowly across the length of his body. As he lay there, Craig began to worry.

How will all this turn out? Am I creating some sort of Frankenstein's monster? Will the clone really be an exact replica of me? Will it live? And if so, will it be blind, crippled, or retarded? The science is sound enough, but the truth is, I don't know what the hell I'm doing!

Craig bid his time in agony. As the scanner continued its slow pass over his person, Craig rehashed the process over and over in his mind. It helped to alleviate his nervous tension and reassure him that nothing should go wrong.

"The approach is based on fundamental somatic cell nuclear transfer—a process in which the nucleus of one cell is transplanted into an egg after its own nucleus has been removed. The egg reprograms the displaced nucleus and after a shock is applied, it begins to divide, creating a blastocyst. The resulting early-stage embryo is basically identical to the original nucleus that was transferred in the first place..."

Craig stared up at the ceiling. He wasn't particularly religious, but for some reason he found himself thinking about the stoning of the apostle Stephen. Craig imagined the ceiling of the Pentagon opening up to reveal God seated on his throne in heaven—just as it did for Stephen when he appeared before the Sanhedrin.

"I wonder what God would say to me right now?"

As Craig lay there wondering, his mind drifted off and he saw the same bloodless hand from before pulling back the veil. Behind the veil a gruesome battle raged. In his mind, he approached a wounded combatant pleading for mercy. As Craig drew his sword, an eerie chill prickled over Craig's skin.

"Pull yourself together," he admonished himself. "Remember why you're here. Think of Graziella. Most importantly, stay focused."

So, Craig turned his attention back to the business at hand. "Instead of an ovum, I'm utilising a bio replica which consists of an organic material capable of reprogramming the nucleus containing my DNA. In theory, this should allow me to produce an adult replica of myself rather than just an embryo..."

Craig's thoughts drifted to all the literature that contested the very premise of his research. "Theory' is the operative term," he sighed with considerably less self-confidence than he'd arrived with.

"Now that I think about it, there are a number of issues that I've only addressed theoretically—such as whether the mitotic division will take place uniformly over the entire bio replica, or whether it will take place at all. I trust my theory, but with no empirical evidence to rely upon, the entire process could end in complete failure. The clone might be only half-formed or grossly misshapen. Anything's possible."

Craig began to despair as he considered the possibilities. "But I've come this far. I can't turn back now."

After photographing Craig's head and torso, the scanner hovered over his upper thighs. Within twenty minutes, the bio replica started to take on human features and colour. Within forty-five minutes, Craig was floored.

"It's *me* laying over there! Unbelievable!"

Careful not to move anything but his arm, Craig reached over and checked the pulse. "It's steady," he breathed a sigh of relief. "That's reassuring. Everything's going well—perhaps too well."

An uncharacteristic pessimism surfaced in Craig that day. He didn't recognise it, but he trusted it. "Either way, it shouldn't be too much longer now."

Craig was beginning to feel nervous again. He'd run out of thoughts to distract himself with.

"Great! Now I have to pee—just what I needed!"

Craig tried to concentrate on the clone to take his mind off of his bladder. "The process is nearly complete. It's actually almost done! The Pentagon data appears to be imaging to the clone's brain without incident as well," he noted optimistically as he glanced at the LED display.

Craig breathed a sigh of amazement and relief all rolled together when a very disturbing dilemma occurred to him. "Oh no! I never once considered how to get the clone back out of the building. I brought the bio replica into the Pentagon in pieces and assembled it here. There's no other way to get the clone back out other than to have it walk out. That is, if it *can* walk!"

Craig paced back and forth inside his head. "I need to think, but I can't. I have to pee! The pressure is unbearable!" The urge to shake his leg or something, anything to relieve the sensation, nearly drove Craig mad! But he coached himself through the agony. "Come on Craig, it's absolutely imperative that you lie perfectly still."

Troubleshooting how he would get the clone out of the Pentagon with no security badge and no identification, it suddenly occurred to Craig. "That's it! I'll give the clone my identification, and I'll keep my badge. The clone will leave first and claim to have lost his badge. That way the evidence will be safely out of the building by the time I leave. If anyone questions me, I'll say that I found my badge in my briefcase. I just pray that it works."

Craig fidgeted nervously as he tried to lie still. "Two more minutes. Come on, you can do this."

When the scanner stopped, Craig waited a second for good measure before he slid off the table. The sight stopped him dead in his tracks as he gawked at his accomplishment. Just an hour ago this fully developed human was nothing more than a blank, lifeless bio replica. It was a lump of genetic material—completely void of any identifiable features at all.

"It's Alive!" He goofed in his Dr Frankenstein voice.

The clone was an exact replica of Craig. All his years of studying and daydreaming culminated in this single, triumphant moment.

Craig glanced at the LED. "That's odd! The data transfer is already finished as well? How curious. It should have taken much longer."

As Craig marvelled over how remarkably fast the information copied to the clone, his celebration was cut short. Two gunmen broke through the door. Both carried nine-millimetre firearms and fired several rounds. Craig dove on to the table to cover the clone and rolled him onto the floor. The fall jolted the clone to consciousness, and he opened his eyes.

Literally an inch from his face, Craig screamed, "Get out of here!"

Both Craig and the clone scrambled to their feet and bound toward the door. One of the agents quickly squeezed off another two shots. The other pushed his arm down to prevent him from firing again.

"What are you doing? The director wants them alive."

Somehow Craig and the clone made it to the elevator. Seeing the doors close at the end of the corridor, one of the gunmen radioed down to security on the first floor to intercept Craig and the clone.

Positioning himself in front of the elevator, the security officer waited for the doors to open. "Don't move!" he screamed, firing into the open elevator.

Chapter Fifteen
Taranto

"That's horrible, Gabriel! Did the agents shoot them?"

"I'm afraid so," Gabriel answered.

"What?" I freaked. "Well, what's the point in that? After everything that Craig and Graziella meant to each other, it's over just like that?"

"I never said it was 'over'. Who said that? The story isn't over."

As Graziella folded laundry in front of the television, she saw live coverage of the Taranto police surrounding their house.

"Oh my God, that's us!" Dropping the sheet in her hands, she covered her mouth and gasped, "Mamma!"

Her mother rushed in from the kitchen, wiping her hands on a towel and shaking her head in utter disbelief. Outside, the sound of helicopters and sirens laid siege to the small family. A single voice rang out over a megaphone. "Everyone step outside with your hands in plain sight."

The police didn't honestly expect Craig to be in Italy yet, of course. They'd come for Graziella. The Taranto police arrested her after searching the house, although no one seemed to know just exactly what they were searching for. When they left, Graziella's mother and grandmother chased them down the street, screaming after them to bring her back.

American federal agents arrived in Taranto soon afterward and interrogated Graziella. When they were convinced that she possessed no information regarding Craig's whereabouts, they placed her into custody 'for her own safety'. An agent by the name of Schriver transported Graziella to a safe house in D.C. where he raped her repeatedly before returning home for the evening.

"Don't worry," Schriver needled her sadistically. "My replacement will be in to visit you soon."

Schriver left Graziella lying half-naked on the cold floor of an empty room. With blood trickling from her nose and her spirit all but broken, Graziella wept bitterly for her husband.

"So, Craig rescues Graziella?" I assumed with relief.

"I'm sorry?" Gabriel responded cluelessly.

"Craig rescues Graziella, right?" I insisted

Gabriel studied my face. My once grey, wrinkled skin now bore the vigour of a man in his thirties. The deep furrows of age and care had faded considerably, and the pain that used to mar my countenance was nearly imperceptible.

"Not exactly," he uttered with some reservation.

Chapter Sixteen
Escape

"Only one security guard had been posted on the first floor," Gabriel explained, "and he was preoccupied at the elevator. Because the stairs were around the corner, the other naked escapee crept right out the front door without ever being noticed."

"They weren't both in the elevator?"

"Fortunately, not. One pushed the button as the other headed down the stairs. When they saw the elevator doors closing, the CIA operatives only assumed that they were both inside. You can imagine their surprise when they arrived at the first floor and found that the security guard had only apprehended one of them."

"Serves them right," I trumpeted. "I knew Craig would get away."

"Did you now? What makes you so sure that Craig was the one that got away?"

"Well, it *was* Craig. Wasn't it?"

Gabriel raised his eyebrows and shrugged one shoulder.

Finding refuge behind a dumpster in an alley, the naked fugitive collapsed in a heap. In the adrenaline of the moment he didn't realised that he'd been shot. Fortunately, the bullet that hit his shoulder passed right through. Still, he'd lost quite a bit of blood. Clearly, he needed medical attention but he couldn't risk being recognised at the hospital. Aesculapius would have to wait. The injured man was able to slow the bleeding by applying pressure to the wound with some rags he'd appropriated from an abandoned shopping cart. After covering himself with some filthy clothes from the dumpster, the exhausted outlaw curled up under a cardboard box and passed out.

When he regained consciousness several hours later, he felt extremely disoriented. The man's thoughts and emotions were all scrambled and discombobulated. As he tried to assemble the broken memories and flashbacks together, certain information stood out as linear and coherent—he knew it just as if it he'd read it in a book only better, sharper and clearer. The disoriented man could speak any language, he possessed detailed knowledge of places he'd never been before and he knew all the dirty secrets of the Pentagon.

I waited impatiently for Gabriel to reveal his identity. "Who was he, Gabriel?"

"Initially, he thought that he was Craig Ryan. But slowly, as he began to remember more, it dawned upon him that he must be the clone."

"The clone? I don't even want to hear the rest," I objected, throwing my hands up in aggravation. "What kind of story is this?"

"It's a very *important* story," Gabriel asserted, "and perhaps it wouldn't take so long without so many interruptions?"

I gritted my teeth, but remained silent.

Once the clone assembled the befuddled memories and emotions into a somewhat cognisant and lucid continuum, he still needed to come to terms with the fact that these recollections were not his own—they were the chemical and intra-amygdaloidal synapses of another man. It also dawned upon him that, strangely, he didn't even have a name. What he did have was an intense longing for Graziella, and his heart ached for her even though he fully appreciated the fact that she was in love with someone else.

The clone called to mind how Graziella used to teasingly call Craig 'Lord Seth' and how Craig used to lovingly refer to Graziella as his 'iris flower'. Graziella liked this. In ancient Egypt, the pleasing and aromatic iris flower used to be placed at the entrance to the most sacred temples. The priests offered it to the gods as a symbol of love and worship. It was a symbol of Craig's love for Graziella as well.

The clone decided to call himself Seth. On the one hand, he felt a little guilty about taking Graziella's pet name for Craig. But on the other hand, something just seemed right about it, and he didn't think Graziella would mind. After all, when it was all said and done, Graziella was his only concern. He obviously felt a strong connection to Craig, but he also felt a measure of jealousy and a certain sense of competition.

There was no time to dwell on all that now. Finding Graziella was his only reason for living. Seth knew that when the time came, he would have to give Graziella up. But for the moment, he needed to find out what happened to the two of them. So, he made his way to the D.C. Public Library.

"You never told me what happened to Craig?"

"Well," Gabriel imparted apologetically, "one got out and the other didn't."

"But what *happened* to him?"

"He didn't make it," Gabriel broke the news gently.

"Oh my God, Gabriel! Does Seth know that?"

"No." Gabriel shook his head. "Seth didn't see what happened because the stairs were around the corner from the elevator."

Seth didn't have a library card or any ID for that matter, but the librarian let him use the computer as she judged from his appearance that he must be homeless. She was accustomed to homeless people passing their time in the library and she saw no harm in allowing them to do so. After the librarian helped Seth log on to the computer, he searched the web for news about the incident at the Pentagon. Oddly, Seth couldn't find any information about the alleged attack anywhere on the internet. He reasoned that the feds must have censored the affair for some reason, and he realised he'd have to hack into the mainframe to find them.

This wasn't a problem, however, as all of the IT records up through the time of the incident were stored in Seth's head. Even though he didn't know where Craig or Graziella were, he could find out because he knew all the passwords which allowed him access if need be from any remote location. But once inside the Pentagon's database, Seth still couldn't locate any information on Craig at all. He took this as a sign that Craig had gotten away, or surely there would be some record of him.

Upon learning of Graziella's arrest, Seth scavenged for clues as to where the authorities might be keeping her. The intelligence in Seth's head suggested that Graziella was most likely being held at a safe house somewhere.

"If it costs me my life," Seth vowed, "I'll never allow any thing to happen to Graziella."

He knew the locations of all the CIA safe houses. But even if Graziella were in a safe house, there were too many to even begin to guess which one it might be. So, Seth tried to sniff out her scent in the mainframe.

"Come on, where are you," Seth stroked the data as he skimmed over hundreds of pages of newly uploaded reports. "Someone must have left a paper trail." Then he traced Graziella to a report that Agent Schriver filed electronically from Taranto immediately following her interrogation. "Bingo!" he exclaimed.

The report indicated that Schriver had taken Graziella to a safe house in DC. Logging out of the Pentagon's mainframe, he left the library and walked the 2.2 miles to Schriver's home in Columbia Heights.

Chapter Seventeen
Schriver

A little past six-thirty am on Friday morning, Seth watched as a maroon Audi pulled into the driveway and parked in the garage. When Schriver entered his home through the back door, he was carrying a brief case and jingling his car keys. Seth loitered behind the garage for a minute and then quietly followed him into the house.

Schriver set the brief case down on the floor and dropped his keys on the kitchen table. He unbuckled his shoulder harness, and laid his sidearm and badge on the table as well. Shuffling through junk mail, Schriver pulled a Heineken out of the fridge and went into the other room.

When he heard the shower, Seth grabbed the brief case and disappeared into the bedroom. After grabbing a pair of socks and some underwear from Schriver's top dresser drawer, Seth quickly rifled through the closet and selected a suit coat, pants, shirt, tie, and some shoes. He couldn't get through airport security posing as a federal agent if he was dressed like a homeless person.

Collecting Schriver's sidearm and car keys on his way out, Seth went downtown to withdraw some cash and have his passport photo taken at a Kinkos. With passport photos in hand, Seth borrowed an Exacto blade and a glue stick from the attendant on duty (who was preoccupied with a jammed Xerox™ 4595). Then Seth went to work in the self-serve area. Moments later, he jumped back into Schriver's car and headed to the safe house.

Pulling into the driveway, Seth found the front door locked and the lights out. Lunging around to the back of the house, he kicked in the back door and quickly searched the premises. He found a traumatised Graziella in the same room where Schriver had left her. She'd clearly been beaten. Bruises lined her arms and legs, and blood crusted around her nostrils.

When she saw Seth, Graziella thought he was Craig. "Baby?" The word barely escaped her throat—parched from screaming.

Graziella sobbed violently as she huddled her arms and legs together, desperately attempting to conceal her violated body. Seth rushed to her side. Pulling off his suit coat, he wrapped it around her and held her close. Graziella frantically latched her arms around him and clutched his wounded shoulder. Seth winced in pain.

"You're hurt?" she distressed.

"I'm fine," he assured her as he rocked her in his arms. "It's just a scratch."

Graziella couldn't even bring herself to face him. Her eyes were filled with humiliation and shame. "Could you ever still love me?" she pleaded and started wailing all over again.

"Shhh…shhh…" Seth held her tighter. "It's alright. It's gonna be alright." Then he put his hands on her face and looked her deep in the eyes. "I could *never* stop loving you."

A vehicle pulled up to the safe house.

"They're back!" Graziella panicked. "Oh my God, they're coming back!"

Two other agents who also planned to take their liberty with Graziella returned from the airport. As the two men plodded from the car toward the safe house, Graziella and Seth scrambled for somewhere to hide. Taking refuge in the darkness, they slipped out the back door and slowly made their way around to the front.

The two agents recognised Schriver's car and expected him to be in the back room with Graziella. Their chattering and laughter ended abruptly when they realised that the house was empty. The sound of Schriver's Audi broke the silence as they frantically darted for the front door.

Chapter Eighteen
Fugitives

Seth quickly negotiated the city streets toward the highway.

"Where are we going?" Graziella screamed over the top of blaring car horns as Seth blew through a stop light at a busy intersection.

"Lebanon," he responded calmly. "Hold on!" Seth jumped the median, pulled a U-turn and just barely missed a motorcycle as he entered the on ramp.

"What's in Lebanon?" Graziella managed to ask while simultaneously working the passenger brake.

"I know a place that's safe."

They were headed to a long-abandoned safe house located in Beirut. Once a CIA haven, few agents even knew about it anymore.

As the two outlaws raced to the airport, Graziella studied her hero as he manoeuvred the speeding vehicle through the DC traffic. His eyes reflected Craig's confidence, kindness, and wit. But something was different somehow. There was a distance between them now.

At the airport, Seth pulled into the parking garage. Reaching into Schriver's briefcase, he produced a pair of handcuffs and clasped them onto Graziella's wrists.

"Is that too tight?"

As the two made eye contact, the chemistry between them was undeniable.

"No, it's fine," Graziella replied, averting her eyes away somewhat awkwardly. The distance had returned, and they both felt it.

The two ran into the airport and dashed to the first ticket counter they saw.

"I need two tickets on the earliest flight to Beirut." Seth flashed Schriver's identification. "This woman is in my custody."

Observing the handcuffs on Graziella's wrists, the ticketing agent entered the destination into her computer and stared at the screen for a moment.

"You're in luck," she disclosed. "There's a flight to Beirut leaving in twenty minutes. It's already boarded, but you can still just make it. The flight stops in Conakry and Cotonou."

Seth and Graziella glanced at one another covertly—each thinking of Mathieu. Seth charged the fares to Schriver's credit card and the airline employee printed their boarding passes.

"Gate seventeen," she directed.

"Call the gate and tell them to wait," Seth called back as they hasted away.

Approaching security, Seth saw the police canvassing the airport. He quickly marched Graziella to the front of the line. Inspecting Schriver's badge, the attendant waived them through. They found their gate and Seth escorted Graziella onto the plane. Just moments after they took their seats, the aircraft was taxiing down the runway. By the time the police managed to track Seth and Graziella to their flight, it had already taken off.

Entirely overcome, Graziella exacted an explanation from Seth. "Why are those people looking for you? What's going on, Craig?"

Graziella tried to maintain a cool exterior, but Seth could see that her eyes were filled with pain and uncertainty. Graziella's demands were more a desperate plea for help than anything.

"This is going to be difficult to understand," Seth began. And then he proceeded to explain everything to Graziella.

"So, you're a *clone*?" The concept was too much for her to wrap her brain around.

"What about Craig?"

"He's most likely in Cotonou at this very moment searching the internet for some clue as to where you might be."

Seth assumed that Craig would seek asylum in Benin. He was also counting on the fact that he and Graziella would be able to stay at the forgotten location for an indefinite period of time while they conducted their search for Craig. Seth wanted to get a message to Craig, but he didn't want the CIA to intercept it.

Graziella focused her eyes back on Seth. Searching for some reassurance, she appealed to him, "Are we really going to find Craig?"

"I promise you," Seth vowed to Graziella. "I *promise* you that I will find Craig even if it's the last thing I do. But right now, I need to find a computer."

Graziella rose to the occasion. She fixed her stare upon the man sitting across the row. He was a thin man who'd been admiring her since she first stepped onto the plane. Graziella sized him up in seconds.

"Excuse me," Graziella flirted with the man, "may I *please* borrow your laptop?"

"I'm sorry," the man resisted pitiably, "but I really need to get some work done."

"Please?" Graziella frowned coyly. "It'll just be for a minute."

The thin man's foray was pointless. He didn't have the wherewithal to resist her.

"Well," he caved, "I suppose I could take a *short* break."

Seth smiled as he looked on. He watched with amazement as Graziella emerged from deep within herself, bursting forth like a delicate butterfly spreading her wings for the very first time. Seth fell smitten with her more now than ever.

Chapter Nineteen
The Power of Love

"This is emotionally confusing, Gabriel. On the one hand, I'm pulling for Craig. I mean, he *is* her husband and he loves Graziella so much."

"But?" Gabriel presupposed.

"But on the other hand," I sighed, "I can't help but feel for Seth. He loves Graziella as well."

Gabriel shared my assessment. "The circumstances surrounding human affection are almost always complicated and confusing, but true love provides clarity like nothing else in the world. When two people *truly* love each other, it's powerful—much more powerful than either of them realises."

"How powerful?"

"Powerful enough to change the universe," Gabriel winked. "It's the closest thing to a miracle that I've ever seen, but it's also extremely rare."

"Why didn't Seth just tell Graziella how he felt about her?"

"Graziella loved Craig. And her marriage to Craig meant everything to her—especially after this encounter."

"You make Seth sound so noble," I noted with admiration.

"Seth's love for Graziella was *very* noble. He respected the sanctity of the vows Craig and Graziella made to one another, and he placed their relationship above his own feelings."

"That must have been hard."

"I imagine it was," Gabriel agreed. "Fortunately, Seth was distracted by more immediate matters."

"Like finding Craig?"

Gabriel shook his head. "He'd masterminded a scheme to contact Craig. It was a long shot, but it was their only option if they didn't want to risk the CIA intercepting the message."

Once he received the laptop, Seth hacked into the Pentagon's mainframe and located Schriver's file on Graziella. Pulling up Graziella's photo, he created a hidden link to a password-protected web page. Seth labelled the link 'Horus' and established the password as 'Seth'. He knew that Craig would immediately associate the two with Graziella but that few others would readily understand. Seth also knew that the CIA would be monitoring the web for any internet activity involving certain key words relating to the Ryan incident—especially the word 'Graziella'. So, in the Meta text to the web page (which is where search engines check for key words), Seth typed a phrase that only Graziella and Craig would know: 'iris flower'. Inside the hidden website, Seth provided the address of the abandoned safe house: 223 Seventh Street in Beirut, and he signed his communiqué 'Seth North'.

Seth reflected on Craig's pet name for Graziella. It fit her so well. Craig had obviously navigated the depths of her waters. He'd studied the weighty forces of her restless tides and strolled the moonlit stretches of her endless shores.

Seth lost himself in the wonder that was Graziella. In his mind's eye, he remembered how Craig used to wonder after her as well. Though he was always discovering some new facet of her personality, Craig never fully discerned the woman from the child. And now Seth couldn't help but feel the awful pain in Craig's heart—compelling him to find Graziella even beyond the horizon of death.

This image of Craig reaffirmed Seth's sacred mission: soon he'd relinquish Graziella to the arms of her true love. The very idea stirred the deepest sadness within him. Seth knew that Craig would never stop searching for Graziella, but he didn't want to take any chances. So, he carefully buried his message to Craig in the very last place the CIA would look—deep in the heart of its own mainframe. He didn't want to risk giving away Graziella's location to anyone but Craig. Seth was confident that Craig eventually would find the link. He just didn't know how long it would take.

When the plane landed at its first stop in Guinea, Seth was not at all surprised to see two air marshals waiting to board the plane. He fully expected the CIA to send operatives to intercept them. But to Seth's great surprise, the flight crew prepared the passengers for take-off and the plane left without incident.

"The CIA let them go?" I thrilled. At this point I was ready for a happy ending.

"Not exactly. The CIA decided that due to the sensitivity of the situation, it would be more prudent to arrange an accident rather than…"

"A bomb?" I interrupted.

"Oh, heavens no! The CIA would never do anything so obvious. It elected to sabotage the plane at its next stop in Cotonou. The plan was to cause the landing gear to malfunction upon landing in Beirut, but instead it failed to fully retract during take-off. So, the plane clipped a building when it departed from Cotonou. The CIA finally eliminated these two 'loose ends' once and for all. Or so it thought."

Chapter Twenty
Humble Beginnings

"We got another one over here," a rescue worker signalled.

"Is he alive?" an EMT questioned as he ran toward the motionless body.

"I don't know—maybe. I think he drowned."

"Let me see."

Rolling the floating remains over, "He's Caucasian!" The EMT remarked with astonishment, straddling the lifeless torso and pounding on its chest. After a few minutes, a gush of seawater spewed from the survivor's mouth and nostrils. "Let's get this one on a stretcher."

Having been resuscitated by the EMT at the crash site, the man remained totally unconscious after he was brought into the emergency room. He arrived at the hospital with twenty-two other survivors of a *Union des Transports Africains* flight that crashed on the southern coast of Benin.

"What happened?" the physician in charge demanded, completely overwhelmed by the onslaught of mangled survivors.

"A Boeing 727 went down just after it took off," one of the ambulance drivers informed her. "Nobody knows why. Most of the passengers were killed instantly. It's a mess! Bodies are strewn all along the beach and even more are drifting in the Atlantic. A bunch are still missing. We're gonna be out there all night."

"Well, I can't handle all this alone! My second physician isn't scheduled to be in for another hour." Calling for the charge nurse, the surgeon directed, "Get on the phone and get everyone in here!"

"Everyone?"

"*Everyone!*" she prompted. "Don't just stand there, a bloody plane just crashed! Let's go!"

Turning to an EMT who was busy wheeling in another body, the physician commanded, "Get on the phone and tell your supervisor to send every available body over here to help out—we need all the qualified personnel we can get right now."

Throwing her hands up in the air, the surgeon bellowed, "I need someone to coordinate triage."

A ward nurse who'd just arrived stepped forward. "I'm on it," he volunteered and began inspecting the survivors. After about an hour of severed limbs and gaping wounds, he reached the white man's gurney. "What do we have here?"

he mumbled as he pulled the sheet back to check his condition. "A Westerner! What are you doing in Cotonou?"

The ward nurse muttered routinely as he examined the patient. "His wounds are surprisingly minor. Skull fracture, damage to the right retina, left femur is broken and second-degree burns over most of his upper body. And what do we have here?" he observed curiously, contemplating a mysterious wound in the left shoulder. "The charred flesh makes it hard to determine what happened. Fortunately, whatever caused this passed right through."

"Alright, this one can wait," the nurse decided. "Get him out of the way. We have more urgent injuries to deal with."

Immersed in chaos, the emergency room buzzed with medical personnel clamouring to help meet the needs of the survivors. In the midst of the bedlam, the white stranger lay still on a gurney in an open ward with nine other victims.

The hospital administrator's name was Mathieu Ahomadegbe. A former Fulbright scholar just recently returned from his studies in America. Mathieu had earned both his M.D. and M.P.A. at Stanford University before returning to Benin to run the hospital in Cotonou.

As soon as Mathieu arrived at the hospital, the assistant administrator advised him that the authorities were already demanding a full report.

"Can't *you* handle that? I'm needed in ER." Mathieu murmured as he unlocked the door to his office. He quickly got on the phone and called the airline in order to get the necessary information for his report to the authorities.

"The plane originated in Prague," the airline spokesperson repeated mechanically. The incident created a media circus and she'd been providing the same information to reporters, regulators, and insurance people non-stop since the crash occurred. "It's a Lebanese aircraft…it made one stop in D.C. and another in Guinea before landing in Cotonou on its way to Beirut."

"What happened?" Mathieu asked rhetorically.

"We don't know. The two black boxes from the aircraft haven't been recovered yet."

"I'll need a copy of the passenger list."

"I'm faxing it to you now," she obliged. "How's it looking on your end?"

"On my end? It looks like a frigging plane crashed on my end. We haven't even begun to account for all the passengers. So far, the few who've survived are in critical condition. It's too early to say anything intelligent at this point."

Once Mathieu received the fax, he started a file and scrubbed up for ER.

Chapter Twenty-One
Suspicion

A few hours later, a Beninese government official arrived at the hospital—poking around and asking questions about the identity of the passengers on the aircraft. Mathieu stepped out of the ER to speak with him momentarily.

The official was a short, podgy man with greasy skin. "An American federal agent named Thomas Schriver was on the plane," the official probed. "Have you seen him?"

"At this point, we're just trying to save as many as we can," Mathieu reported. "We haven't had a chance to identify the survivors."

"I see," the bureaucrat clenched his jaw. "Be sure to inform me the minute you have something. The Americans are riding my ass on this."

"Of course," Mathieu consented. "Now if you'll excuse me, I have to get back to work."

After the first thirty-six hours, much of the pandemonium in the emergency room subsided. Suddenly, with a bitter and mournful tone, Seth screamed out in Fongbe, *"Ekpo kpede! Ekpo kpede! Noté! Noté!"* This means "Not yet! Not yet! Wait! Wait!"

Astounded by the outburst, Mathieu considered the anomaly. *Caucasians rarely speak Fon,* he reasoned to himself. *And when they do, it usually means one of two things: they're either a missionary or a spy.*

It hadn't escaped his attention that this may be the missing American agent. If he wasn't, then who was he? Mathieu began to take quite an interest in this Fon-speaking Caucasian, and he made regular visits to his bedside in one of the decrepit, crowded wards.

The country had only at best been a shaky democracy since the early 1990s. Most could still vividly remember the bloody repression of the PRPB: Kérékou's Marxist regime that dominated Benin in the 1970s and 1980s. Horror and violence riddled the tiny African nation and left a legacy of fear and distrust in its wake. By and large, the locals were still extremely suspicious of outsiders—particularly white outsiders. And the government showed little toleration for uninvited guests.

Protocol required that Mathieu alert the authorities when any unidentified persons turned up in the hospital. Harbouring undocumented strangers was strictly forbidden, but this was no ordinary white stranger…he spoke Fon and this intrigued Mathieu considerably. With no identification and no one to come forward to claim him, he remained unexplainable. Mathieu chose not to contact the authorities in this instance—a move that could have cost him his job and quite possibly his freedom.

For the next several weeks, the foreigner's unconscious screaming intensified and he always screamed in Fongbe. Most times he wailed the same thing, *"Ekpo kpede! Ekpo kpede! Noté! Noté!"* At times he also shrieked, *"Bo yi!"* which means "Get out of here!" But he never uttered a single word in English.

Chapter Twenty-Two
Where Am I?

As Gabriel droned on about Benin and the hospital in Cotonou, I was daydreaming about my love's eyes: deep, oval portals so full of light that they sparkled. It was then that I made a startling discovery: my love's eyes weren't as full of light as I thought they were. Something was reflecting in them. It was bright and beautiful like the sun, except it moved back and forth from one eye to the other.

While I tried to figure out what it might be, Gabriel casually slipped in, "Your heart's desire is beautiful beyond description. She's truly a gift from heaven."

"You've seen her?" I thrilled.

"As a matter of fact, I have. But I didn't need to see her to know how beautiful she is—I can see how very much you love her."

Now that caught my attention. "Where does love come from, Gabriel?"

I was still trying to conjure up a face and body to go with my beloved's eyes when Gabriel added, "Love doesn't *come* from anywhere. It's the infinite source of all things, and it's your love that allows you to see true beauty in the first place."

I lost myself for a moment in the possibilities...and the paradox. Gabriel continued the story as I listened with consummate fascination—not realising that my years of care and worry were being wiped away with each passing sentence.

For three weeks after the stranger arrived, he remained unconscious in the dingy, crowded ward. The foul odour of faeces and sweat, masked by antiseptic, hovered in the air. A Kenyan nurse's aide named Wafa was busy attending to the patients' daily hygiene and changing their bedding when suddenly the man gasped and awakened.

"Where am I?" He demanded in a spate of episodic consciousness.

Startled by his sudden awakening, Wafa backed away from the bed. "Nurse! Nurse!" she called out in a thick Swahili accent, frightened because she didn't understand what the foreigner had said.

Thinking a patient was expiring, the ward nurse came running. "What is it?" she questioned apprehensively.

Wafa pointed at the stranger.

"Where am I?" He insisted again.

Realising that he was speaking English, the nurse motioned with her hands, "Quick Wafa! Go get Dr Ahomadegbe."

Mathieu was the only other one in the hospital who spoke English, and he had been waiting three weeks to speak with the outsider. Brimming with questions, mostly he wanted to know how this white man learned to speak Fongbe.

Upon entering the ward, Mathieu approached the bed. Bandaged from head to waste, the patient reclined with his left leg elevated and in a caste.

"A se glensigbe we a?" Mathieu asked him in Fongbe. This translates roughly as "Do you speak English?"

"Yes," he responded.

"A se Fongbe a?" which means, "Do you speak Fon?" Mathieu intended to wait before asking this question, but the temptation got the better of him.

"No."

Speaking in English, Mathieu asked, "What's your name?"

"I don't kn…I don't remember," the patient asserted—his eyes revealing that he'd only just realised this himself. Suddenly, a flood of confusion swept over the man and a slew of questions stormed his brain at once: "Where am I? Who are you? What's happened to me?" The stranger became more agitated with each question, and he made a pathetic attempt to sit up by leaning his weight on his right arm.

"Hold on now," Mathieu said softly in an effort to appease the stranger. "There will be plenty of time for all of that. Just calm down now, all right? Just calm down."

The fact that the foreigner understood Fon but continued to speak only in English intrigued Mathieu.

"Poly vu Français?" Mathieu asked for no reason in particular.

"No," the patient replied quietly as he turned his head in utter despair.

He stared at the half-person lying on the gurney next to him. Missing both of her legs and half of her right arm, what flesh she still retained had been burned so badly you could barely recognise her as human.

The man hadn't even thought to check his own condition. A rush of pure adrenaline surged through his very core. Again, he toiled to sit up. Reaching to feel his legs, he discovered his own bandaged torso.

"Oh my God! Give me a mirror!" He screamed in horror. "What happened to me?"

This time Mathieu spoke with a distinct sternness in his voice that hadn't been there before, and he spoke in English so that no one else would understand him.

"You're in Cotonou. You've survived a terrible plane crash, and you're lucky to be alive. You've no identification and no one has come forth to claim you. If I cannot discover the truth of your identity, I'll be forced to report you to the government. You do *not* want me to do that. Do you understand?"

Struck by both the harsh tone of Mathieu's voice and the dire meaning of his words, the stranger cast his eyes upon Mathieu in shock and amazement.

"Do you understand?" Mathieu pressed.

"Yes," he answered obediently.

"Good." Mathieu's voice reverted back to its quiet, reassuring tone. "Now, can you tell me what happened to your shoulder?"

Chapter Twenty-Three
A Name for the Authorities

By the time the stranger fully regained consciousness, he spoke only in English and claimed to remember nothing of his past. At first, Mathieu thought this might be a charade—nothing more than a deliberate attempt on the part of the foreigner to conceal his true identity. He found it very difficult not to be suspicious. In fact, even though he was the wrong height to be Agent Schriver, Mathieu strongly considered the possibility that this white visitor might be some sort of an agent or a spy.

As the days passed, however, Mathieu became convinced that the newcomer truly did suffer from amnesia. Even given the tremendous risk that Mathieu took by not immediately reporting him to the authorities, he believed he'd made the right decision. So, Mathieu committed himself to learning more about his guest. He wanted to learn the true identity of this Fon-speaking white man. Also, Mathieu knew what the authorities did to illegal aliens upon learning of their presence in Cotonou. He'd seen first-hand the corpses of those who'd been interrogated by the government.

The day the doctor removed the white man's bandages, Mathieu could hardly wait to see him. That evening before he went home, Mathieu slipped into the ward. As he stepped through the door, his countenance changed from excitement to utter shock.

"What is it? The scars are bad, huh?"

"Oh, it's nothing, my friend," Mathieu pretended as he beheld the face of the stranger. Visibly moved and choking back his emotions, he added, "You're healing well! The scars will be gone in no time. I'm just so happy to see that you're alright."

A week later, the man's memory was no better than it had been on the first day that he opened his eyes. Lying in bed one afternoon, he had the strangest experience: in his mind's eye he watched as a pale hand reached for a veil of some sort. Just then, Mathieu walked in.

"The doctors are planning to release you in the next few days. Soon you'll be discharged from the hospital. Can't you tell me *anything* about yourself?"

The stranger held his hand to his mouth. Rubbing his dry knuckles with his thumb, he contemplated the mystery of his existence. "*Honestly,* I can't remember anything," he insisted—half fearing that Mathieu didn't believe him.

"Well, you'd better come up with a name for yourself. You'll need one for the discharge papers if you don't want to attract the attention of the authorities."

"Yeah, you're right." He rubbed his temples and let his mouth hang open as though the very thought of being discharged gave him a headache. "I hadn't even thought about that."

The patient closed his eyes and escaped to a place in the back of his brain. He didn't know what it was, but it was dark and comfortable and familiar—like it had always been there. After a minute or so, his eyes opened mechanically like one of those ventriloquist dolls and he beamed, "How about Seth?"

When Mathieu heard the name, his eyes lit up. "Whatever made you think of that?"

"I don't know. It just popped into my head."

Mathieu smiled and chuckled to himself, *perhaps you remember more than you think.*

Over the next couple of days, Seth racked his brain trying to remember his true identity and what might have brought him to Cotonou in the first place.

"I believe that you probably don't have any business in Benin at all," Mathieu speculated. "Most likely you were just passing through from some other place. Yes? Besides, who could *you* possibly know in Cotonou? Hmm?"

In their daily conversations, Mathieu regularly asked Seth a variety of questions hoping to trigger his memory. Every response presented the same scenario: Seth remembered nothing of his own past. But when asked specific questions regarding virtually anything else, he knew a lot—usually more than Mathieu himself. Mathieu soon discovered that in addition to Cotonou, Seth also possessed extensive knowledge about Benin and the broader region of West Africa.

The past remained a complete blur. Seth's entire life remained elusive. Sometimes he thought he could remember having a mother, but Seth couldn't remember what she looked like or anything about her. Seth possessed no other coherent memory prior to waking up in that squalid hospital in Cotonou.

Chapter Twenty-Four
A Sad Goodbye

After his release from the hospital, Seth stayed with Mathieu and Bangoura.

"You're always welcome in our home, my friend. However, this arrangement places the three of us in great jeopardy. If the authorities discover that you're here, they'll arrest us all. So, we have to stay alert for opportunities to move you to a safer place as quickly as possible."

Shortly after taking Seth in, Mathieu arranged to have him meet with Ed Herrington, the Fulbright representative there in Cotonou. Mathieu knew Ed well and trusted him unquestionably—Ed had helped Mathieu receive his own Fulbright scholarship several years earlier. Reasoning that this may be the safest way to get Seth out of the country, Mathieu wasted no time in setting up the appointment.

After the interview with Ed, Mathieu lingered behind as Seth crawled into the back of a cab. "So, how did our friend fare?"

Ed shook his head as he lit a cigarette. "I've never seen anything like it. I'm definitely going to write a letter of recommendation. I'll be in touch. You can count on that."

"That's very good news!" Mathieu delighted. "Thank you! Thank you so very much."

After shaking Ed's hand and thanking him again, Mathieu joined Seth in the cab and the two left.

"Fortunately, I also know the American Foreign Service Officer here in Benin. I once helped him with a delicate matter. He owes me a substantial favour."

So, Mathieu called in his favour and obtained an American passport and social security card for Seth.

Examining the passport with curiosity, Seth read the name out loud. "Seth North. How'd you come up with the last name?"

"*You* came up with it," Mathieu countered. "That's the name you wrote on your discharge papers. Don't you remember?"

"No. I must have forgotten." Seth dismissed, flipping through the blank pages and fantasising about travelling to exotic destinations.

With Ed's help and a generous scholarship from Fulbright, Seth also secured admission for the spring term at a prestigious university in New England. Before he knew it, Seth was on his way to America.

At the airport, Seth hugged Mathieu and Bangoura good-bye. "Thank you both so much for your help," he acknowledged gratefully. "I'll never forget you."

The solemnity of the moment was interrupted by giggles as Seth and Mathieu broke into laughter.

"What's so funny?" Bangoura puzzled quizzically.

"The amnesiac will never forget us!" Mathieu translated.

"Aww," Bangoura smiled as she reached her hand around Seth's neck and kissed him on the cheek. "*E na ce nu we,*" she whispered, which means, "God bless you."

As Seth walked away, Mathieu called after him, "*Hwetenu a na leko do Benin?*" ("When are you going to come back to Benin?").

Seth stopped. Shaking his head sadly, he sighed, "I don't know." As their eyes met, the finality of goodbye pierced Mathieu's heart. A great emptiness expanded deep within him as he watched Seth walk away. Bangoura squeezed his hand gently.

Chapter Twenty-Five
Four Years Later

Once in New England, Seth's brilliance went unnoticed. He kept to himself and excelled just enough to maintain his Fulbright scholarship. Being an older, non-traditional student, no one thought it very odd that he distanced himself from campus life. Seth's interests were simple: dwelling on his past and wondering how he'd arrived at this particular place in his life.

Four years had passed since Seth first arrived in New England. It was now March 17, 2003, and on that particular morning, Seth woke up to an uncertain future. It had been three days since he took his comprehensive exams, and it would still be a few weeks before he defended his dissertation. But what would he do after that?

He'd completed his PhD in Biosciences with almost no trouble at all. Like so many other things in his life, Seth sensed a mysterious cognisance about it—almost as if he'd studied it all before. One would think that this might have afforded him a distinct advantage over his colleagues. But Seth was lost. He was lost and alone.

"You know what your problem is?" Seth chastised himself as he stared in the mirror. "You've never made any decisions on your own."

Talk about hitting the nail on the head. Ever since that fateful day when he woke up in the hospital in Cotonou, every course of action in Seth's life had been more-or-less laid out for him. He simply went with the flow.

"You've spent the past four years deliberately ignoring any concept of the future," he admonished his mirror image. "But what are you going to do now?"

Patting his face dry with a towel, Seth wandered out of the bathroom and stretch out on his bed. He stared at the ceiling and contemplated what in the world he would do next. With the exception of a few random trips to the kitchen and the bathroom, Seth spent the entire day in his bedroom doing absolutely nothing. As evening cast its shadow, Seth closed his eyes in passive acceptance of the inevitable.

The Monsoon rains eased the West African heat and the evening breeze gently whispered the nocturnal secrets of bliss. But Seth couldn't sleep. As he lies awake listening to the downpour, his mind drifted off. Seth envisioned a picturesque, young lady with flowing long hair and a wonderfully soothing voice. She whispered something to him, but he couldn't make it out. No matter how intently Seth tried to listen and read her lips, he just couldn't comprehend what she said—her words were too faint. Seth's head felt like it would explode he concentrated so hard, and the young woman's eyes signalled the utmost urgency. But before Seth could understand, he woke up.

Sitting straight up in his bed, Seth struggled to catch his breath. He'd been having this same dream almost every night since he arrived in the U.S. But Seth only retained consciousness of the dream for a split second before falling back to sleep. He always dreamed the same thing: As he reclined on the couch in Mathieu's living room, a comfortable breeze blew through the open window. The sound of the monsoon rains on the roof were hypnotic and soothing. Then the mysterious woman appeared. She whispered something—something urgent. But Seth always woke up before he could make out what she said. How maddening! Fortunately for Seth, he never agonised for long. He always fell right back to sleep and forgot the dream by the time he woke up again the next morning. This night was no exception.

Chapter Twenty-Six
The First Memory

Seth passed the entire next day doing absolutely nothing. He was thoroughly institutionalised. As long as there were classes to attend and deadlines to meet, Seth could function just fine. But now that classes were over, he was clueless as to what to do with his time. While Seth was cognisant of his need for some kind of a game plan for the future, he honestly just didn't care enough to make any effort whatsoever. He reasoned that either way, the future was coming—with or without his participation and consent.

The digital clock on his computer displayed only four-eleven p.m. But already, Seth felt completely worn out. It wasn't long before Seth felt the cold blade of emotional evisceration returning to disembowel his will to live. The acute, dull aching gnawed at him like an intense craving but with no appetite. Seth gave in to the apathy as he had so many times before. Staring at the ceiling, he collapsed from chronic mental and emotional exhaustion.

In a surreal escape that he subconsciously waited for every day, Seth found his way back to Mathieu and Bangoura's sofa. He felt at peace and at home there. The comforting breeze blew across his body as he listened to the torrent descending from the sky. But the enchanting damsel in distress didn't appear this evening.

In his dream, Seth left the sofa. He walked into the bedroom and watched as Mathieu and Bangoura embraced one another. In the dim light of evening, Seth could just barely distinguish one from the other. Mathieu's tall, lean frame accentuated his muscles. His chocolate-brown skin paled in comparison to Bangoura's espresso-black hue, and Mathieu's nearly shaven head teemed with closely cropped, grey hairs. Bangoura's voluptuous body fit Mathieu's perfectly, and her natural black hair sprouted in short, kinky spirals. Bangoura's soft face matched her intelligent, caring eyes.

The couple didn't notice the voyeur in their room. Mathieu held Bangoura in one arm while she rested her head on his chest. She smiled sleepily and enjoyed Mathieu's long, slow caresses and tender kisses. Suddenly, Seth felt a hand on his shoulder. Turning around, he saw the captivating young woman from his dream.

"Did you find him yet?"

Immediately, Seth was transported to the crash site. Carnage lurked in the horizon. Black smoke, hideous screaming and the smell of burning flesh permeated the landscape. Corpses and body parts were strewn about everywhere as were incendiary hunks of metal and debris from the disintegrated aircraft. Badly burned and bleeding, Seth couldn't see out of his right eye. He strained to make sense of the writhing and pain that clouded his field of vision. Squint-eyed and sidelong, he combed the blazing beach until he spotted the elusive maiden lying on the shore with the waves crashing over her. Seth strove to go to her, dragging his broken leg through the burning sand. When he finally reached her, he could see that she was bleeding from her abdomen and on the verge of death.

Whispering faintly and peering straight into his eyes, she summoned the strength to speak his name, "Seth."

Covered in sweat and desperately groping to find the light, Seth's thoughts were erratic. They didn't make any sense, and they were racing faster than he could keep up with them. Seth didn't realise it of course, but this was the longest he'd ever retained any memory of the reoccurring dream. The bearing and manner of the intriguing stranger that haunted his subconscious mind had never permanently burned into his conscious memory before…not until tonight. As he inhaled the memory of his mysterious acquaintance like the scent of fragrant nard, a remarkable sense of familiarity washed over him.

"I don't know how, but she knew my name! Could this be my *real* name? Am I really Seth North?"

Clenching his hair with his fists, he half wanted to yank a handful of it out. *I can't remember even being on that plane!*

Dropping to his knees, he collapsed into a prostrate position and pressed his face deep into the carpet. "Oh God!" he screamed. "Who am I?"

Chapter Twenty-Seven
The Secret Link

Seth awoke around midnight in the same prostrate position on the floor.

"My head is pounding!" he groaned as he rubbed his neck. Seth's barbed facial hair cast a red-speckled shadow across his face. "Geeze that itches," he complained, frantically clawing at his chin. Seth staggered as he made his way to his computer.

He Googled his name only to retrieve a number of hits that meant absolutely nothing to him. Then he searched just his first name and found a web page explaining that Seth is the Egyptian god of chaos, storms, and foreign lands.

Thought to rule over foreigners and particularly people with red hair, Seth reigned from the north: the realm of darkness, cold, and death. His brother Horus…

"Seth has a brother?"

Typing the name Horus, a number of hits turned up in the search. Seth clicked through them randomly. He'd nearly lost interest when he came across the phrase 'iris flower'. He didn't know why, but he felt a strange tugging at his heart. When he clicked on the link, it opened to reveal a photo of the most intoxicating woman Seth had ever seen. He instantly recognised her as the woman in his dream. Racing out of control, Seth's heart felt like it would explode.

Staring at the photo for what seemed like hours, it suddenly occurred to him to save it so that he would always have it. As Seth moved the mouse over the picture, the word 'Horus' appeared. Curious, he clicked on it. A text box popped up requesting a password. Seth stared at it for a minute. Taking a wild guess, he typed in 'Seth'.

As soon as he pushed the enter key, a flood of data came streaming in. Hundreds and hundreds of pages containing calculations, dates, figures, and prophecies opened up before his eyes. Much of the information came from ancient texts: writings long since lost to the world.

Since angel DNA is comprised of both pairs of chromosomes, an interesting phenomenon appeared in the interspecies breed. When the rebel angels impregnated human women, they bequeathed their progeny with a full pair of chromosomes rather than just one as humans do. The resulting embryos possessed three sex chromosomes instead of two. However, since the full pairs of angelic DNAs didn't separate, the sex of the child was determined by whether the angel imparted an XX pair or an XY pair. The single X chromosome supplied by the human mother proved superfluous. For the male offspring, the additional

X chromosome contributed to extraordinary size, strength, intellect, creativity, and ingenuity. The most brilliant generals, artists, composers, and thinkers in earth's history are the derivatives of this gene pool. For the females, however, the additional X chromosome produced immeasurable beauty.

"What *is* this?" he wondered in amazement. Seth spent the next several hours poring over archaic prophecies describing a fierce future uprising in which the great king would finally be overthrown. Sifting through intricate battle plans for laying siege to the kingdom, he stared in curious wonder at blueprints that revealed the construction and location of a massive tower reaching all the way to the stars.

"The Tower of Babel?" he couldn't believe what he was reading. "Can this be real?"

Seth discovered detailed genealogies extending all the way back to the toppled angels. Chronological records indicated the names, births, and deaths of every ruler since the beginning of the world along with the histories of the most prominent ancient empires:

Egypt, Babylon, Media-Persia, Greece, and Rome...all of them were governed by descendants of the transgressors. Every one of these vast empires amassed immeasurable wealth and enslaved entire human populations with the single goal of building another tower that would reach to the gates of heaven.

"They wanted to build another tower?"

Seth stared at a sketch of a massive structure that disappeared into the clouds. Tiny figures that looked like winged humans were climbing up it. Seth clicked on the image to enlarge it.

"The Tower of Babel?" I demanded—the tone of my voice a mixture of scepticism and cynicism.

"I fought beside Michael in the Great War," Gabriel mourned in a tone much too sincere to scoff at. "An insurrection beyond description. No human words capture the abomination of that terrible tragedy. No mortal construct evokes the wasting desolation that followed. The carnage was just too great."

"My God, Gabriel! The war in heaven was real?" My question was more of an apology of sorts. "I had no idea. I always assumed it was just a metaphor for sin or something..." Fortunately, my voice possessed the good sense to trail off before my foot made it all the way to my large intestines.

"The war was more real than you can ever imagine," Gabriel assured me. "And yet at times, it still seems so unreal." A deep sadness scarred his countenance. It struck me as kind of odd, but I guess angels get sad like anyone else.

"The scourge of war held no place in our vocabulary until then. At no time before did the savage slaughter of our brothers darken our thoughts—the opaque notion of death completely eluded us."

"So, you're saying that *war* literally broke out in *heaven*? How does something like that even happen?"

"It's difficult to comprehend," Gabriel agreed, "and even more difficult to explain. I still haven't managed to fully wrap my own brain around it. Try to imagine an infinite number of celestial beings, majestic as whales and lofty as trees, living together in tranquil repose since before the universe began. Ours was a world beyond the dimension of time, and the Ancient of Days reigned eternal."

"It sounds wonderful."

"At once, our gentle peace ended when the rebels laid siege to the kingdom." The pain in Gabriel's voice was unmistakable.

"The rebels?" I gasped wide-eyed.

"The rebels," he repeated, swallowing back his tears. "But we're getting ahead of ourselves." Gabriel offered one of those reluctant expressions that people give when they're being gracious.

For anyone who's never seen an angel on the verge of tears before, it's awkward to say the least. But it also made me conscious of the fact that maybe angels and humans aren't that different after all.

Chapter Twenty-Eight
War in Heaven

A dark, foreboding hue collected on the horizon. Illuminated by great flashes of lightening in the distance, the ominous formation became visible through the morning midst. Then the ground started to quake as the thundering horde approached like a furious deluge. Billions advanced upon the capital with Lucifer in the lead.

The watchmen sounded the alarm, "Rebels at the perimeter! Secure the gates!"

As I looked out over the sea of rabid angels, a throng so vast and angry, my knees gave way like water beneath my weight. High above, the dawn revealed a scarlet sky just waiting to rain death down upon our heads.

Our attackers chanted in unison as they approached, "Sack the city! Take the throne!"

Lucifer further incited their lust for destruction. "Today we end the tyranny of the old order!" he shouted—his voice cutting through the blackness. "When I am king, you shall know true freedom!"

The mass applause advanced on the wind. Hurled at the city like colossal boulders, their war cry curdled my blood. Then a firm hand grasped my shoulder.

"Prince Michael," I saluted, standing at attention.

"At ease, Gabriel," Michael spoke softly. "Take courage, you still have much to do when this day has passed."

His message, and the mercy behind it, relieved my anxiety like a stay of execution. It also emboldened me to lay down my life for the King if necessary. With a gaze that penetrated my soul, Michael mounted his white stallion and trotted over to address our foremost column. Gripped with horror, they awaited his encouragement.

"This is a moment of great urgency," Michael exhorted. "The royal throne depends upon your loyalty and dedication. Outside these gates, our own brothers approach to attack us, but we must never let them near the city. Fight Valiantly! We ride at once!"

Michael himself led the counterattack. Gripping the reigns of his steed with one hand and waving his sword high in the gleaming radiance of the throne with the other, Michael issued the command: "Guardians of the eternal kingdom…warriors…faithful citizens of the celestial citadel…Attack!"

As we charged the approaching army, I served my King as second in command.

Breaching their forward line, I shouted, "Don't lose heart! Be courageous! Secure the victory! Pray for peace!"

Clouds of dust enveloped us as the clash of steel rang out among the hideous wails of the dying. Cold blades and hot anger waged merciless violence upon flesh and bone. The thick darkness obstructed our vision, but it was a blessing. For when the sky cast its angry glances, fearful bolts of lightning flashed over our heads revealing the debris of limbs and bodies everywhere—terrifying even the most courageous among us. The universe itself joined in the conflict. Decimating both royal forces and rebels alike, great hailstones pelted the battlefield and pockets of flames ignited about us. The cosmos convulsed and spasmed, and the very fabric of space appeared to be unravelling.

Stumbling over the dead and injured, our ranks pressed on. We attacked ferociously, but the fear and uncertainty in our eyes betrayed us. No one ever imagined this could happen.

Drawing his sword, Michael unleashed his fury on the insolent horde. "May the Lord God stretch out his mighty arm against the anger of our foes!"

When the last heretic in their forward line fell, the ruthless throng retreated—trampling the desecrated corpses of our brothers in the mud.

"Pursue them!" Michael commanded.

Our horses brayed and strained as we pushed them harder and faster to the farthest corners of the universe. By the end, many in our ranks were lost. The rest staggered in despair. Innumerable casualties littered the expanse as far as the eye could see and beyond.

Among the columns, I heard them wail, "Who is left? Who is left? Which of our brothers has survived the awful calamity of this crushing blow?"

Michael consoled their faltering courage. Riding among the formation, he spoke in sombre brevity. "The cost is overwhelming, and the forsaken are incalculable. We'll never forget the faithful we've lost this day. But you, devoted bulwarks of heaven, you have gallantly defended both the honour and the sovereignty of his Majesty on High." Raising his sword above his head, Michael rallied his battle-weary troops with the acclamation, "Champions of God Almighty, we return to our King victorious!"

Gabriel stared off into the distance for a moment—his thoughts lost in another place and time. Then he turned to me and smiled sadly, "The ensuing battle raged for over one thousand earth-years. Your world has seen its share of escalations over the millennia, but mankind has never witnessed anything of this magnitude. Even Earth's most horrific conflicts wane in comparison. The hundreds of trillions who perished in the Great War are several tens of thousands of times more than the total population of all who've ever lived upon the earth to this day."

"Hundreds of *trillions* were lost?" I stammered. "I can't even imagine such a number."

Of course, literally speaking, a hundred trillion is a one followed by fourteen zeros. But figuratively, it might as well have been a gazillion. Who can imagine so many casualties? The thought that such unthinkable violence took place *in heaven*—itself supposedly the very source of peace and love—left me without any frame of reference whatsoever. It literally turned everything else upside-down. The more I tried to make sense of it, the less anything made sense because of it.

As though he were reading my mind, Gabriel agreed and then elaborated upon my thoughts. "Even beyond the unfathomable death toll, what made the war in heaven so difficult to comprehend is that it threatened to change the destiny of all eternity…and it has. Before the Great War, none of us ever once entertained the possibility that the infinite order could be altered. But that's the peculiarity of free will: you can never truly know what another is going to choose. The Great War is the perfect example. Lucifer was once the most glorious of all the created ones. He commanded the highest position an angel could occupy. But still, it wasn't enough. Lucifer wanted the throne. That's why the war in heaven began in the first place—Michael defended what Lucifer attempted to take by force. And all throughout the earth's history as well, brother has risen up against brother: Cain and Abel, Isaac and Ishmael, Jacob and Esau…that legacy began in heaven with Lucifer."

Gabriel's revelation changed my entire perspective on reality. And this was only the beginning.

Chapter Twenty
Nine Fallen

After the insubordinate angels were driven out, they were destined to eventually grow old and die. Lucifer was no exception. Once the most illustrious creature in all the universe, his radiance began to vanish and he no longer shone with heaven's immaculate glory. His ivory wings were now soiled by sin and war, and his skin sagged from his bones with the weight of his guilt.

"Already, our power is diminishing significantly!" Lucifer seethed, his anger flaring like a supernova. Pounding his fists in outrage, he incinerated the massive stone table the council gathered around. The others cowered in fear. Despite his declining capacity, Lucifer was by no means powerless. And they'd all seen his anger flare up before.

Lucifer scowled with unholy discontent. "Without access to the holy city, our immortality will gradually fade as well. We have only one hope: either we ascend to heaven and take the kingdom or we'll all perish!"

Summoning his top advisors, Lucifer opened the floor to suggestions. When no one came forward with an idea, Lucifer cursed them vehemently, "I'll skin you all alive! Worthless! That's what you are—completely worthless!"

"We could construct a vast tower that reaches to the gates of the citadel," the chief engineer proposed timidly.

The dark prince cracked a scheming grin. "I like that. Anyone else?"

"Well, if we *were* to build such a tower," his chief astronomer cautioned, "it would be absolutely imperative to time our attack according to the earth's rotation around the sun. Otherwise, we may miss Orion altogether."

"Are there any other contingencies we need to consider?"

Lucifer searched the faces of his sulking subjects. When no one spoke up, Lucifer's eyes glowed with satisfaction.

"Very well, then. When the earth's rotation nears Orion, we'll ascend the tower and storm the gates. We'll lay siege to the city and this time we will *not* fail! Draw up the plans and get to work. I loathe this miserable planet."

When the others left, Lucifer sat alone, admiring the timeless locket that hung around his neck. It had been crafted by the King himself, and Lucifer twisted and turned it in his hand to take in its exquisite excellence.

Initially, the fallen angels were careful to conceal their existence from the inhabitants of the earth. Residing in the secluded mountains of what was later called Tibet, they drew up the blueprints to their tower and mapped out their strategy for the second assault. When the plans were drawn and the coordinates plotted, the council assembled before Lucifer.

"We're ready to begin construction," the chief architect reported.

"How long will it take to construct the tower?"

"Approximately three hundred and fifty earth-years, my lord. Roughly seven generations of slaves will be required to complete the task."

"And what of our alignment with Orion?" Lucifer pressed the chief astronomer, his tone exacting and forceful.

"In three hundred and fifty rotations, the earth should near Orion on the new moon following the spring equinox."

"Then all we have to do is make certain we finish the tower *and* allow ample time to ascend it prior to our window."

"But we have a much larger concern."

"What?" the tenebrous sovereign snapped pensively. This is not the sort of thing he wanted to hear. Lucifer was still licking his wounds over their great defeat in heaven. All he could think about was another stab at the throne—his lust for glory nearly drove him mad. In Lucifer's eyes, the small measure of success the rebels enjoyed so far was shallow enough already. He had no patience for added delay.

"The earth's rotation around the sun is just one factor to consider, my lord." The astronomer's voice quivered with hesitation. "The sun is also traveling around the galaxy. My calculations suggest that in three hundred and fifty earth-years, the planet will be on the very outside edge of Orion's astral plane."

"Explain yourself. How does this affect us?" Lucifer knew he couldn't very well discount critical information, but he also didn't want to entertain mere excuses.

"If we miss our window by even one day, the earth won't pass heaven's gate for another two hundred and thirty million years, assuming the planet survives that long."

"Then there's not a moment to waste!" Lucifer screeched. "Call the captain of the guard!"

When the captain appeared before him, Lucifer stipulated the urgency of the situation. "Enslave the nearby peoples and imprison them in forced labour camps in the valley. That's where we'll build—between the mountains. Move!"

Once outside, the captain of the guard assembled an elite team and charged the members with their mission. "Leave immediately. Attack the surrounding villages and bring back everything you find: people, animals, food…everything! I want you back within three earth-days."

Chapter Thirty
The Place of Remembrance

At the next council meeting, Lucifer was in better sprits. Construction of the tower progressed on schedule and all appeared to be in order.

"Brothers," he greeted the assembly, "at last we near our destiny. Soon we'll fulfil our purpose and storm the capital city once again. It's our right!" He pounded his fist in his open palm. "It's our inheritance!" He hammered both of his fists against his chest. "And it's our duty to topple the dictatorship and despotism that currently occupies the throne!"

At this point, Lucifer flung his head back and threw his arms up into the air like an enraged madman. Shouting at the sky, he appeared to be daring heaven itself to strike him dead. Meanwhile, the group of assembled angels cheered excitedly and applauded his sacrilegious defiance.

Lowering the intensity of his speech, Lucifer continued his address. "But we also need to plan ahead. We can never forget those we lost in the first battle. While our numbers are still strong enough to take the kingdom, we cannot afford to be decimated further."

The others solemnly shook their heads in agreement.

"What are you proposing?" asked one.

"Yes, what is it you plan to do?" queried another.

"We need a contingency plan for replenishing those among us. Somehow we must uncover the great tyrant's secret of creation."

"Creation?" they all mumbled and murmured under their breath. A great stirring arose among the wicked throng. Even among the leaders of the rebellion, none had dared to imagine such heresy.

"How would we do such a thing?" one prominent council member inquired.

"While we're infinitely superior to these filthy earthlings, there are similarities that we share with them as well. Dissect them, study them, and discover the most basic building blocks of their existence. Work quickly and report back to me as soon as you've learned something."

The council adjourned, and the fallen ones busied themselves with the task of studying the humans they'd enslaved. With demonic indifference to their victims' suffering, the rebel angels dissected thousands. Those once forced to labour without rest now served as human guinea pigs, and the labour camps echoed with the screams of living cadavers. Digging and clawing through intestines, organs, brain matter, and reproductive systems, the rebels eventually discovered both the secret of human procreation and the structure of human DNA.

At the next council meeting, Lucifer inquired, "So what have you learned? What can you tell me?"

"We've discovered much," one of the members answered. "The humans have the ability to procreate, my lord. We've seen how they do it, and we've engaged in this activity with them."

"Is it possible for humans to procreate with angels?"

"It *should* be possible, my lord. However, the human females take about three new moons to reveal that they're with child. It's been nearly four new moons since we first attempted to procreate with them, but none that have survived reveal any change as of yet."

"Cut to the chase! Do you know why?" Lucifer's tolerance for incompetence had plummeted to well below zero during his stay on the earth, and the angel risked lighting a very short fuse with his incomplete answers.

"Possibly. The other information we've collected concerns the basic physiological traits of the humans such as skin colour, eye colour, height, etc. All are determined by a nucleic acid that transmits a sequential code from the parents to the offspring. It's possible that the human females don't conceive by us because, having been created, we don't have such a code. Or..."

"Or what?"

"Or perhaps we do. But there's only one way that we know of to find out."

"Take him! Learn what you must."

The others seized their fellow councilmember and dragged him out of Lucifer's presence while he screamed for mercy, "Please, my lord! I beg you, please spare me!" But Lucifer ignored his pleas, staring instead at the mysterious inscription on the locket hanging around his neck.

As the angel begged for his life, a colleague cut him open with one of his long, sharp claws. The others pulled open his rib cage and removed everything, from his oesophagus to his colon, to dissect and study.

Holding the shrieking angel's heart, one of his fellows looked into his pleading eyes and laughed sadistically before yanking it out. Then the mob of malignant angels left him with his detached arteries gushing blood into the dirt. Staring in disbelief and horror at his own empty chest cavity, the mutilated angel suffered horribly.

As his life force ebbed away, he thought of his King and the timeless perfection of his life in the capital. He remembered the new moons and feast days when all the sons of God assembled before the throne on a majestic sea of glass. For the first time since before the rebellion, he recalled the joy of his innocence and found a temporary reprieve from his mental anguish. But then he relived the horror of the Great War.

Looking on as if a great, bloodless hand were removing his cloak of self-deception, the angel saw himself through the eyes of all the innocent angels he'd hacked and chopped to pieces. Vile and malignant, his guilt spread throughout his bones like a cancer, riddling him with unbearable remorse and deep regret.

"Oh, how Lucifer deceived us!"

With agonising grief, he cried bitterly for forgiveness, "I'm so sorry, Father."

"One of the fallen angels asked God for forgiveness?" As I reflected with fascination, an almost imperceptible sadness tugged at my heart. "Did God forgive him?"

"Oh yes!" Gabriel affirmed with certainty. "The King not only forgave him, he showed him tremendous mercy. Summoning him from that very spot, his Majesty brought him home. Then he entrusted him with a very important mission. All of heaven celebrated that day."

"What kind of a mission?"

"No one knew—only the King. But it was a very great honour."

Feeling a sense of my own guilt, I ventured, "Will God forgive anyone?"

Smiling compassionately, Gabriel promised, "As long as you really want him to."

I felt relieved by Gabriel's answer, but something inside me doubted as well. Sceptically, I tested him, "But what about Sodom and Gomorrah? How do you explain that?"

"The same way I explain Nineveh," Gabriel answered gently. He seemed genuinely impressed that I knew anything about the Bible at all. Then with a gentle smile he added, "Your great love has brought you great forgiveness."

Surprised but with sincerity, I wondered, *how does he know about my love?*

As though he'd read my mind, Gabriel peered directly into my eyes. And with a tone that sounded almost envious, he revealed, "I'm the one who led you to the place of remembrance."

Chapter Thirty-One
Gabriel's Mission

When long at last the great tower was finally complete, Lucifer addressed the council. "Leaders of the rebellion—brothers—as you know, the new moon approaches and the second assault is close at hand. We ascend the gates of the city in just a few days and I want everything to be in order. Thanks to the sacrifice of our brother, we've uncovered the secret of our own sequential code. We've also since learned that procreating with the humans *is* possible, and today we have an enormous army of crossbred warriors that we'll send up the tower as our vanguard."

"Kill the tyrant!" The members of the council applauded approvingly.

Speaking over their boisterous shouting and gesturing for them to be quiet, Lucifer deflated their overblown jubilation. "Quiet! Quiet!"

When the raucous subsided, Lucifer continued, "Unfortunately, we've *not* yet learned the secret of creation—so we cannot yet create more of our own kind. This means that we *must not* kill the tyrant until he reveals the secret to us. Without it, we're lost. Is this understood?"

Grumbling, the council members reluctantly agreed.

"So, this is what we'll do. We'll safeguard detailed records of the structure of our sequential code along with vials of our seed here on Earth. If victory comes to us quickly, we'll force the tyrant to reveal the secret of creation and use that knowledge to reign for all of eternity. But if we should fall, the brothers we leave behind will have the code and the vials with which to replenish our forces and begin anew."

Then, with a final sidelong glance, Lucifer ordered, "Prepare the troops. We attack on the next new moon."

Soon, Lucifer and his minions began the arduous climb to the gates of the citadel. Had the Almighty One not intervened, the mutineers would have yet again laid siege to the garden of God. Rather than destroy the recusant angels, however, his Majesty devised another way.

"Gabriel, I want you to confuse their language and demolish the tower. We've endured enough slaughter. Isolate the seditious forces from one another. Without the strength of their numbers, the blessed elysian fields lay beyond their reach."

"Yes, my Lord. May it be as your mercy allows."

Departing from the celestial capital, I carried out my orders immediately. As I approached the tower, its sheer stature and girth intimidated me instantly.

Constructed of cypress and banyan, the base of the tower extended more than a mile in each direction from the centre. It narrowed incrementally with each level, and gangplanks ascended up the middle.

The rebels were well on their way to the top of the tower with the units of crossbred soldiers in the lead. They kicked the bodily remains of human labourers over the edge as they marched upward toward the holy city. The corpses flipped and spun as they dropped out of sight—some hit the edges of the tower on their way down and others fell like chestnuts on an autumn day. From a distance, the tower looked like a vast wooden beast with ants scurrying up its spine.

As I neared the rebels, Lucifer spotted me first. "What do you have to do with us, Gabriel? Have you come to throw in your lot with the traitors?"

"I come with orders from the King," I responded. "This tower is hereby condemned."

"No! Stop him!" Lucifer screamed.

The crossbreeds shot arrows and flung stones with slings while the fallen ones lunged after me in the air. Narrowly escaping the arrows and rocks, I easily outpaced the rebels due to their diminished speed. Rushing to the earth, I stomped on the orb with all my strength until the force generated an earthquake so powerful that the mountains themselves moved. Then, as the crust of the earth cracked and split, I pried it apart, causing the orb to open its mouth and swallow the tower along with all the records of the fallen ones.

The tower crumbled and the vast army fell to the earth. The rebel angels survived but the crossbred troops were ripped to pieces. Most were buried in the rubble along with the tower.

"Regroup and fight!" Lucifer commanded; his face now beet-red from shouting. But there was no one left for the fallen angels to battle. I'd already left.

Acting quickly from another location, I rained confusion down upon the entire populace. Garbling the idiom of the mighty seraphim as well as the speech patterns of all the earth's inhabitants, I plunged them deep into chaos.

"Hold your ground! Maintain your ranks!" Lucifer bellowed in a hopeless attempt to exert authority. But the lawless angels fled in confusion.

Returning from my mandate, I reported to the throne. "Great King, live forever! I've carried out my mission according to your instructions."

"And what is the result, Gabriel?" The King's demeanour was patient but direct.

"The tower is demolished and sealed up in the earth along with the records of the fallen ones."

"Very good. And the other matter?"

"Scattered across the earth by the severity of the quake and unable to communicate with one another, the factious angels defile themselves even more by dwelling among ordinary humans."

"I see," the King responded. "Go and record what happens, Gabriel. But do not interfere. Your service and loyalty is invaluable as always. Thank you."

"My Lord," I extolled and bowed in obeisance. Then, excusing myself from his presence, I departed to diligently examine the earth and document my observations.

Chapter Thirty-Two
Jack and the Beanstalk

Up until this point, I'd grown so fascinated by the story itself that I'd lost sight somewhat of who was telling it. Gabriel's gentle demeanour made me feel so welcome and comfortable that I'd totally forgotten that he was the second in command of all the universe. Instead, I'd begun to view this mighty colossus as a friend. But now Gabriel sounded angry. It wasn't a fly-off-the-handle, out-of-control kind of anger. This was more like moral outrage.

A deep, vertical crease appeared smack dab in the centre of Gabriel's forehead. The furrow stretched out so wide that it looked like an extension of his nose. And remember the gentle waterfall in his voice? Well, let's just say that I suddenly wished I had a barrel to hide in. It made my little angry voice sound like one of those sprinklers that toddlers play under.

I felt like a five-year-old listening to my kindergarten teacher reading from a picture book. Children have no interest in knowing the goose's motive for laying the golden eggs, nor do they care why the giant lives in the sky in the first place (much less how). It's enough for them to understand, albeit implicitly, that the beanstalk offers Jack a chance to view the world from a perspective outside of his own reality. That's what Gabriel was offering me.

To be sure, some of the character development was lacking considerably and I found the dialogue somewhat flat and passive, but Gabriel did the voices so well that it completely made up for it. Besides, I didn't get the impression that Gabriel's main purpose in telling me all this background information was to make Lucifer's personality convincing. He seemed to be glossing over all that in service of a greater end. Exactly what that greater end was eluded me for the longest time, as the story twisted and turned like the Ganges. Gabriel did eventually bring the story back on track—although it took him considerably longer than I would have liked. Still, there was a method to his madness.

Before I could truly understand 'the story', I had to learn to listen. Not the way most people listen: information goes in, their brain processes it, matches it to what they think they know, and disregards the rest—that kind of listening only works when ninety-nine percent of what you hear matches what you already think you know. I definitely wasn't in Kansas anymore, and I'll be the first to admit that I wasn't always very happy about it.

I probably should have disclaimed this right up front—the story of the ages is *long*. I promise to keep it as short as possible. Keep in mind however, I'm no

Dostoevsky. I'm just a dead guy with a tale to tell. Of course, some people might argue that there's no difference.

Chapter Thirty-Three
Worm Holes

"It wasn't long before the fallen ones began to assimilate with the humans. With intense curiosity, I bore witness as the depraved celestial creatures took the most desirable women for themselves and killed anyone who challenged them—whether it be husbands, fathers, sons, or brothers. Amassing great harems, the fallen ones easily commanded the obedience of the lowly masses."

"I'm curious. Did the angels ever have more children?"

"As a matter of fact, they did." Gabriel gave me one of those polite smiles. His tiny dimples offset the lines around his mouth, making him look like he had a sad, one-eyed clown embossed on each side of his face. "I was just about to get to that, too. When the angels copulated with common terrestrial mortals, they engendered a superhuman race that inherited the beauty and grace of heaven itself. Taller than humans, and often referred to as giants in folklore, the prodigious offspring stood head and shoulders above the rest. Possessing a complexion so radiant as to be mesmerising, the luminescent ones elicited the most solemn reverence from Earth's awestruck, plebeian soil dwellers. But the most telling trait of this sanguine breed continued to be its unmistakably red hair."

"Red hair, huh?" My voice twisted in a quirky inflection. "That's not the kind of thing you normally associate with power, is it?"

"Not in your day, it isn't." Gabriel sounded kind of grandfatherly. I imagined him with a pair of bifocals and a cardigan sweater. "But in the first few millennia after the fall, red hair comprised the very symbol of power. Like their angelic ancestors before them, those claiming this majestic lineage easily dominated the lesser inhabitants of the earth, and they ruled over mighty empires as god-kings, magicians, wise men, and astrologers."

"Did they rule over any of the empires that we know about today?"

"All of them," Gabriel re-joined matter-of-factly. "All of the *ancient* ones that is—except for ancient Israel."

"Seriously?" I spouted. "Which ones?"

"Pick one," Gabriel dared me—sounding like a magician about to perform a card trick.

"Alright. What about Egypt?" I suggested for no particular reason.

"*Egypt?*" The emphasis Gabriel placed on the word made me feel stupid for even asking. "Egypt was the most notorious of them all! Built on the backs of slaves and yet ruled by first-generation sons of stardust, Egypt extracted the most precious resources of the earth and funnelled them into this topmost priority."

"Didn't they know how to get back to heaven anymore?"

"No. The path to the portal of eternity remained veiled in secrecy ever since I confused the dialect of the renegades and destroyed their great tower. Remember? The rebel angels hurried to build the tower because if they missed their window, the earth wouldn't pass Orion again for another two hundred and thirty million years."

"Oh, that's right," I recalled, chewing on the thought for a minute. "But wait a minute. They did miss their window, right? If it was going to take so long for the earth to pass Orion again, why did the Egyptians even bother?"

"Because the universe is an unfathomable expanse. In many ways, it's as unsearchable as the King himself. The passage through Orion merely represented the only *known* way back to heaven. But the cosmic order is a delicate balance between natural law and free will. Do you understand?"

"Not at all," I admitted, staring blankly back at Gabriel while I grappled with the concept.

"Let me try to explain it this way," he offered patiently, breaking it down into words a first-grader could understand. "The universe itself is alive and changing. We first truly realised this during the Great War when the elements around us reacted to the rebel's lawlessness."

Once again, Gabriel's storytelling abilities transported me from my safe little corner in the void directly into the heat of battle.

"Intense explosions transformed the expanse into a minefield as stars went supernova and engulfed billions in their rage. The disruption of the natural order caused immense singularities that sucked everything—even the light—into obscurity."

"You're talking about black holes?" I chimed in.

By the way, why do people do that? I knew that Gabriel was talking about black holes. But for some reason, I felt compelled to ask him anyway. It's not like I needed to clarify what he meant or anything. It was more like a power play to establish the superiority of my term over his. The seeds of hegemony had definitely taken root. I found myself wondering if I'd ever thought about these things while I was still alive, but my little exercise in self-discovery was cut short as Gabriel indulged my pernickety human nature.

"Yes, entire companies of rebel angels were lost to these 'black holes,' as you call them—his Majesty alone knows what happened to them. Those that managed to escape groped through entire galaxies in darkness. When the battle was over, the universe itself had changed. If not for Prince Michael, we would've never found our way home."

"I'm stunned, Gabriel. The little I learned about the universe was never put to me quite like that before." Actually, I was beginning to suspect that very little of reality was as I understood it to be. "But I'm still not clear how that affected the window of opportunity regarding the earth and its position relative to Orion."

Transfixed in an empty stare, as if his mind was still back in the war, Gabriel broke out of his trance with a blink and refocused his eyes.

"Like all living creatures, the universe breathes and thinks and remembers. As it breathes, it expands and contracts. And as it thinks, synapses fire and connections develop between disparate points in space and time. These connections are what you humans refer to as worm holes."

"Are you saying that worm holes are the universe's memory?"

"They play a crucial role in its memory function, yes. And the passage through Orion is just one of an infinite number of such worm holes."

"Angels travel via worm holes? This is starting to sound like science fiction."

"It's a little more involved than that, but yes, in a manner of speaking we do. You see," Gabriel paused as he searched for the right human words to express the celestial concept, "worm holes aren't roads in the conventional sense as you would understand them on Earth—they're constructs. The universe is just a tiny portion of the mind of God, and worm holes represent a minute fraction of his memory and also his will."

"I think I'm too stupid to understand this," I groaned as I rubbed my temples to alleviate the oncoming headache.

"It's really not all that difficult to understand. Angels 'travel' through wormholes like thoughts in the mind of God as we carry out the King's decrees. It's his will that guides us. In fact, it's only through fulfilling the will of the King that we exist at all because we're nothing more than the instruments of his will. This is why the fallen angels eventually died. Have you ever heard that the wicked will perish?"

"Yeah, I think everyone's heard that at some point or another."

"That's because it's true," Gabriel educed, "but not for the reasons that Lucifer told everyone."

"I'm not following you."

"Lucifer instigated the rebellion by deceiving a large percentage of the angels into believing that the King was a cruel tyrant who would destroy them if they disobeyed."

"And...?"

"And his lies created a self-fulfilling prophecy."

I curled my lips up under my teeth and squinted my eyes. But it didn't help.

"Don't you see? Lucifer caused them to fear their own father, and that fear developed into hatred. Their hatred eventually caused them to rebel, and through their rebellion they brought about their own demise. Lucifer also deceived himself into believing that he could recover his immortality by returning to the holy citadel. But there's nothing inherent about heaven that spawns immortality. You see, it isn't *where* you are that matters, but *who* you serve, because we have no immortality of our own. We certainly can't recover it by going here or there, or doing this or that. It's only by obeying the King's will that we partake of eternity, because it's the King's will that we inherit eternal life in the first place. But his Majesty never forces his will on anyone."

"Still," I resisted somewhat defiantly, "those who don't obey him *will* die, right?"

"Yes, that's true," Gabriel conceded agreeably. "And those who don't breathe will die just as readily."

I had already opened my mouth to drive home my point when Gabriel's response took the wind right out of my sails. "Oh," I mumbled. "That puts things in a slightly different perspective." The idea that God wasn't a vindictive judge was kind of new to me. It caught me off guard, but Gabriel's point really got me thinking.

"Perspective is everything. Wouldn't you agree? As for the worm holes, especially after the Great War, Lucifer realised the risks involved in trespassing through the King's realm—let alone on uncharted territory. This is why the rebels laboured so arduously to finish the tower before the earth passed Orion's astral plane. But afterward, Lucifer poured every ounce of his energy into charting a new course."

Chapter Thirty-Four
The Offer

Seth considered applying to a post-doctoral program in biotechnology. He'd received a brochure concerning such a program from his dissertation advisor. A small number of fellowships were awarded each year, and Seth figured, "Why not?" It would answer the problem of what to do after he finished his Ph.D.

Shuffling through a stack of mail on his kitchen table, Seth racked his brain. "Where did I put that brochure?"

Finally locating it under a pile of take-out menus, he declared the victory, "Aha! Found you!"

Seth skimmed over the program requirements and considered the application deadline. The brochure stated that all application materials for the summer session must be postmarked no later than…

"March 30th? That's in three days!"

Worse yet, it was already Thursday.

"March 30th is Sunday. Mail doesn't even go out on Sunday, and I need to get three letters of recommendation by tomorrow."

Staring at the brochure, Seth almost didn't apply. "Why even bother," he reflected in a defeatist tone. But then he threw caution to the wind. "What do I have to lose? It's not like I'm doing anything else right now."

Seth emailed the three professors serving on his dissertation committee and requested letters of recommendation. "I apologise for the late notice," he read out loud as he typed the email, "but could you *please* prepare and mail the letter immediately. The deadline is March 30th. The address is…"

Seth stopped typing. "What *is* the address to this place? Hmm—that's curious," he mumbled as he spied the address. "A post office box in Washington DC? Why would the return address be a P.O. Box?"

A strange, silent warning began to go off in Seth's brain, but he shrugged it off and provided the address to his advisors. After sending the emails, Seth called the records department at his school.

"Records and registration," The clerk answered.

"Hello?"

"Yes? This is records and registration. How may I help you?"

"I need a copy of my official transcripts sent to a fellowship program that I'm applying to."

"Are you currently enrolled as a student here?"

"Yes, I am."

"Alright. What's your social security number?"

"386-67-1374"

"Can you verify your name and address, please?"

"Seth North. 158 Prospect Street, New Haven, CT. 06511."

"Alright, Mr North. That will be five dollars. Where would you like me to mail those?"

"Well, that's the problem. I just realised that the application deadline is March 30th, and I was hoping—"

"March 30th is Sunday," the clerk interrupted.

"Yes, I realise—"

"But today is Thursday," the clerk interrupted again.

"Yes, ma'am—I realise today is Thurs—"

"Well, how do you expect it to get there by Sunday? The post office doesn't even deliver mail on Sunday."

"I know that, ma'am. Isn't there some way that I can have the transcripts expedited?"

"USPS will overnight it for $16.50, but it's already past eleven. There's no guarantee I can get your request processed in time. Next day delivery is only guaranteed if it goes out before noon."

"Oh please, will you try?"

"What's the address?"

"It's a P.O. Box in DC."

"You have two problems," the records clerk informed him. "First of all, I can't send official transcripts to a P.O. Box."

"What can you send?" Seth petitioned desperately.

"I can only send unofficial transcripts to a P.O. Box, but you also have another problem—overnight delivery only applies to physical addresses."

"Oh," Seth muttered. Figuring the entire venture was a lost cause anyway, he decided to punt. "Well…would you just send the unofficial transcripts in the mail then?"

"Certainly," the clerk agreed. "The first three copies are free. What's the address?"

After giving the clerk the information, Seth typed up a letter of intent. The bulk of the letter entailed a detailed complaint about the program's lack of a physical mailing address disguised as an explanation as to why the *unofficial* transcripts would be forth-coming. Seth signed the application letter, sealed it in an envelope, and sent it off.

Within about two weeks, Seth received a response. "That was really quick!"

He almost didn't even bother to open the envelope. "It must be a rejection," he concluded. But his curiosity ultimately got the better of him, so Seth opened the salmon-coloured envelope and retrieved the matching letterhead. Unfolding it, he skimmed past the pleasantries to the meat of the answer.

"Full tuition waver, room and board, and a stipend allowance of ten thousand dollars!" Seth screamed with delight as he skipped through his apartment and waved the acceptance letter in the air. After a few celebratory cheers, he settled down and read more of the letter.

"Summer session begins on April 13th. Oh my God! Most spring sessions aren't even out by then." But then Seth remembered that the brochure specifically required that all course work be completed prior to application. "I guess that's why," he reasoned as the light bulb began to flicker.

"But wait, April 13th is *Monday*! Today's already the 10th—I need to get my act together!" Seth finished the letter, "Please check your email for e-tickets and flight itinerary. If you need help obtaining a passport please don't hesitate to contact us. Congratulations and welcome!"

Seth's exuberance immediately turned to confusion. "Passport? I thought I was going to DC." Seth logged in to his email account. "Maybe that's just there for international students." Seth found the email and opened it.

"Congratulations! Yeah...whatever, ya-dee-ya-dee-da..." Seth skimmed quickly through the superfluous verbiage to the location of the school. "Prague? It's in Prague? But the P.O. Box is in D.C."

"That's really strange," Seth mumbled as he thumbed through the brochure scanning for any reference to Prague. "There's not even a name for this place. I can't believe I never noticed that!"

The strange warning in Seth's brain was not so silent anymore.

"No name anywhere." Seth didn't know what to make of it. He couldn't even research the school! "Talk about blind faith," he winced sceptically.

Seth felt both excited and overwhelmed at the same time. "There's so much to do!" And the fact that the school turned out to be in Prague really nagged at him. The prospect of going to Prague seemed like a substantially greater commitment than DC.

"Get over it," Seth counselled himself. "You'll be attending a different school either way. Besides, it's not like you have any reason to hang around here."

Seth sat down in front of his computer with a note pad and pen. "Where should I begin?" Seth checked his notepad with a heavy sigh of resignation. Reading off his list, he began to feel overwhelmed. "Tomorrow's going to be a busy day. I need to pack, print out my tickets and itinerary, find my passport, notify my landlord, forward my mail and exchange some currency for my layover in Rome. I still have a lot to do—I'd better get some sleep."

Stretching out on his sofa, Seth stared at the acceptance letter.

On the one hand, he felt extremely fortunate to have been awarded a post-doc. Still, he felt uneasy. It had all happened so quickly.

Chapter Thirty-Five
Prague

"It's hard to believe I'm on my way to Prague!" Seth chattered enthusiastically. "This will be my first trip anywhere since Cotonou."

Seth jittered excitedly, but he also yawned excessively. He'd stayed up the entire night packing and tying up loose ends. Seth's mind was still preoccupied with last-minute details. Had he forgotten anything? As Seth contemplated these very questions, the captain's voice came over the intercom.

"Good afternoon everyone and welcome aboard US Airways flight #4507. It's currently three forty-nine p.m. here in New Haven. This flight services the Philadelphia International Airport. We'll be taking off in just a moment. Travel time is approximately one hour and fifteen minutes, and we should be landing in Philadelphia at approximately five-fourteen p.m. Thank you for flying US Airlines and enjoy your flight."

Fidgeting compulsively, Seth watched out the window while the plane taxied down the runway. Those inevitable butterflies began to flutter just as soon as the aircraft embarked on its ascent.

"Do you like to fly?"

Seth turned and looked at the elderly gentleman sitting next to him. "I'm sorry?"

"I asked you if you like to fly."

"I like the taking off part," Seth conversed as he looked back out the window, "but I get terrible pressure in my ears when the plane lands. At least that's what happened the last time I flew—the only time I remember flying. My ears blocked up something fierce and I..."

Seth turned his head mid-sentence to look at the man, only to realise that he was speaking to an empty seat. "Now I'm hallucinating, great." Seth ruminated soberly about the plane crash in Cotonou as he looked around for any sign of the mysterious passenger. "I wonder what it would be like to fly," He whispered to himself. "Just imagine, soaring through the sky without a care in the world." Seth let out a heavy sigh. As he exhaled, his breath fogged up the glass. Fantasising about flying got him meditating on the plane crash in Cotonou again. "No, I'm not going to think about that," he determined in a bastioned state of mind. "Today is not a good day to die." Having resolved the issue once and for all, Seth wiped the fog from the glass. "Oh my God!" he jumped in terror—the old man's face was looking back at him through the glass.

"What's wrong with you?" the elderly man derided.

Seth turned to find the elderly gentleman back in his seat. "Where *were* you?"

"I just went to the bathroom."

"During take-off?" Seth chastised him.

"What? Are you the head stewardess?" the man chided with a grin that revealed his oversized dentures. "Do I need your permission to take a leak?"

"Very funny," Seth rolled his eyes as he adjusted his position with his back to the old gentleman.

I really want to take a nap, he contemplated, *but the flight is just a little over an hour. Maybe I can tough it out until the connecting flight to Rome.* Seth checked his itinerary. *Yeah, that would be good. It's eight hours and forty minutes from Philly to Rome—I'll have plenty of time to sleep then.*

Staring out the window, Seth breathed on the window again and calculated the length of his flight with his finger. *Let's see, an hour to Philly and eight hours to Rome…after a three-hour layover, it's another two hours to Prague…*

The venti peppermint-mocha cappuccino with four extra shots of espresso he drank on the way to the airport barely affected him at all. Seth's motor function continued to operate out of pure adrenaline and a nagging fear of missing his flight. After tallying his numbers, Seth yawned with exhaustion. *The hardest part is going to be staying awake right now.*

Exhausted as he was, Seth was nervous and there was no getting around it. He didn't like thinking about the plane crash—especially at 15,000 feet—so he deliberately tried to clear his mind. Looking out the window, Seth fixated on the open expanse. Still, try as he might, he just couldn't put the plane crash out of his mind.

Seth decided to face his fear head-on. "You know what they say about falling off a horse," he asserted with a false sense of confidence. Just then the plane encountered a bit of turbulence. Seth clutched the armrests with a white-knuckle grip and exhaled slowly. "But no one ever says that about airplanes."

To divert his attention from his dread of dying in a plane crash, Seth obsessed on how really stupid the flight plan seemed. "Excuse me," he asked a flight attendant as she passed by with complimentary headphones, "why are we heading more than an hour *west* to Philadelphia before going *east* to Rome? We're actually flying about two and a half hours out of our way."

"Well, I suppose that's one way to look at it," the flight attendant responded disinterestedly. "Of course, another way to look at it is that there are no flights that fly directly from New Haven to Rome. Not to mention, you're probably the only passenger on this flight that's actually going to Rome—most are just going to Philadelphia. If you wanted a direct flight, perhaps you should have left from a different airport."

"Hmm," Seth postulated. "The more I think about it, the more convinced I am that I made the best choice after all. The New Haven airport might be small with only one airline, but it's still more convenient than leaving from Hartford or Bridgeport—even if it does mean flying two and a half hours out of my way."

"I'm really happy for you," the flight attendant patronised him. "Would you like a pair of headphones?"

Thirty minutes into the flight, Seth was straining just to maintain control of his mental faculties. But as the short flight to Philadelphia neared its destination, he experienced a second wind. In fact, by the time the plane landed, Seth was feeling a little giddy. During the flight, he'd taken advantage of the complimentary headphones in an effort to stay awake. First, he listened to a comedy channel that featured some of Bill Cosby's older material.

"Are you high?" the old man berated him as Seth laughed hysterically.

After being tortured by his co-passenger for about ten minutes, the elderly gentleman switched seats. When the Cosby material ended, Seth decided to listen to some music. Scrolling through the channels, he came across a 'best hits of the '80s' channel. Seth liked it. He felt a sense of nostalgia—although he had no idea what for.

'Hungry Like the Wolf' had just started playing when the pilot interrupted, "Welcome to Philadelphia International Airport. Please remain in your seats until the aircraft comes to a complete stop. The time is five-thirteen p.m. and the temperature is a balmy sixty-two degrees. We're experiencing a little inclement weather here locally so those of you that are driving, please do allow for slippery conditions. We hope you've enjoyed your flight—it's now safe to exit the aircraft. Thank you for flying US Airlines and have a wonderful evening."

After about twenty minutes, nearly all of the passengers seated in front of Seth were exiting the plane. Meanwhile, the peppermint-mocha had gone right through him.

"I really need to pee!" he agonised.

Watching in tortured anticipation, Seth engaged in a middle-aged rendition of the potty dance. One by one—as if in slow motion—the passengers ahead of him walked that lackadaisical airplane walk to the front of the plane. An extremely obese lady with a huge bosom sat in the row directly in front of Seth. Struggling to get out of her seat, she noticed Seth shaking his leg desperately. He wanted to dart out in front of the woman, but he didn't want to be rude.

"Why don't you just go ahead of me," she offered.

"Thanks!" Seth smiled graciously and quickly followed the rest of the passengers to the front of the plane.

Once inside the Airport, Seth's first stop was in front of a urinal.

"Sweet Jesus, that feels good!"

Seth had no clue where he'd picked up certain cherished phrases such as "Sweet Jesus!" But he found himself using them from time to time—usually when he was operating on autopilot. Debouching from the men's room into the bustling airport, Seth located a flight teleprompt. Shuffling through his e-tickets and spying his flight number, he searched for it among the list of departing flights and secerned his gate from the hundreds of others.

"US Airways flight #718 departing at six-fifteen p.m. Found it!"

As Seth headed for his gate, he experienced a sense of Deja vu. From time to time, the conviction that he knew a lot more than he could remember haunted him—it stalked him. This was one of those times.

Seth reached his gate only minutes before a phantom voice announced, "US Airways flight #718 is now boarding."

Seth found the end of the line. He did the airplane walk through the gate and onto the aircraft, and then he found his seat. He waited for one of the flight attendants to pass by with pillows and blankets, and he requested a pillow. After adjusting the flat, starchy cotton-lined piece of foam a few times behind his head, Seth double-checked the window for the old man's face, closed the window shade and shut his eyes.

Seth hoped to sleep the entire way to Rome. He yawned one of those yawns that—once you start—it takes on a life of its own and feels like your eyeballs are being sucked into the back of your head. Seth suffered through it and hoped it would pass quickly. Once his lungs expelled every last molecule of carbon monoxide from his fatigued frame, Seth curled up and fell asleep.

Awakening suddenly from his slumber, Seth found himself engaged in a fierce battle. He recognised the look of sheer terror in the eyes of the dying as though he'd witnessed it many times before. Their haunting wails were nothing new to his ears. To the West, Seth peered out at a familiar stretch of sky. Obscured in thick blackness, angry flashes of lightening revealed the horror of the moment.

Everything appeared in black and white, like in a memory or an old photograph. Seth realised that the place had always been inside his head. It had been part of his identity all along. Like childhood—it was vivid and real, yet transparent as a pane of glass. The bloody conflict served as a lens through which he's viewed the outside world his entire life. He'd been a fish in water, never even noticing it was there.

The strange intimacy with which he related to this scene haunted Seth. For some reason, the dead and dying have also always been with him like relatives he's never met—cluttering the photo album in his brain.

Suddenly, Seth was transported to a different battlefield. The mighty colossus shook the orb while a platoon of demons advanced against him.

"Stop him!" Lucifer bellowed between vile epithets of anger and rage.

With every stomp of his celestial feet, violent seismic waves ravaged the earth—forcing cracks in its crust and producing massive tsunamis that deluged the antediluvian world.

"Hold your positions!" the dark prince demanded as thousands and thousands abandoned their ranks. "Stay in formation!" But his efforts were futile. His insistent injunctions fell to the ground wholly unheeded. Pandemonium usurped his authority, and terror commanded the hearts of his fallen host. Pangaea, once stable in its revolution, now wobbled—erratic and out of control.

Humans fled for their lives, and angels cursed their creator as fissures split the defecting ground beneath. Deep fiery chasms spewed scalding-hot geysers while steaming yellow sulphur blocked out the sun. Acid rain clouds corroded the expanse and pelted the insurgents with excruciating pain. Torrents of agony descended like locusts that crawled on their skin and consumed their flesh.

The screams of the desperate shot like arrows across the slumbering plains. Ravenous funnels scoured the horizon in search of victims to quench their bloodlust. Rocks became cannon balls and trees became spears that crushed and impaled all who crossed their path. Splinters and stones became deadly projectiles—visiting wrath upon the unholy horde.

"Run! Hide! To the mountains! To the sea!" But nowhere was safe. There was nowhere to go. Chaos and horror enveloped mankind—bedlam and mayhem reigned as their new kings. Those who sought refuge in mountain retreats were entombed in a mausoleum of igneous rock. And those who managed to escape to the sea were pulverised by the relentless invasion. Wave after wave of displaced fury pummelled them back to the merciless shore.

P waves, induced by the behemoth's blows, emanated out in every direction. Traveling as fast as the speed of sound, they spread like pandemics and penetrated stone. Rupturing eardrums and shattering teeth, they haemorrhaged tissue while eyes burst in their sockets. Those nearest the tower collapsed in a heap as their bones disintegrated into dust.

"Retreat! Retreat! The tower won't hold..." the rebels panicked and languished in dread. As the titan structure swayed and buckled, the damned—gripped with fear—embraced their last stand. Splintering beneath its own weight and girth, the proud, defiant obelisk knelt. Then, as with a clap of thunder, it capsized and sank deep into the earth.

When the turbulence ended, a mushroom cloud of earth and debris settled over the camp—burying its many secrets away for a day and a time not yet disclosed.

Jolted back to consciousness by the sounds of screaming and confusion, Seth sat straight up and clutched the arms of his seat with a white-knuckle grip. The nose of the plane aimed straight down towards the earth—the force of the descent throwing everyone back in their seats. Lights flickered as an eerie, pressurised dirge filled the cabin with lament. Debris caromed about and luggage—shaken loose by the turbulence—tussled around the plane. Oxygen masks bounced and swayed as they ricocheted off the ceiling. But no one even thought to use them—the impact came so quickly.

Seth screamed! He didn't know what, but he knew he must have screamed something because everyone was staring at him.
One of the crew rushed over to him.

"Sir? Are you all alright?" she mothered him with a comforting hand on his shoulder.

Seth exhaled hard. He sat perfectly still for a moment—holding his chest like he'd just swallowed a jawbreaker. Once the disorientation passed, he realised that he'd been dreaming.

"Yes. I'm fine. Thank you," Seth shook his head spiritedly. Then, with a laugh that betrayed his reticence he added, "Bad dream I guess."

"Well, everything's alright now," the kindly airhostess reassured him as a smile of embarrassment spread across his face. A sigh of relief mixed with anxiety came next.

As his surrogate mother returned to her duties, Seth imposed, "Excuse me. Can I get a drink or something?"

"Certainly. What would you like?"

"I don't know," Seth averred as he turned up his palms, "I don't drink."

"I'll be right back," she promised with a crinkle of her nose.

Seth put his hands over his face and leaned forward in a position reminiscent of 'crash mode'. He would have prayed, but he honestly couldn't remember if he believed in God. Stretching out as best one can in coach, Seth tried to reposition himself and get comfortable.

The flight attendant returned with a little bottle of Meyers's rum and a glass of Coke with ice. "Is this okay?" she probed confidently as she offered it to him.

"Oh yeah! Thank you," Seth accepted the drink appreciatively. "Thank you so much."

"You're very welcome, Sir." And with a wink, she went back to work.

Seth put the bottle down on his lap and opened the tray table with his free hand. Then he put the glass of Coke on the tray table and opened the bottle of rum. He poured the contents of the tiny bottle into the glass and drank it down quickly.

"Mmm, that's good! I wonder why I've never tried that before." He shook the glass to free any remaining cocktail from the ice and tipped the plastic cup to his lips.

"Should I have another one?" Seth tempted himself. "Maybe not, I don't want to show up at the program intoxicated." Seth literally never drank, and he didn't know how long the effects of alcohol would last in his system. So, he decided to error on the side of caution.

The 'fasten seatbelts light flashed, and the captain made his announcement as the aircraft approached the Leonardo da Vinci Airport.

"Already?"

Seth didn't realise it, but he'd indeed slept nearly the entire flight. He returned his tray table to its original and upright position and fastened his seat belt. Then he opened the window shade and watched as the plane circled the runway and proceeded to make its descent into Fiumicino.

"I'm starving!" Seth grumbled.

After exiting the aircraft, he wandered around the airport on a quest for something to eat. Gazing into the windows of the extravagant bars, restaurants, and cafes, Seth began to lose heart.

So many places to choose from, but not one opens before nine a.m. What time is it now? Seth wondered, looking at his watch. *Eight-forty a.m. I have a three-hour layover until my connecting flight, so I guess I'll find my gate first and then find someplace to eat close by. Something should be open by then.*

After he'd gotten hopelessly lost, Seth became even more discouraged. "Easier said than done," Seth mumbled dejectedly. "This airport is huge!"

After wandering aimlessly, he finally pinpointed his gate.

"Czech Airlines flight #4729 to Prague, finally!"

Seth still had a couple of hours, so he searched for someplace to eat. Perusing the many high-end restaurants, Seth spotted a McDonalds.

"Welcome to McDonalds. May I take your order?" the manager greeted Seth—looking somewhat annoyed to be there.

"Yeah, can I get a ninety-nine-cent double cheeseburger?"

"It's too early to get a cheeseburger, sir. We're only serving breakfast at this time."

Glancing over at the 'value' menu, Seth quickly realised that it didn't matter anyway because a ninety-nine-cent double cheeseburger actually cost three euros in the airport.

"Four dollars and fifty cents for a cheeseburger?" Seth exclaimed.

"We're not serving cheeseburgers yet, sir," the manager reiterated.

"Yeah, I heard you the first time. Hmm, I'm not sure what I want then," Seth vacillated as he studied the breakfast menu.

Since McDonalds was so 'affordable', a very long line had already formed.

"Sir, there's a line behind you. If you don't know what you want, I'll have to ask you to step aside."

"How about a steak and egg bagel meal with hash browns and coffee?" Seth quickly read from the menu.

"How about it?" the manger brattled under her breath as she rang up the order. "Twelve euros."

Seth calculated the cost in U.S. currency.

"Eighteen dollars!" he objected as he pulled out twenty euros and reluctantly paid the cashier. "I thought I was at *McDonalds*!"

"Thank you." The manager smiled and handed him back seven euros. She held up the other euro and asked, "Would you like to donate a euro to the Ronald McDonald House?"

"No, I would not!" Seth enjoined, snatching the euro from her hand.

As he was herded through the roped corridors to the other side of the counter, Seth inspected the Vitruvian Man imprint on the Italian one-euro coin.

"Number 44." An overdressed man at the counter announced as he set Seth's order down on a plastic tray.

"What happened to my shake?"

"We're not serving shakes yet, sir." However, since the shake machine was ready, the employee took Seth's word for it and asked, "What kind of shake did you order?"

"A large chocolate shake," Seth asserted glibly.

The associate made the shake for him and placed it on the tray next to his coffee. "There you are, sir."

"Thank you," Seth beamed and walked away with his food.

On the large menu hanging overhead, Seth saw that a large shake cost six euros and some change. Feeling a little less like he'd just been jacked, Seth went and sat down.

Immediately after he scarfed down his food and inhaled the chocolate shake, the combination gave him brain freeze and indigestion. Seth also suddenly felt an acute case of nausea from the onslaught of fat and sugar that now travelled through his blood stream.

As Seth searched out the nearest restroom, he sipped his coffee. "Ouch! That *is* hot!" Seth protested incredulously. *They're not kidding,* he thought to himself as he read the warning on the cup.

Imagining a huge class-action lawsuit against McDonalds, he cracked up over the mental image of a courtroom full of claimants screaming "it's too hot" as they pathetically endeavoured to enunciate their words with no lips. The graphic portrait made Seth decide to let his coffee cool awhile.

Seth occupied a stall in the restroom and waited for the nausea to pass. Then he found a seat in his gate near a large window overlooking the tarmac. Sipping his coffee, he watched the planes take off and land.

Back on the airplane, Seth settled into his seat. *With any good fortune, I'll have the entire row to myself,* he surmised. The plane seemed curiously empty for an eleven-forty a.m. flight. Seth found this peculiar, but *when in Rome...*he chuckled to himself.

"Eager to help," an elderly woman across the aisle interjected, "young man, you *are* in Rome."

Seth smiled and nodded politely, trying to ignore how sick he felt from the chocolate shake he'd ingested two hours earlier.

"Good morning and welcome aboard Czech Airlines flight #4729. Our first stop will be Prague. We'll be landing in approximately two hours…"

As the plane taxied down the runway, a slim, boyish-looking woman in her late teens slid into the seat next to Seth.

"*Ahoj*!" she asserted confidently without actually looking at him.

"*Ahoj*," Seth replied, not really certain if the airline allowed passengers to switch seats—especially during take-off.

Seth examined the slender gamine. He expected her to introduce herself and perhaps explain why she was suddenly sitting next to him.

"What?" she retorted snidely.

"Nothing," Seth murmured as he turned away.

It feels odd to be speaking first in Italian and now in Czech. I can't remember ever speaking in either language before.

Seth could read and understand just about any language, but he rarely enjoyed the opportunity to speak anything other than English (except with Mathieu, who always spoke to him in Fongbe. Mathieu got such a kick out of the fact that Seth could speak Fon. He never really got over it).

"So, why are you going to Prague?" the young woman probed—her ill-concealed attempt to strike up a conversation seemed obvious even to Seth.

"How do you know I'm going to Prague?" Seth dodged her slyly. "I could be staying on to the next connection."

"Whatever." The soubrette sarcastically relinquished the victory with a role of her eyes. "Where *are* you going then?"

"I'm going to school in Prague," Seth admitted with a smile. "You?"

This time the flirtatious minx didn't have an answer. Instead, she surveyed him up and down and inquired, "What are you going to school for?"

Cutting directly to the chase, Seth reached out his hand, "I'm Seth."

The young coquette considered his hand with absolutely no idea what he wanted from her. "Are you trying to shake my hand?" she taunted after a prolonged silence.

Seth withdrew his hand and tried to shrug off the embarrassment.

"I'm Amber," she said mockingly in a deep voice as she reached out to shake his hand—her infectious giggling supplanting her very business-like allocution.

Amber's blonde hair wrapped around her chiselled face like a pair of parentheses—it matched her tanned, athletic physique. Seth estimated Amber to be about nineteen. Flattered by her company, he sensed something mischievous about her easy smile that made him uncomfortable.

"So where are you from?" Seth noticed just the slightest twinge of sadness in her eyes when he asked her.

"Here and there," she jawed—avoiding the question. "You?"

Suddenly, Seth's eyes were the traitors. Avoiding eye contact, he turned toward the window and stared out at the empty sky. "I honestly don't know."

Amber thought he was joking. Seth's wit enticed her, so she flirted back, "Mystery Man: how sexy!"

Seth blushed as Amber stroked his arm playfully. He really liked the attention, but clearly, Amber belonged to a league of her own. One of the flight attendants rolled up with a trundling drink cart.

"Would you like a drink before we land?"

Seth started to say 'No, thank you when Amber pre-empted him, "Yes, we'd love one."

Squinting suspiciously at Amber through her bifocals, the fifty-something female insisted, "I'll have to see some ID."

Amber folded a piece of chewing gum into her mouth and handed her the wrapper. "There's your I.D." And with that she went back to her seat four rows back and across the aisle.

The plane landed in Prague on schedule, and much to Seth's relief, he'd secured a seat toward the front of the plane this time. Seth attempted to get Amber's attention, but her eyes were closed and a bulky pair of headphones were clamped down over her ears. Seth almost went over to her seat, but he lost his nerve.

Happy to be one of the first people off the aircraft, Seth hoped to accompany Amber to the baggage claim area on the lower level. But Amber disembarked last. Presumably, she waited in her seat until everyone else departed. Seth didn't want to come across like a stalker, so he loitered near the gate as long as he could without actually remaining stationary. This amounted to ambulating extremely slowly and making a point of stopping at every shop and newsstand between their gate and the escalator.

Seth 'ran into' Amber in an odd sort of way: she walked right past him.

"Going to get your bags?" Seth proposed invitingly after lunging forward to keep pace with her.

"No. I don't have any bags. Bye!" Amber motioned a little wave and disappeared into the crowd.

Seth surveyed Amber's diminishing soma as she became one with the throng. Begrudging the fact that he'd squandered his sole remaining opportunity to ask Amber for her number, Seth accepted his fate as a loner. Staring into the horde—indeterminately hoping to spot Amber but not knowing what he would do even if he did—Seth eventually decided to lumber over to the line at the turnstile.

Everything in the Ruzyně International Airport was labelled in English, Deutsch, and of course, Ĉesky. Seth understood them all. He located the luggage carousel for his flight and waited about forty minutes—marking the time by watching people and fantasising about the woman from his dream.

The carousel started up with a clank and proceeded to hum noisily as various pieces of baggage slid down onto the metal plates. Seth grew dizzy gawking at the revolving conveyor as he scrutinised each miscellaneous trunk, suitcase, and satchel. Finally, his small, black overnighter flew out of the opening at the top of the slide and tumbled down onto the spinning platform—producing a cloud of dust when it landed. It appeared as though someone had dragged it behind their car for a few kilometres. Waiting in anticipation for it to come around, Seth held his arm out ready to snatch it up as it passed in front of him. Then, doing his best to brush off what resembled tire tracks, Seth nudged his way through the crowded lower level toward the exit.

Besides the few clothes he'd packed, Seth didn't have much. His only other item was the notebook computer he'd stuffed inside his carry-on bag. With his badly soiled tote in one hand and his valise in the other, Seth flagged an approaching cab by extending his leg. Initially, the cab passed by him. But then the driver stopped, backed up, and waited for Seth to get in. When he read the address to the driver, her eyes engaged him through the mirror.

"That is far," she informed him in broken English. "Around one hundred and fifty CZK."

Seth suddenly realised that he'd forgotten to exchange his currency in the airport. "Will you accept U.S. Dollars?" he petitioned desperately.

The driver glared at him through the rear-view mirror. "Yes. Alright," she agreed in a reluctant tone. "I'll exchange them later when I'm off duty."

Seth felt bad for inconveniencing her. He calculated in his head that the fare would be about twelve dollars. He handed her two twenty-dollar bills to compensate.

"*Děkuji,*" he thanked her.

She accepted the generous tip with appreciation. Seth noticed on the driver's license that her first name was Vlasta.

"Vlasta, that's a pretty name," he complimented.

"*Děkuji,*" she answered—her big green eyes smiling back at him.

Vlasta's perfume smelled like plumeria and apricots, and her nails were perfectly manicured. This impressed Seth as uncommon for a cab driver.

"How long is the drive?" Seth asked as he settled into the seat and got comfortable.

"Mm…forty-five minutes," Vlasta estimated with a tilt of her head and a purse of her lips.

"Will you wake me up when we get there?"

Vlasta gestured with her hand that she would. Stretching out in the back seat, Seth drifted off to sleep.

The car made its way west on the E50 Expressway toward Plzen. Vlasta exited at the Křivoklát cut-off and drove along the Berounka River on Highway 116. After about forty-five minutes the car arrived at Křivoklát Castle. Seth woke up to a bumpy grinding of the tires as Vlasta pulled the cab over. Her eyes sparkled at him through the rear-view mirror.

"You don't mind sharing the fare with someone, do you?"

Before Seth could answer, a young woman opened the door and sat in the back seat next to him. Hiding behind sunglasses and a large sun hat, Seth recognised her all the same. She could be wearing a nun's habit, or even a full burka, and he would still instinctively discern it was her.

Seth spoke first, "You remind me of someone."

The woman didn't respond.

"Her name is Graziella."

Startled, the woman searched Seth's eyes. "How do you know my name?" she asked curiously in her lovely accent.

"I've always known you," Seth vowed, "as long as I can remember."

Even through her sunglasses, Graziella's eyes penetrated right into his soul. She removed her glasses and revealed the tears in her eyes.

"Have you found him yet?"

Chapter Thirty-Six
The Castle

"Excuse me, sir...sir!" Vlasta's voice penetrated Seth's slumber. "I'm sorry to wake you, but we're here."

Seth woke with a start. His neck hurt, and drool dribbled from the corner of his mouth as Vlasta eyed him through the rear-view mirror.

"Sorry. I'm sorry!" Seth yawned hard. "This is it?"

Vlasta shook her head impatiently. "I've got to get back."

"Of course! Okay." Seth continued to apologise as he handed her his last twenty-dollar bill. "Thank you."

"My pleasure," Vlasta smiled gracefully.

Seth grabbed his belongings and stepped out of the car. He watched as the cab drove off, and then he walked toward the front entrance. The building bore the likeness of an old Bavarian castle complete with grounds, gardens, and stables.

What is this place? Seth wondered dubiously.

He opened the door slowly and found himself standing in a great hall with eight doors on each wall—each door about twelve feet from the other. An illustrious chandelier hung from what must have been at least a twenty-foot ceiling while a lush, embroidered tapestry decorated the far wall and another carpeted the centre of the floor all the way to the entrance. Two large corridors broke in each direction immediately inside the monumental front door.

An innocent-looking young rosebud exited through the first door to the right and an older distinguished gentleman in his seventies followed after. Donning a tailored, blue business suit and a crisp white shirt, the well-dressed executive gaited with a limp and leaned on a cane. His blue and charcoal necktie bulged in a full Windsor knot just below his prominent Adam's apple. Smiling shyly, the *juene fille* pressed past Seth and saw herself out.

The gentleman eyed Seth keenly. "Seth? Seth North, I presume? I'm very pleased to make your acquaintance." He proceeded confidently toward Seth with his free hand extended. Seth reached out his hand and the man clutched it—nearly crushing it—and shook it firmly. "You made it!"

Seth didn't even try to disguise his bewilderment.

"I'm Dr Zahradnik. But please, you must call me Gabek. Welcome!"

Seth swallowed hard. "Thank you," he accepted somewhat reservedly.

"You must be weary. Oh! Where are my manners?" Dr Zahradnik strode over to a table by the wall and picked up the telephone. He spoke in a low, quiet tone. Seth couldn't perceive what he said. "Fiala will be here in a moment to assist you."

Literally one moment later, quick, light footsteps echoed from the corridor to the right. A stunning professional with long slender legs approached. "You must be Dr North. It's such a pleasure to meet you. And congratulations! Full fellowship—you *must* be someone special! My name is Fiala. If you prefer, you may call me Violet. I'm your personal assistant. I'll be at your beck and call for the next twelve months."

Fiala ended her sentences with a quick, upward inflection. It matched her bubbly and bouncy persona. Fiala's bronze skin and her silky, chestnut hair radiated the soft glow from the chandelier above her.

"If you'll follow me, I'll show you to your quarters."

Fiala turned and walked back down the same corridor she'd appeared from. Her hair bounced as she walked and her cream business skirt rose and fell softly over her svelte curves with every step. Fiala's sleek, refined appearance underscored the marked easiness about her—creating a contradiction of sorts that Seth found intriguing. He didn't feel inadequate around her at all like he usually did in the presence of women who looked like Fiala. And he couldn't believe that *she* would be at his beck and call for the next twelve months!

Maybe this was a good move after all, Seth considered to himself.

"I think you'll really like it here," Fiala replied confidently.

The corridor opened into the most spectacular sight: a room—easily the length of a football field and just as wide—with angles that aligned like a giant cube. Its marble walls supported great stained-glass windows depicting scenes from the Genesis account of creation—and the entire ceiling formed a single magnificent skylight. But by far the most amazing aspect of this room was the spotless parquet floor, which sparkled like pure crystal. A huge vacant expanse, it shimmered like a great sea of glass beneath Seth's feet. On the far side of the room, a palatial fountain added to the illusion that an infinite bottomless ocean extended beneath the floor's placid surface. Seth stopped in awe when he saw it.

Fiala stepped in close to Seth. "It takes your breath away. Doesn't it?"

"It's beautiful," Seth melted—mesmerised with admiration.

"I think I'm going to like you!" Fiala surmised promisingly. Her compliment came at the end of a very peculiar day for Seth, and he didn't know quite what to make of it.

"Follow me," Fiala beckoned as she led the way across the stately parquet floor.

Feeling a bit like Jesus walking on water, Seth followed close behind. The two sojourners traversed the great expanse to an enormous open staircase that led to an extravagant balcony with leather sofas and a pewter elevator.

"This is you." Fiala reached out her hand. As Seth placed his hand in hers, she squeezed it gently and offered invitingly, "call me if you need anything."

Then with a wink, Fiala spun around in her perky fashion and sashayed off. Seth could still hear her footsteps long after she'd disappeared out of sight.

"Oh my God!" Seth eyeballed the stairway. "This is *me*? I could fit my entire apartment complex into these stairs alone!"

Seth bolted up the first flight to the grandiose landing. Then, attempting to take it all in, he proceeded slowly up the second half of the stairway as if he were ascending the side of a great pyramid. Arriving on the balcony, Seth leaned over the banister and instantly became woozy. The veranda towered above an expansive courtyard below—the view made Seth dizzy. Like the spacious room with the parquet floor, the courtyard must have been at least a hundred yards long and just as wide. Seth could barely wrap his brain around it.

"I feel like King Nebuchadnezzar," he boasted.

Turning back inside, Seth wandered about the deluxe terrace. Bulky leather sofas faced each other on either end. In the centre of the room—against the back wall opposite the banister—a hulking pewter elevator figured ominously.

Seth approached the elevator. After a few minutes of complete awe, he hesitantly pushed the button. The polished doors opened slowly to reveal the spacious interior. Brass rails and carved oak mouldings dressed the custom carriage. A lush Persian rug sprawled out on the floor, and Mahogany benches topped with thick velvet cushions lined the walls. Seth stepped inside and found that, curiously, there were no numbered buttons to choose from. Instead, the doors simply closed automatically and the elevator slowly ascended on its own. When the doors opened again, Seth was beside himself.

"Can this get any better?"

Seth rambled through the rooms and took it all in. The suite came complete with its own study and a library. Inside the study, warm embers glowed in a ponderous stone fireplace. Another fireplace dominated an entire wall in the massive master bedroom, and the master bath featured a large Jacuzzi tub. The living and dining rooms were both splendid with scintillating onyx floors and a terrace that extended out over an august lake.

"As imperial as this all is, right now I'm only interested in two things: the shower and the bed."

Seth dropped his meagre belongings to the floor, found the shower, and turned on the water. As he undressed, a young gentlewoman entered.

"Here, let me get that for you," she offered softly. "I'm Zuzu, your bed maid."

Embarrassed by his ignorance, Seth asked anyway, "What's a bed maid?"

"That's funny!" Zuzu giggled. "Now, let's get you out of *those* clothes." Zuzu's inflection gave Seth the distinct impression that she thought there was something wrong with his clothes. She checked the water temperature and then bid him entrée. "All ready."

Seth stepped into the shower expecting to find a shower. Instead he entered a steamy, chasmal chamber more cavernous than the elevator he'd just been in. The shower towered ostentatiously like a great stone monolith—smooth, luxurious, and swanky. Granite benches adjoined the walls with Jacuzzi jets all around about twelve inches above the seats. Four showerheads protruded from the parapets—one centred on each wall. After the hot water washed all of Seth's stress away, he turned off the water and patted himself dry with a thick, thirsty towel. Climbing into bed, he fell into a deep sleep.

Seth woke up to the smell of coffee and bacon. Laying in a commodious bed surrounded in sleepy luxury, he voraciously inhaled the aroma. "Mmm, that smells so good!"

Zuzu bounced over to him and stopped somewhat startled. "You're awake?" she observed in a pleasantly surprised tone. "Would you like breakfast?"

"I'm starving!" Seth admitted. "Breakfast sounds great."

"Okay!" Zuzu smiled happily and sprang back out of the bedroom—her pigtails making her appear even more chipper than usual.

Seth dropped back deep into the ductile feather pillows. Floating in his plush accommodations, he stared at the vaulted ceiling. Within ten minutes, Zuzu returned with a breakfast tray containing more food than twenty people could eat. She set it on the bed and placed her arm behind his back.

"Okay, sit up," she bubbled.

As Seth leaned forward, Zuzu propped his pillows up for him.

"Okay, lean back."

Seth sunk comfortably back into the downy pillows as Zuzu folded the thick comforter down around his legs. She placed the breakfast tray over Seth's lap and poured his coffee.

"Do you need anything else?"

"No thank you, Zuzu," Seth acknowledged appreciatively.

"Alright. I'll be back in a little while. Enjoy!" Zuzu bounced out of sight, and soon Seth heard the sound of running bathwater.

"This is amazing! Fresh mango, tangerines, English saffron cakes, Canadian bacon, eggs, coffee and guava juice." Seth couldn't remember ever being so excited over breakfast before. After hesitating a moment to take in its visual splendour, Seth scarfed it down like a ravenous animal.

It's odd, he thought to himself. *I'm normally not that hungry in the morning. Is it still morning?* Seth wondered. With the heavy embroidered curtains pulled shut, it was impossible to discern the time.

When Zuzu returned, Seth asked her, "What time is it, Zuzu?"

"It's seven thirty," she chirped.

"Seven thirty *a.m.*?"

Zuzu reached for the breakfast tray. "No silly! It's seven thirty *p.m.* You've been asleep all day."

After his bath, Seth received word that Dr Zahradnik wanted to see him. As he approached the office off the main hall by the front door, Seth saw that the door was open. Knocking on the door jam and poking his head inside, Seth found the doctor busying himself with paperwork of some kind.

"Seth, please come in. Have a seat."

Seth stepped inside the office and sat down beside Dr Zahradnik's monstrous zebrawood desk.

"Would you like anything?" Dr Zahradnik offered, collecting his papers and setting them aside. "A drink, a cigar?"

"No thanks. I'm fine."

"Do you remember this place?" The elderly man stared at Seth inquisitively.

"How can I remember it when I've never been here before?"

"Oh, but you *have* been here, many times before."

"What are you talking about?" Seth objected with a thinly veiled lack of confidence.

"Do you remember this?" Dr Zahradnik held the outline of Craig Ryan's doctoral dissertation in his hands. "Please, take it," he implored as he offered it to Seth. "Study it."

"What *is* this?" Seth puzzled as he flipped through the pages—skimming over bits and pieces.

"That?" Dr Zahradnik laughed cynically as he rose from his chair. "That's how I found you." His words were punctuated with the sound of his cane tapping on the floor. "It's only the single-most important scientific discovery in modern history. *Your* research easily qualified as the most insightful work I'd ever read, Seth—it was truly cutting edge. But *this*? This is *brilliant*."

Extending his arm toward the long corridor to the right, Dr Zahradnik gestured for his guest to accompany him on a little walk. "Please, there's something I'd like to show you."

"Something else?" Seth cracked uneasily—still examining the outline. As the two of them continued down the corridor, they approached the impressive room with marble walls and the magnificent fountain.

"Stroll around. Familiarise yourself. You really don't remember this place?"

Wandering about amazed, Seth made a startling discovery. "There's no echo," he noted with surprise. "What is this place?"

"This is one of your greatest contributions to mankind," Dr Zahradnik beamed. "This is your brainchild."

"I don't understand," Seth puzzled suspiciously. "It's a room."

Dr Zahradnik became visibly agitated. "It's not a room, Seth. It's an *incubator*." The doctor's tone grew even more intense. "You applied to this very program nearly twenty years ago. You were fresh out of medical school and green—but with ideas that no one's ever thought of before. Your vision and insight turned the literature of the day on its head. So, I brought you in and I gave you everything you needed."

Pounding his fist into his open palm with the rhythm of his words, Dr Zahradnik elaborated. "When you needed materials, I gave you materials. When you needed money, I gave you money. And when you needed bodies, the Committee supplied you with all the human subjects you could maim, mutilate, and dismember. And *you*, Seth! You paid attention to every meticulous detail. You showed such promise—*such* an eye for detail."

Seth did his best to block out the words by holding his hands to his head and trying to plug his ears. This capacious room now somehow started closing in on him, and everything was spinning. "No! You're lying! That wasn't me. That wasn't me!"

"Oh, no?" Dr Zahradnik insisted. "What do you make of this?"

Fiala handed him a large binder filled with notes. The binder detailed horrible and cruel experiments on human subjects—failed experiments that went back nearly two decades. Men, women, and children horribly disfigured, mutilated, and ultimately discarded.

Dr Zahradnik opened it and read the last entry dated January 10, 1990:

At last, I've attained my greatest success: I've achieved perfect adult replication. I am now ready for stage two.

Seth's mind split in half. "Adult replication? That's absurd! It's not even possible. This can't be true."

"Oh, but it is true," the doctor remonstrated. "When you first proposed your ideas to the Committee, the others thought you were mad. But *I* believed in you. I convinced them to let you conduct your research. And when you needed more time and more participants, I arranged that as well."

"What Committee?" Seth protested. "What *research*?"

"Don't tell me you can't remember, Seth! You were working on the ultimate soldier: strong, ruthless, heartless, and brutal. Together, we promised the Committee an insurmountable army that would enable it to rule the world and beyond!"

"Rule the world?" Seth ridiculed, "Are you mad?"

"At first, you worked day and night. You never slept! You never gave up! The Committee could barely keep up with your demand for more and more flesh. Secret prison camps were set up all over the world to cage your victims until they could be flown here."

Dr Zahradnik pointed in the direction of the vast courtyard Seth had seen earlier. "That very courtyard used to be filled with thousands of captives. They were *your* captives, Seth. Standing on the banister, you presided like a god—deciding who to carve up next. You kept your victims alive as you dismembered them because you needed living tissue. The monstrous beasts that you created tore open pregnant women and ripped the heads off of little children. Each creation emerged more aggressive and vicious than the last, but none of them met your rigid criteria. You fed each successive replica more and more innocent blood to test how long it would continue to kill without remorse. And when one failed, you sacrificed scores of men to create another—only to go through the entire process all over again. Once you finally did achieve the ultimate warrior, you planned to replicate thousands at a time right here in this very room."

Looking like a proud father, the doctor boasted, "You successfully mapped out the sequence for mass-producing human clones, Seth! You discovered the precise algorithm. Together we could have built the ultimate army! But I couldn't do it without you. Nobody could."

Seth thought he was going to pass out. "I need to sit down," he petitioned as he closed his eyes and braced the weight of his upper body against his thighs. Breathing in through his nose and out through his mouth, Seth's eyelids twitched and his head trembled as he struggled not to swallow his tongue.

"Dr North!" Fiala exclaimed as she rushed to his side. "He's choking!" she alerted Dr Zahradnik.

"He's fine," the doctor related calmly. "It's only his imagination. His cranial nerves are overwhelmed, and his major motor functions are becoming impaired."

"Oh my God!" Seth abhorred, "What's that smell?"

"It's the smell of death. One never forgets it. Now, just breathe deep, Seth. In and out, that's it, in and out…"

Seth obeyed D. Zahradnik's instructions until the psychosomatic incident passed. Meanwhile, Fiala offered Seth a chair at a table with a large computer screen and three binders.

"The Committee funded your work by the billions, Seth. Just look at this place! You lived here like a deity with no limitations or laws of any kind. You held the very power of life and death over all who entered these walls. No one else has ever been so cruel! Never has anyone been so evil. But after only three years *you were the one* who succumbed to remorse."

Seth listened in horror. Like a zombie, he remained speechless and motionless. Teetering on the verge of a nervous breakdown, he reluctantly believed what the doctor was saying, but he didn't remember any of it.

I'm a monster, he convinced himself. *I must be the worst kind of monster!*

Dr Zahradnik seized Seth by the arm. "Listen to me, Seth. I'm your friend, you can trust me. You're no monster—you're a *genius*. Morality and laws don't apply to men like you. This is your gift. It's your calling."

Letting go of Seth's arm, he confided in a far less grandiose tone, "The Committee wanted its army. And it still does, Seth! I did all I could to convince it to give us more time, but you disappeared and left me holding the bag."

Dr Zahradnik held up the outline of Craig Ryan's dissertation. "It wasn't until a certain dissertation came to my attention that I found you again. Craig Ryan's dissertation claimed to be able to transfer and retrieve data between a digital storage device and a living organism. He'd discovered the perfect solution to controlling the collective mind and will of our army, Seth. This provided the answer to instilling the will to kill without remorse in every last soldier! Most importantly, Craig Ryan's dissertation offered us the key to the great mystery we'd been working on."

"So why don't you get Craig Ryan to help you?" Seth suggested—still unsure as to why he was there.

"I know of only one mind capable of writing this dissertation, Seth. There's never been the slightest doubt in my mind who it belongs to. But when I traced it back to you, I found that you'd completely snapped and taken on an entirely new identity as Craig A. Ryan. You wanted to start over completely pure and free of the abominations of your past. You studied medicine at Stanford University, and you were naturally drawn to biotechnology."

Dr Zahradnik pulled up a photograph on the computer. "Do you recognise this woman?"

Seth stared in total amazement. It was the woman from his dream. He closed his eyes to get a better look.

"Graziella." The name emanated from somewhere deep inside his core.

"Yes, Graziella," the doctor related affectionately. "I see you haven't forgotten everything."

"I don't actually remember her," Seth confessed. "She's been haunting my dreams."

The warm smile faded from Dr Zahradnik's face. "Once I found you at Stanford, I hardly recognised you. Your hair had turned completely grey. The Committee planned to kill you, Seth. It demanded nothing short of a miracle to make the members reconsider. But I believed in you. So, I exacted every ounce of my influence to ensure that you received another chance. I convinced the Committee that *you* were the one who would ultimately lead the ten members of the Committee in world domination, and I made up the cover story about the Pentagon needing to back up its files because of Y2K."

"Y2K?"

"That's how I convinced you to come back to work for us. I approached you—rather I approached Craig Ryan—with an offer I knew you couldn't refuse: the opportunity to test your theory by backing up the Pentagon's mainframe. The Committee never worried about Y2K, Seth. Who do you think dreamed up the Y2K scare in the first place?"

"You made up Y2K?"

"We wanted to heighten Americans' perception of vulnerability in order to justify more military spending. It's our bread and butter, Seth."

Dr Zahradnik leaned in close. "You have to understand, the Committee spent *a lot* of money on you. It never stopped searching for you ever since you disappeared from the program thirteen years ago. When you turned up the first time in '99, the other members insisted that you were too much of a liability. They all wanted you dead. I had to put my own neck on the chopping block to save your ass. It wasn't easy, but I persuaded the others that it wouldn't be prudent to kill you just yet. If not for the brilliance of your dissertation, I would never have succeeded in convincing them. Fortunately, the genius of your work spoke for itself, and the Committee agreed to postpone your assassination at my request. Still, it certainly wasn't about to let you out of its sight again."

An expression of loss pervaded the doctor's countenance. He looked like a gambler reduced to his last dollar—his obscure smiled vaguely, concealing the desperation behind it. "Can you imagine my alarm when you disappeared *again*? Seth, you put me in a terribly difficult predicament. The Committee ordered you dead on sight—no questions asked. After it sabotaged your plane, the Committee thought that it had finally eliminated you once and for all. But when it was unable to recover your remains, the standing order for your assassination remained. When you turned up alive in New Haven, I fully expected that to be your swan song. The fact that you're still alive is a miracle in itself."

"Why *am* I still alive, then?"

"I believe it's your destiny, Seth."

Seth felt a distinct impatience. "Where's all this leading? Where's Graziella?"

Dr Zahradnik smiled reminiscently—the way one does when they've narrowly escaped disaster. "Back in '99 when you hit a brick wall on the Y2K project over *the ethics of cloning another human being*—of all things Seth—I really started to squirm. I realised that the Committee would kill us both if you didn't produce. Fortunately, like all geniuses, you have idiosyncrasies. One of yours is that you think out loud."

"You mean I talk to myself?"

"Unceasingly!" the doctor taunted. "Not the best practice when you're doing highly-classified work for the Pentagon. Wouldn't you agree?"

Seth half-heartedly agreed with a shrug of his shoulders.

"When it became clear that you were unwilling to clone another human being because of *ethical* concerns, I realised that you were *not* the same Seth North I once knew. When you decided to pitch your pathetic little software solution to the Committee instead, it became obvious that we were both dead men if I didn't do something quick. Thank heaven, you revealed that you needed to make a sample back-up file, upload it, and check it for accuracy. I anticipated that you'd have to physically read the data in order to verify its quality, so I planted the notes from your research into all of the Pentagon's mainframe files. It's a handy trick I learned from the spooks for framing someone. The virus infiltrates every single file in the network and then simply erases itself after forty-eight hours. This way, you were certain to be exposed to your own notes."

A rather cocky smile betrayed the good doctor's overall satisfaction with the concept. "When you called and made your appointment to access the main frame, I had my window. I deliberately removed security from the premises to encourage you to take your time. I didn't want you to feel inhibited by the concern that you were being watched, even though you were, of course. I hoped that your own notes detailing all the people that you'd personally slaughtered would trigger something in your memory—anything. But it didn't work. Instead, when you read about all the horrible atrocities that *you* committed, you decided to clone yourself and use the data as evidence against us."

Zuzu approached with a tray containing two drinks: a Meyers's rum and Coke and a Macallan's thirty-year-old single malt scotch.

"We allowed you to go through with the data transfer procedure just to see if you could actually do it. And damn it, Seth! You really pulled it off!"

Fiala presented a cedar humidor, lifted the lid and held it before the two men. Inside were twenty La Corona cigars—hand-made in 1937.

Dr Zahradnik offered one to Seth. "Please, you used to really enjoy these."

"No thanks," Seth declined, "I don't smoke."

Dr Zahradnik selected a cigar for himself and sipped his scotch. Waving his hand to Fiala, he quietly asserted, "You don't seem to do much of anything anymore."

Seth tasted the rum and Coke. Instantly reminded of the one he'd had on the plane he reminisced, "This really *is* good."

"We were all very impressed that you perfected the digital data transfer to living flesh. But knowing what you planned to do with it, we needed to stop you before you got out of the building."

Unable to conceal his irritation, the doctor slammed his empty scotch glass on the table. "We simply asked those idiot CIA operatives to take you into custody. You'd think they could get that right! Instead, they killed your clone and shot you in the shoulder. And still, they let you get away!"

Tossing a quick, confident glance toward Seth, he admitted, "At first we thought that you'd only transferred the data to the clone. It wasn't until after I checked your Fulbright record that I realised you must have transferred the Pentagon data to your own brain as well. How else could you have mastered so much in the few short years you'd been missing?"

Seth's eyes brightened with newfound understanding. "That's how I learned all those languages?" Quickly however, Seth's enlightenment turned to doubt. "But if I can access all the data from the Pentagon mainframe, why can't I remember anything from my own past—not even the research notes that you say you uploaded?"

Dr Zahradnik discounted Seth's inquiry regarding the notes with a brush of his hand. "The files I added containing your notes were temporary. They'd already erased themselves by the time you successfully transferred the data out of the mainframe. As for the reason you can't remember anything else from your past, I believe that you don't *want* to remember. Another side of you has sequestered your will, and it refuses to share control with the Seth North from the past."

The usurper stared back with an empty, unknowing gaze.

"After those incompetent CIA agents shot your clone, they tortured the poor creature. The damn thing told us secrets that were so old, we needed to go back and look them up just to verify them. This is the main reason that we were initially so convinced that we'd captured the clone and not you."

Rolling the cigar between his thumb and forefinger, the doctor reached into his pocket and retrieved a double-bladed guillotine. After severing the end of the cigar, he lit it and puffed it several times until the end blazed with a red-hot cherry. Drawing the smoke into his mouth, Dr Zahradnik twirled it around with his tongue before releasing it with a smack.

"One thing I have to say about the CIA: they certainly are effective at getting information. But the fools killed the clone in the process!"

"They *killed* the clone?" Seth gawked.

"Yes, unfortunately." The doctor ashed his cigar into a lead crystal ashtray. "And once you got away, you were as good as dead yourself. You'd become a liability, Seth. You knew too much."

Biting on the end of his cigar and squinting with one eye from the smoke, the doctor chuckled, "Of course, little did we realise just *how much* you actually knew! But since we had absolutely no way of knowing what you'd tell or to whom, the Committee wanted you dead. It couldn't risk the information falling into the wrong hands. When the agents failed to apprehend you, the Committee decided to kill you against my wishes. It's a ruthless game that we play, Seth. You knew the rules when you joined in the first place. Now there's only one way out." The doctor's eyes were hollow. He stared emptily with a flat affect.

Seth focused sombrely on the fountain. *Who are these people?*

The warm smile returned to Dr Zahradnik's face, "I don't want you dead, Seth."

"What *do* you want, then?"

"I just want you to remember who you are. I want you to remember your work."

"What happened to Graziella? Why won't you tell me?"

Leaning back in his chair, Dr Zahradnik folded his arms and broke the news to Seth gently. "Graziella's story is intricately wound up in your own. If you'll bear with me, I promise to answer all your questions at the proper time. Do we have a deal?"

"That means you're not going to tell me?"

"It means I'll tell you at the *proper time*," the doctor repeated. "Do we have a deal?"

"What choice do I have?"

Dr Zahradnik puffed his cigar and eyed Seth with his best poker face—as if to call his bluff.

After a moment or two, Seth capitulated, "Alright, we have a deal."

Dr Zahradnik shook his head. "Good. After we discovered the link that you made…By the way, what a terribly clever idea! I was most impressed! After we discovered it, we understood that either you actually believed yourself to be the clone, or you simply wanted us to believe it. We took great interest because, as far as we knew, the CIA eliminated the clone back in Washington. Of course, you can imagine our suspicion when you signed the entry with your real name! Honestly Seth, most of us thought you were playing a game of cat and mouse."

Dr Zahradnik sat back and rolled the remnants of his cigar between his thumb and index finger. Then he gazed at Seth as though he knew a great secret that he just couldn't keep to himself a moment longer. "Do you know how you did it, Seth? Do you know how you transferred the Pentagon data to your own brain?"

"What makes you think that *I* did? How can you know for certain that I'm not the clone?"

A huge boisterous laugh exploded from Dr Zahradnik's frail, bony frame. "Now there's the Seth North that I know—always considering every possibility."

The doctor collected his thoughts as he put out his cigar. "Quite honestly?" he admitted in a more serious tone, "from an empirical standpoint, I don't know. We only assumed we'd apprehended the clone back in DC because of all the secrets it disclosed. After the operatives tortured and killed it, the stupid bastards disposed of its body in the incinerator. So, we no longer possessed the means to verify whether we'd killed the clone or the original. We were left with no choice but to assume that the CIA killed the clone and that the real Seth North remained at large."

As if right on cue, Fiala inserted the surveillance video from the Pentagon recorded the day of the data transfer.

"As you can see, the surveillance tape reveals that the operatives entered the room shooting. In the chaos that ensued, it's impossible to tell which one of you is the clone and which is the real Seth North. Signing the link with your real name led us to think you were making sport of us by *pretending* to believe you were a clone. But when I discovered your Fulbright record, it gave me considerable reason to doubt that conclusion."

Seth curled his lips and raised his eyebrows. "So, what are you saying?"

"I'm saying that reviewing your Fulbright record has convinced me that you weren't *pretending* to be a clone. You honestly didn't know who you were."

"But if we both received the Pentagon data; I still don't understand why you're so convinced that I'm Seth North and not the clone."

"I've watched the tape of your replication procedure again and again. You were conscious the entire time. The data in the Pentagon mainframe should have taken days to write to the clone's brain, but it only took an hour! And it should have left the clone in a vegetative state. I racked my brains trying to comprehend what happened. And then it came to me! The human brain is nothing more than a vast supercomputer, right? What happens when you write files to a hard drive?"

"No clue," Seth shrugged in ignorance.

"The computer makes a temporary cache first, sort of a photocopy, and then it writes the data in the new location. But since the clone's brain wasn't fully formed, the data needed an external hard drive as it were—somewhere the cache could be stored temporarily until the clone's brain developed the capacity to receive it. That's why the data transferred so quickly. The mainframe wrote it to a temporary cache in your brain first."

Dr Zahradnik glowed with satisfaction over his own cleverness. "Once the clone's brain was fully developed, the temporary cache copied to his brain as well. It only required an hour for the temporary file to be stored in your brain and then copied to the clone's. But the actual writing of the data to its new location in both of your brains necessitated days. You and the clone both enjoyed full access to the temporary cache while it transcribed the permanent file. And while the clone didn't live long enough to display any significant memory loss, you did! You didn't lose your memory in the plane crash, Seth. The Pentagon data wiped it out. Or should I say, the Pentagon data *should* have wiped it out."

Dr Zahradnik beamed like a child on a Ferris wheel, excitedly waving to his admiring parents below. "For nine years you masqueraded as Craig Ryan. But Craig Ryan is the alter ego of Seth North. Your unconscious memory remains, Seth. Don't you see? Your pain won't let you remember, but your love won't let you forget."

Chapter Thirty-Seven
Seth's Father

Dr Zahradnik stood up and motioned for Seth to follow him. Turning toward the large staircase, he cautioned, "Not everything is as it seems, Seth. The best that I can tell, there's no scientific explanation as to why you shouldn't be able to remember everything."

Leaning on Seth's arm, he began to hobble up the stairs. "Your father collaborated with the Nazis...a brilliant man! I see a lot of him in you. The war broke out just before his thirty-second birthday. He originally came from Budapest, but in 1939 he went to Poland to work at Auschwitz. Your father was a genetics man just like you, Seth. We owe much of what we know today to his early work."

When the two men reached the top of the stairs, they continued toward the elevator. "After the war ended, your father left to work in the United States. His work never changed that much over the years. This is one of the reasons you remind me so much of him. You were both so driven—so obsessed!"

Seth was growing impatient. "Look, I'd like an answer. Where's Graziella?"

"I was under the impression that we'd come to an understanding about that."

"There is no fellowship program, is there?"

"Seth, have you been listening to anything that I've said? If there were a fellowship program, *you'd* be leading it. Now, can you remember anything about your work?"

"I don't want to talk about that."

"Your father wanted to bury the secret as well."

Seth could barely conceal his angst. "*What* secret?"

"What secret? Well, my boy, the very same secret that you've buried deep inside yourself."

At that point Seth became indignant. His heart palpitated wildly and his breathing intensified. "Look! I have no interest in trying to figure out your riddles. I demand three straight answers. *Straight* answers—do you understand? No more rhetorical questions. No more vague, obscure answers. And no more strolls down haunted memory lane."

"What are your questions?" Dr Zahradnik countered in a tone that sounded like he'd just pulled out his checkbook.

At first, Seth just eyed the doctor with suspicion. "How do I know I can trust you?"

"Try me."

Inhaling slowly through his nose and exhaling through his mouth, Seth regained his composure and averted his stare. Then, looking back at the doctor, he complied, "Okay…Where is Graziella? Why am I here? And when can I go home?"

"Graziella is here. You're here for Graziella. And you can leave whenever you choose."

"Graziella is *here*?" Seth implored excitedly. "Here in Prague, or here in this place?"

Dr Zahradnik remained silent.

"Well?"

"Seth," the doctor pacified, "you have to listen to me. You're not ready to see her."

"This is exactly what I'm talking about!" Seth exploded. "You keep talking in circles. If Graziella is here, why can't I see her? What is it that you want from me?"

"I want you to come back to work."

"You want me to commit more of the butchery you were talking about last night? Absolutely not!"

"No, Seth. I want you to focus on much more important work right now."

Dr Zahradnik reached over and handed Seth a notebook from his bookshelf. "Your father used this as a journal while working at Auschwitz."

Seth opened the notebook. The notes and sketches were sickening. "Why are you showing me this?" Seth slammed the notebook down on the desk.

"You know, you used to be an expert on your father's writings. I would always find you studying his work."

"Here we go again." Seth closed his eyes and shook his head.

"Your grandmother came from the Ukraine. She gave birth to your father in 1907 and named him Krzegosz after your grandfather who froze to death in the winter of 1918—he died trying to return home from Siberia after serving in the Czech Legion. The legion successfully forced the Bolsheviks into retreat after capturing a large portion of the railway during the summer. But winter came early, and the one and only rail system moved slowly and often fell under attack. Many died including your grandfather."

Seth vented his agitation by chewing on his lip and nodding his head obnoxiously after every syllable.

"Your grandmother raised your father alone. The two were very close."

"What does any of this have to do with Graziella?"

"There's a method to my madness, Seth. Just indulge me a while. What do you say?"

"Fine." Seth crossed his arms and grit his teeth.

"Shortly after your father turned eighteen, your grandmother gave birth to two boys—identical twins. Your grandmother loved these boys. They brought her great comfort. But your father manifested extreme jealousy towards them. When the Nazi's rose to power, your father wanted to join the party. However, being an East European made this very difficult. The Nazis denied your father again and again, but he persisted. He volunteered at Buchenwald when it first opened and he demonstrated enormous talent. After some time, the Nazis offered him a position. He stayed on at Buchenwald until 1939. After the war broke out, your father earned acceptance into the Nazi party by betraying two of his own blood relatives. These were, of course, his two twin brothers."

A masked intensity appeared in Dr Zahradnik's stare. The tone of his voice remained calm, but the anger in his eyes betrayed him. "The brothers were sent to Auschwitz," he recounted without emotion.

"What kind of person," Seth stammered, "sends his own flesh and blood to Auschwitz? I don't want to hear anymore!"

"Well then, I suppose we're through here." Searching his breast pocket for his trifocals, Dr Zahradnik stood as though he were about to leave.

"Wait! What about Graziella?" Seth interjected anxiously.

Expostulating very matter-of-factly, the doctor demurred, "We haven't gotten to her yet."

"Well, when *will* we get to her?"

"When it's time, of course."

"Can you please make it quick?"

"Because it's you," the doctor quipped like a used-car salesman. And with that, he sat back down and proceeded with Seth's family history. "Your father actually met Adolph Hitler once. Did you know that?"

"I'm not at all surprised," Seth cogitated. "At this rate, I was half expecting him to be 'Uncle Adolph.'"

Dr Zahradnik let out an infectious chortle. "Very funny—really, that's quite witty. But seriously, the war started going badly on the Eastern Front. It got to where the Germans were losing more troops to the bitter cold than to the enemy. Your father's acceptance into the party required the approval of some very high-level Nazis. Evidently, the Fuhrer was so impressed by your father's devotion to the party that he personally commissioned him to pioneer a new program at Auschwitz. Your father couldn't have dreamed of a greater honour, and he threw himself into his work—experimenting with a variety of possibilities."

"What kind of a program?"

"A cutting edge, top-secret program. Legend has it that it was the brainchild of Hoess, but since the death camps fell under the purview of the SS, your father answered directly to Himmler."

"Do I want to know what my father did for this cutting edge, top-secret program?"

"Initially, the Nazi's enlisted him to prove the superiority of the Aryan race."

"How was he supposed to do that?"

"That," Dr Zahradnik raised his eyebrows, "the Nazis left for him to figure out. And let me tell you, Goebbels had *nothing* on your father! If he hadn't devoted his life to science, he could have managed the entire Nazi propaganda machine single-handedly in his sleep."

"So that's how he *proved* the superiority of the Aryan race—with propaganda? Not very scientific," Seth objected.

"Oh, but it was very scientific," Dr Zahradnik insisted, "and ingenious at the same time! First, he set out to document the physical inferiority of other races by taking precise measurements of prisoners' bodies and paying great detail to their imperfections. Then he measured the biggest, the strongest and the most symmetrically perfect Germans he could find and focused on all their positive physical qualities."

"But the imperfections of the prisoners in the death camps must have been extensive. The Nazis were working and starving those poor people to death!"

"Exactly! Of course, when your father published his results, he deliberately failed to mention that particular independent variable as a potential causal factor. Instead, he presented his 'hard scientific data' as evidence of the superiority of the Aryan race."

"So, is that it?" Seth sounded a little relieved. "Is some sloppy, biased research all that my father did for the Nazis?"

"Not quite. As with all high-ranking Nazi officials, your father had to earn Hitler's trust gradually. He soon learned that proving the superiority of the Aryan race was only secondary to his mission. After demonstrating his competence and efficiency in tackling his first assignment, your father was commissioned to design the perfect soldier: invincible, immune to suffering, and…"

"Immortal?" Seth chimed in cynically.

"Well, let's just say as immortal as a soldier could be in the 1940's. But because the field of genetics still wallowed in its embryonic stages, your father was forced to rely strictly on empirical observations alone." Dr Zahradnik referred to the sketches in the notebook—praising Seth's father for his keen attention to detail.

"I don't want to look at those again," Seth refused.

"Oh, come now," the doctor rationalised. "They're only sketches."

Seth reluctantly perused the contents of the notebook with revulsion. Page after page unveiled how his father's work gradually advanced.

"Your father became obsessed with perfection, Seth—just like you. But genetic mapping and splicing were not available to him. Back then, no replication of any kind existed. Your father did everything 'the old-fashioned way,' as they say, 'with needle and thread'." His futile attempt to interject a little humour into the conversation fell on deaf ears. Seth didn't find it amusing in the least.

"Your father's work resembled your own in many respects. Of course, he could only slice and sew." Dr Zahradnik proceeded to recount the details of a number of failed attempts to extract superior body parts from one prisoner and use them to replace inferior body parts on another. "The prospects were beyond comprehension," he expounded. "Your father essentially laid the groundwork for *your* future accomplishments."

Pushing a large photo album across his desk, Dr Zahradnik's eyes beamed with intensity. "Initially the experiments produced hideous results, and your father photographed every last monstrosity. Here, have a glimpse for yourself."

Seth reluctantly reached for the album. After hesitating momentarily, he opened the front cover. "Oh!" Seth vomited in his mouth. His gag reflex forced the vile excretion back down but the burning sensation lingered in his throat.

The photos revealed men, women and children with arms, legs, and a host of other body parts missing. Horribly disfigured, they looked like lepers—their flesh appearing to have rotted right off of their bodies.

"You've really lost your edge, haven't you?" the doctor observed with disappointment.

"Yeah," Seth agreed, "and you've lost your mind! What's wrong with you people? This isn't the kind of thing you keep a scrapbook of."

"There are far worse things to remember."

Neither said a word for what felt like an eternity. The old man studied Seth's face with deep interest. Then with a sigh of exasperation, he confessed, "Up until now, I've been indulging myself in the hope that you were the same old Seth North after all. Right up until this *very moment*, I've continued to entertain the remote possibility that you really had been just toying with us all along. At the very least, I'd hoped my former colleague was still inside you somewhere and that I could somehow draw him out. But I can see now that's not the case. The old Seth wouldn't have so much as blinked at something so benign."

"Benign?" Seth disputed. "You call those photos benign?"

"I've watched you eat a sandwich while you were up to your elbows in someone else's guts—the fowl stench of their excrement nearly thick enough to choke out their blood-curdling screams."

"That wasn't me."

"Clearly not," Dr Zahradnik agreed. "Clearly not."

"So, what happened to those people in the photos?" Seth inquired—eager to change the subject.

"Their bodies rejected the grafted flesh." The doctor's monotone voice sounded detached and clinical. "But this led your father to the discovery that would change the course of medical science right to this very day. You see, he eventually realised that a much lower level of rejection occurred if the harvested body parts came from a blood relative. I know it seems quite obvious to us now, but we owe this common knowledge to your father."

Seth turned cold and pale. Some might have been proud to learn that their father discovered such an important medical breakthrough. But Seth's skin crawled over what he'd just heard.

"Your father stumbled upon this discovery quite by accident." Scooting his chair around the desk to sit next to Seth, the doctor flipped through the photo album to a section with photos of identical twins. "He enjoyed very few occasions to work with identical twins in the camps. But when he did, he found that often the imperfections in one were not present in the other—and vice-versa. Since twins are usually very similar to one another in size and skin tone, employing the body parts from one twin to correct the flaws of the other precluded the time-consuming necessity of suitably matching donor to recipient. This is where your father's work became very interesting."

Making a muscle with one arm and clutching his bicep with the other hand, Dr Zahradnik alluded metaphorically, "This is where the real 'muscle' of his work began to develop."

"How clever," Seth extolled sarcastically.

"After measuring a given set of twins' physical features in great detail and deciding which imperfections could be corrected via the body parts of the other twin, your father decided which twin would be the donor and which would be the recipient."

"So, the twin with the fewest flaws became the recipient?"

"Hardly. More often than not, the recipient was simply the twin that survived—and this test incorporated much of his other research. You see, in the course of his work, your father exposed his subjects to a variety of stimuli: excessive blood loss, hypothermia and pressure chambers as well as more basic forms of torture such as multiple fractures, concussions, and amputations. Ultimately, the twin that survived the longest became the recipient. Your father would then attempt to put it back together. Once he nursed the surviving twin back to health, he'd subject it to a new round of testing: punctured eardrums, severe abdominal wounds, infections—even decapitation in some instances."

"Why?" Seth asked abhorrently. "*Why* would he do that?"

"To determine how long they could survive a multitude of battlefield wounds and conditions. Do you realise that your father pioneered procedures that were decades ahead of the medical technology of his day? Combat surgery would never be the same *because* of him."

Seth closed his eyes in sickened outrage. Extending his arms with his open palms out, he motioned for Dr Zahradnik to cease and desist. But it proved to no avail. The zealous doctor held steadfast to his speech—resolute in his discourse, indicating no intention of stopping. And while it may be true that Seth could leave at any time, he knew that Dr Zahradnik would not tell him what he wanted to know unless he stayed. So, Seth patiently endured the doctor's repugnant exaltation of his father's legacy and his despicable Nazi deeds.

Hobbling to the window and tapping his cane, Dr Zahradnik drank in the night sky. With a puzzled expression on his face, he wondered out loud, "Do you think there are other life forms out there?"

"I have no idea," Seth admitted indifferently as he dropped the photo album back on the desk and pushed it as far away from his physical person as possible.

Peering at Seth through his trifocals, Dr Zahradnik recovered his original train of thought. "When the recipient twins accepted the transplants much more readily, your father made a pre-eminent medical discovery. From then on, he continued his work exclusively with recipients and donors who were blood relatives of one another. It became common practice for him to graft bones or transplant limbs and organs from father to son, mother to daughter or brother to sister. Your father greatly advanced our knowledge of a number of medical procedures common today such as bone grafting and organ transplants."

Seth put his hands up as though he were being robbed and backed away toward the door. "This has been very enlightening, doctor. Thank you. I'm just going to go slit my wrists now."

Dr Zahradnik removed his eyeglasses. Folding them and slipping them back into his breast pocket, he took a few feeble steps toward Seth. "Don't you want to hear about your father's visit with the Fuhrer?"

Fearing the doctor would start repeating himself, Seth ascertained, "Hadn't he already met with Hitler back when he first received his position at Auschwitz?"

"No! Heavens no—he had to prove his worthiness first. It wasn't until after Himmler reported your father's tremendous successes that Hitler invited him to *Das Kehlsteinhas* to meet with him personally. This was the one and only time your father ever met with the Fuhrer, but he never forgot it. During this private luncheon, Hitler entrusted him with the work that would consume the rest of his life."

Chapter Thirty-Eight
Seth's Mother

"Since the Germans were losing as many troops to the cold as they were to the enemy, Hitler enlisted your father to experiment on undesirables in search of a means to increase the human body's resistance to freezing temperatures. Your father accepted the commission, and he viewed it as a very great and sacred honour. First, he exposed men, women and children to sub-zero temperatures. Ever so carefully, he meticulously monitored and recorded even the slightest incremental changes in body temperature, metabolic rate and discoloration in the extremities. Your father notated with absolute precision the exact amount of time it took for each subject to lose consciousness and ultimately die. Then, he thawed them out in a number of fashions: quickly, slowly, at room temperature, in boiling water...he even tried boiling-hot enemas. Afterwards, your father autopsied the corpses and attempted to discern any biological differences that might explain why some demonstrated a greater resistance to the cold than others."

Sickened with disgust, Seth blurted out, "Look, Doc, I don't want to hear any more about my father's experiments, ok?"

Startled somewhat by his sudden outburst, the doctor reluctantly agreed. "Very well. We'll skip over the rest. After the war, the Committee commissioned your father to continue his work on the ultimate soldier. He truly was the most advanced bio-theorist of his day—light years ahead of everyone else."

Sensing another digression, Seth rolled his eyes. "Can we please get to Graziella? I just want to know where she is."

"As you wish, Seth. Graziella is an expert on Egyptian mythology. Did you know that?"

"Graziella? No, I didn't know that at all." Seth sat up and leaned in as he contemplated the implications.

"Oh yes!" Dr Zahradnik affirmed enthusiastically. "She studied under one of the greatest minds in the field back in Budapest."

"Budapest!" Thinking back to the soft, faint voice in his dreams, Seth gleamed, "I knew her accent was Hungarian!"

"Indeed," the doctor agreed, sensing that he'd finally piqued Seth's interest. "As for Graziella, her interest in Egyptology is itself inexplicable beyond all human comprehension."

"How do you figure? Everyone's interested in something, aren't they?"

"Yes, I suppose that's true. However, if you'll indulge me, I'm certain that you'll find the coincidence to be far more compelling than you presently suspect."

Already hooked, Seth dug in his heels and waited for more.

Dr Zahradnik threw him a knowing grin. "It's simply uncanny! You could *be* your father." He boasted as though he were a proud uncle.

Seth didn't know how to take that particular compliment—especially having just learned about his father's history as a ruthless, Nazi war criminal. What he heard next definitely tipped the scales in the wrong direction.

"Your mother was an incomparably captivating woman," Dr Zahradnik sighed. "She came to America from Italy as a teenager in search of the American dream. Instead, she initially found hunger and unemployment. Arriving in New York with English so poor that she could barely communicate, it appeared that fortune smiled upon her after all because within a week or so she secured a very good job with a well-to-do family as a housekeeper. The lady of the house was the only surviving child of a very wealthy and powerful judge. She got married against her father's wishes. The two lived alone in an estate owned by the wife's father, and they supported themselves with a monthly allowance that he reluctantly arranged for them. Without his wife, the man would have been essentially penniless."

"Didn't they have any children?"

"No. The man of the house hated children—he never wanted any. It became a huge point of contention with the woman's father who desperately wanted grandchildren. But that's beside the point. One day, the man told his wife that he'd decided to surprise her with a housekeeper as a gift to show his love and appreciation. The truth of the matter turned out to be quite different altogether. What actually transpired is that your mother, fresh off the boat, wandered the streets of New York aimlessly looking for work. After some time, she stumbled into the red-light district. Because she mixed among the other prostitutes soliciting their services, they mistook her for a prostitute as well. However, because of her language barrier, she didn't understand what the men were shouting at her from their cars."

Sitting with his elbows on his knees and his fingers clasped together, Seth wondered, *what were they shouting?*

"I'm fairly certain you can figure that out for yourself, Seth. The man of the house frequented the red-light district often. Seeing your mother, he instantly set his mind upon having her. Naturally, he also took her to be a prostitute. At first, he called out to her in a manner not unlike the rest of the men were doing. But when she didn't respond to his advances, he got out of his vehicle and approached her on the sidewalk. Once the man realised that your mother didn't speak English, he gestured to her to get into his car. He convinced her by showing her the very large quantity of money in his wallet. At that point your mother understood exactly what the man wanted. Cold, hungry and desperate, the sight of all that money tempted her. So, she agreed to go with him."

"That's a flattering image of my mother. Thank you for that."

"The man expected his wife to be away at the dressmaker until early evening. So, he brought your mother back to their home where he planned to have his way with her and then send her away. Once inside the manner, your mother became inebriated with its grandiosity. She'd never seen a mansion from the inside before, and it naturally aroused her desire for affluence and splendour. After the two philandered about, the man couldn't bring himself to send your mother away. He desired her more and more with every touch. Plummeting into a desperate infatuation, he didn't want her to leave at all. Your mother might have been intoxicated with his wealth, but the man of the house fell deeply in love. Needless to say, he completely forgot about his wife."

"This guy sounds like a real catch!" Seth sighed sarcastically, shaking his head in despair. "Way to go, Mom!"

"To be certain," the doctor indulged him. "When the man's wife came home, he faced a very awkward and inexplicable predicament to say the least. The man quickly dreamed up the lie about hiring your mother as a housekeeper. He explained that he'd sent her into the bedroom to strip the bedding and launder it. The man's wife appeared to believe him at first. But after only a few days, she became so jealous of your mother's unparalleled beauty that she threw her out on the street with no notice and no pay. Given any real say in the matter, the man would have kicked out his wife and begged your mother to stay."

"You mean if he truly loved her."

"No, Seth," the doctor conceded, "he probably didn't love her. But you shouldn't judge him too harshly either way. Your mother cast a beguiling spell over the man—he couldn't help himself. As for your mother, who can say? Perhaps if she would have stayed in New York, she might have found respectable employment among the large Italian-speaking population there. However, she didn't stay on in New York. As she walked down the empty street, it grew dark and began to rain. Your mother's prospects seemed scarce on that cold evening. But she could always earn a living in the red-light district, so that's where she headed. Your father just happened to be driving down that very same street at that very moment. In a rare but sincere gesture of compassion, he offered your mother a ride. Thinking that your father wanted the same as the other man, she got into his car. Once your father laid eyes on her, he fell hopelessly in love with her. He'd never met a woman so young and vulnerable and yet so mesmerising."

"Another nice image. Do you have anymore?"

"The weather turned miserably cold and damp, and your mother had nowhere else to go. Since the two couldn't communicate with one another, and since she indicated no desire to get out of the car at any point along the way, your father continued to drive. He didn't live in New York. By coincidence, or fate, your father drove right past your mother on his way home from a meeting with the Committee. It threatened to cut off his funding, and he travelled there to personally try and convince them otherwise."

"Where did he live?"

"Minneapolis."

Aside from his acrid interjections, Seth had held his tongue for the most part and let Dr Zahradnik do all of the talking. He'd been preoccupied with sucking all the remaining rum out of the ice cubes from his drink. The combination of jet lag and alcohol made it hard for him to take any of this seriously—insulting depictions of his mother and all.

"What a heart-warming romance," Seth flipped caustically as he slipped into an imaginary dialogue. "How did your parents meet, Seth? My Parents? Well, my mother used to be a prostitute. One day she went out looking for a trick. She got into a car with a complete stranger, and it turned out to be my father. The two lived happily ever after…or not."

"Yes, that's very clever, Seth. You can be quite humorous when you're in the right mood. You must get that from your mother—your father certainly didn't have a joking bone in his body. Being considerably older than your mother, your father was also very set in his ways. This proved to be problematic at times. Still, grateful to find a man to take care of her, your mother stayed with him through the hard times."

"What kind of hard times?"

"Oh, you know, the usual things that couples fight over: infidelity, money, those sorts of things. But they argued about other things as well. For instance, when you were born in 1958, your mother wanted to name you Craig Ryan North after your father. But you had all this red hair, so your father flatly refused to give you his name because of your non-Aryan appearance. Your mother's indiscretions were many, and your father doubted whether you were even his son. I believe that your father might have been perhaps the only man to possess any measure of resistance toward your mother at all, and she stayed with him because of his great strength. But your mother was *so* magnetic and passionate as to be largely irresistible even to your father. And so, you were named Seth Craig North—a compromise destined since the dawn of the immortal age."

The remark about the immortal age reminded Seth of something he'd read on the hidden website. "I remember reading that supposedly the fallen angels procreated with humans to create a superhuman race called the redheaded ones."

"How much about that do you remember, Seth?"

"I don't know. I remember that the redheads supposedly ruled the world, more-or-less. Oh! And that the women were unimaginably desirable. That part especially caught my attention…"

"Yes, Seth," the doctor chimed in, "the women *are* breath-taking."

"Isn't this just ancient folklore?" Seth insisted sceptically.

"You've read the book of Revelation, haven't you? The war in heaven? A third of the angels cast out?"

"Yes, I've read it. At least, I'm pretty sure that I have. But that doesn't mean that I believe it! I remember skimming over some prophecies on the website as well, but I didn't take them seriously."

"You should, Seth. You should take them very seriously."

"Why? What could any of that have to do with me?"

"I'm convinced that you play a critical role in how the prophecy will ultimately come to fruition."

"What *prophecy*?" Seth scoffed, over-enunciating the word to demonstrate his complete and utter disbelief.

"The prophecy of the second war."

"Are you referring to that nonsense about building another tower? Because if..."

"It's not nonsense," the doctor related coldly. "The Committee has invested countless billions toward this very end."

"But didn't the website say that the redheads had all died out?"

"Died out but destined to rise again."

"Oh, please," Seth chided sceptically. "You sound as though you actually believe all this..."

Studying his face for a moment, Dr Zahradnik wagered a gamble. "I'm just going to lay it out on the table, Seth. During the war, the Committee chanced upon the archaeological find of the millennium: the oldest and most complete artefacts ever recovered."

"Artefacts of what?"

Retrieving his trifocals out of his breast pocket, Dr Zahradnik perched them back over the bridge of his nose. A most solemn expression encased his countenance. "Seth, this information is so top secret that it's never been documented anywhere. I need you to swear that it won't leave this room."

Intrigued by the doctor's earnestness, Seth complied, "I swear."

"During the war, we found intact records of the fallen angels along with roughly half a million vials of their seed."

"Angels? The seed of *angels*? Are you crazy? I flew all the way to Prague for you to tell me this? How many of those single malt scotches have you had tonight, Doc?"

"Please, Seth," the doctor petitioned, "I need you to take this seriously. About the same time that Hitler enlisted the services of your father, the Committee engaged in its own experiments with artificial insemination. The procedure had been used for some time with animals but never successfully performed on a human being before. Once the Committee perfected the process, it attempted to impregnate a fertile, young test subject with the angel seed from one of the vials. Even with every last variable methodically controlled for, the recipient didn't conceive—or so the Committee thought. After three months, it discharged the woman."

"What do you mean, 'or so the Committee thought'?"

"The Committee didn't realise it at the time, but because of the unique structure of the angel DNA, the gestation period took about twice as long as that of ordinary humans. The woman did become pregnant, but she didn't experience any symptoms for over six months. She didn't even start to show until after nine months. Since she'd been sexually active in the months following her discharge, she believed it to be a normal pregnancy."

"If the mother didn't even know, how did the Committee find out?"

"Now there's a story for the history books," Dr Zahradnik gleamed. "The Committee never did find out. It's been my secret all this time."

Chapter Thirty-Nine
The Proposition

"Since the Committee didn't know whether any more of these vials existed or into what hands they might fall, if they did, it needed a new plan of action. Believing the problem to be one of incompatibility, the Committee stockpiled the remaining vials in its possession and decided to invest heavily in research and development in search of a way to make angel DNA compatible with human DNA. That's when the Committee brought me on board, and I started the program here in Prague."

"You've been with the Committee that long?" The inflection in Seth's voice aired a counterfeit sincerity that made him sound really interested in the doctor's career—even though he wasn't.

"Yes, Seth, it's been a good many years. Some have been better than others, but all in all I have to say that…" Suddenly Dr Zahradnik caught himself. "You don't really want to hear about that, do you?"

Seth bit his lip.

Clearing his throat, the doctor regained his train of thought. "The Committee eventually terminated your father's funding. But still, your father remained engrossed in his work and adamant about continuing it. With no research grants and no assistants, he elected to move to a one-room cabin out in the Canadian wilderness where he supported his family by hunting, trapping and fishing. He continued his research up there as well. Your father left traps for other hunters. After he trapped them, he shackled them in the river and kept detailed records of incremental changes in body temperature, metabolic rate, etc. until they froze to death. Then he attempted to thaw out them again and resuscitate them. The more he failed, the more he drank. The more he drank, the more he beat you and your mother. Needless to say, you hated your father."

Seth didn't know what to make of the doctor's words. On the one hand, it seemed too outlandish to even take seriously. But on the other hand, the possibility that it just might all be true afflicted him. The implications were startling.

"Early one morning when you were just fourteen years old, you attacked your father. He easily repelled your attempt and beat you severely. Your father humiliated you by laughing at you and calling you weak. Given that he already suspected you were an illegitimate child, he seized the perfect opportunity to throw you out of the house and told you never to come back. You ran away in disgrace. But you vowed revenge."

It seemed to Seth as though Dr Zahradnik were making the entire story up as he went along. He couldn't remember any of it. Not to mention that it all seemed so cruel and unusual—not at all what he'd envisioned his past might be like. Seth often wondered who and what he might have left behind. But still, he never imagined anything quite so sick and demented as what the doctor was sharing with him. Seth concluded that perhaps it would have been better not to know the truth about his past at all.

"I want to make you a proposition, Seth. You must realise by now that it's no accident that you're here. When I saw your dissertation, I sent the brochure on the fellowship program."

"Yeah, I kind of figured that out already."

"I brought you here to test you. Do you want to know the full story of who you are and why you're here?"

"I don't know anymore," Seth admitted honestly. "I really don't know."

Dr Zahradnik watched as Seth fidgeted nervously. "I think you do," he surmised. "Here's my proposition: I'll tell you everything, then you decide for yourself what you want to do. What do you say?"

"When do I get to see Graziella?"

Dr Zahradnik stood up. Gesturing with his cane rather like Moses, he said, "Follow me."

The two strolled across the magnificent hall and down the corridor to the left. "This is the East Wing. There are more than a hundred suites in this wing." The doctor reported—sounding a bit like a tour guide.

The long hall—replete with the usual epicurean trappings—reminded Seth of a five-star, luxury hotel. Being after midnight, the entire place slumbered in quietude.

"What are the suites used for?" Just as Seth asked the question, the two men came to the end of the corridor. Two mirrored glass doors stood closed before them.

"She's right through there."

No sooner did the words leave Dr Zahradnik's lips when Seth darted for the door. He didn't hesitate a minute.

As Seth reached for the door, the old man cautioned him, "I don't think you should go in there yet."

Seth let go of the handle. "Why not?" he cursed in frustration.

Seth didn't know why he listened to the doctor, but he did and it really aggravated him. Still, a certain logic to the whole fiasco resonated deep within his core. Dr Zahradnik knew so much more about everything than Seth did—at least that's the way it appeared. Seth couldn't remember anything, and the doctor had all these stories. He alone seemed to offer the explanations and the answers that were key to unlocking the mystery of Seth's past. The problem is that Seth didn't like any of them.

Pointing to a sitting area a few feet away, Dr Zahradnik suggested, "I think you should sit down."

Seth stole one last discouraged glimpse of the glass doors and agreed to go sit down. His heart ached for Graziella, still Seth began to have doubts. All this talk about his past really disturbed him. Also, a strange new sentiment began to take over inside of Seth.

Even if just a small fraction of what Dr Zahradnik said is true, Graziella is better off without me. Maybe I'm just being selfish. Maybe I should listen to him.

The doctor kept his comments to himself as the two walked over to a bench and sat down.

"Do you remember anything, Seth? Anything at all?"

"It's all a blur," Seth conceded. His speech grew more disassociated with every syllable. "I remember a few dreams...about the plane crash...and Graziella..." Seth's stammer faded into a mumble. The glass doors were clearly distracting him.

Dr Zahradnik watched Seth closely—examining his every twitch. "What do you remember about Graziella, Seth? Can you tell me?"

Seth wrestled with that very question every single day of his pathetic and lonely life. "I can only remember what I've dreamed."

"No Seth. Do you remember *her*? Do you remember the real Graziella?"

Seth stared vacantly at his folded hands. He felt hollow and empty. "No. I don't remember her at all."

Adjusting his position so that he faced Seth directly, Dr Zahradnik steadied his eyes on Seth. "I need to impress upon you how imperative it is that you remember who you are *before* you go through those doors."

"What is it about my past that makes that so imperative?"

"Let's talk," Dr Zahradnik propounded therapeutically. "After you fled from your home in Quebec, you wandered in the snow until you almost died of hypothermia. You were very fortunate, Seth. Some hunters found you wandering in the woods. If they'd not come along, you would have most certainly froze to death. They turned you over to child protective services, and the courts placed you in a foster care home in Winnipeg."

Seth half listened and half restlessly watched the doors.

"Over the next four years, you vowed that you would one day go back to your home in the wilderness and defend your mother's honour. But it was your own honour that you sought to defend, Seth. You felt a burning need to prove to your mother that you were *not* weak and that you could defend her. Your father's words and the memory of him laughing at you echoed in your brain—it nearly drove you insane. You plotted to precision your plan to return and murder your father. Experiencing severe behaviour problems at home and in school, you often got yourself thrown out of both. You saw a psychiatrist regularly who medicated you heavily. But it didn't help. Developing a paranoid personality disorder, you eventually became delusional. The court moved you about quite a bit during those years. Neither foster parents, schools nor the courts knew how to handle you."

Seth shook his head slightly. He searched the darkest recesses of his mind, but still, he came up blank. With a sigh of frustration, he bellowed, "I don't remember any of that."

Dr Zahradnik placed his hand on Seth's wrist. "You don't want to remember," he asserted conscientiously. "When you turned eighteen, you were no longer a ward of the court. At first you searched for work—here a while and there a while, but you always knew what you needed to do. Eventually, you went back to your father's house. As he checked the temperature of one of his subjects, you snuck up behind him with an axe and knocked him to the ground. After chopping him into a dozen or so pieces, you left him there by the river."

Seth reacted with shock and remorse. "I *killed* my own father?"

"I'm afraid you did, Seth. Afterwards, you hid in the woods for several hours building up the courage to confront your mother. Just before nightfall, you went back to the cabin, found your mother and confessed that you'd killed your father. But before you could revel in your victory over him, she ran down to the river. You followed her, promising to take care of her. But she was in shock, wailing over the mutilated body of her husband. You tried to console her, but she rejected you. In her grief, she cursed you and said she hated you. She told you to leave and said she never wanted to see you again."

Seth ran for the double glass doors screaming in denial. Dr Zahradnik caught him by the shoulders with both hands. "Don't go in there, Seth. You're not ready!"

Seth shook himself free with a violent shrug. "Does she even know I'm here? Can she see me?" He hit himself over and over on the head. "Why can't I remember any of this?"

Dr Zahradnik put his hand lightly on Seth's shoulder. "Come on, Seth. Come on, let's take a little walk."

The two passed back through the East Wing, along the glittering hall and down the corridor leading to the exalted marble room with the fountain. Neither said a word the entire way. The only sounds resonated from their footsteps and the continual tapping of the old man's cane against the argillaceous tiles. As they neared the end of the corridor, the doctor picked up his story where he'd left off.

"After leaving your mother in Manitoba, you wandered aimlessly. You were running and you didn't really care where to. Wanting to get as far away from the ghost of your father as you possibly could, you eventually hitch-hiked all the way to Ann Arbor where you applied for admission to the University of Michigan. As fate would have it, you gained acceptance on a full scholarship. Managing to control your paranoid delusions at school during the day, you were terrorised at night by the ghost of your father. You also became convinced that your father's research finally came to fruition and that one day his posthumous offspring would seek revenge."

"What?" Seth stammered in frightened denial.

"Believing that your mother conceived in this way, you harboured this obsession for eight long years. You finished your M.D. at the age of twenty-six, but the fear of your brother terrorised you more so than ever. He'd come for you one day—in your heart you knew it."

When they reached the grand room, Dr Zahradnik reminisced fondly, "You and I first met right here in this very room. It looked totally different then, of course. Yet even then, you envisioned it completely as it is now. I remember you describing it to me in great detail and explaining how it would work."

The two paused momentarily in the centre of the room. "When you applied to my fellowship program here in Prague, your application letter astounded me. You were either a genius or a madman—I honestly couldn't tell which. But when you arrived, I could see that you were possessed by the same obsessive-compulsive nature that possessed your father. You were running from something Seth, but I didn't know it at the time. I assumed that you were just edgy and driven by your genius like your father before you."

Opposite the fountain on the far side of the lavish room, the outline of a door appeared undiscernibly flush against the wall. Seth hadn't noticed it before. It wasn't hidden per se, but you'd probably never notice it without it being pointed out to you. Dr Zahradnik opened the door, and the two stepped outside onto the terrace.

"Do you know what's beyond this terrace?" he ventured rhetorically in a cold, solemn tone.

It the dim moonlight, Seth could only make out a fallow field. "I don't know…a field of some sort?"

"It's a land fill, Seth—a mass grave."

Chills crept up Seth's spine, and it quivered biliously. "I want to go back in now," Seth protested. "Why are you showing me this?"

"I told you, Seth. I'm testing you."

Dr Zahradnik typed in the code and the electronic lock buzzed. He swung open the door and motioned for Seth to go in first.

"Seth, I want to show you something. It's over here."

The two made their way back over toward the staircase to the table they'd sat at the night before.

Dr Zahradnik reached for one of the thick binders next to the computer. Opening it, he read aloud, "He's coming!"

Removing his glasses, the doctor articulated, "You wrote that just two weeks after arriving here. I found it nestled within your research notes. I remember reviewing your notes and being surprised when I came across it. But at the time, your work had already progressed substantially. We were all deeply impressed with your achievements thus far, so I disregarded it. As time went by, however, the entries became more disturbing, more paranoid and clearly more delusional."

Chapter Forty
Celestial DNA

"I'm afraid I haven't revealed everything to you, Seth."

"There's more?"

"Yes," the doctor admitted clinically. "Just as we kept the information regarding the vials top secret, we maintained the DNA records as strictly classified as well."

"DNA records?" Seth mocked with undeniable curiosity. "Are you telling me you have DNA records of angels?"

"Yes, Seth. We discovered them along with the vials. Of course, no one had any idea at the time what a game changer the discovery would turn out to be. It wasn't until after the Committee spent a large sum of money funding research grants on genetic sequencing that we finally made a breakthrough in 1953."

"The double helix."

"Francis Crick and James Watson." Dr Zahradnik smiled approvingly. "But their discovery was nothing compared to your work."

"My work?"

"Yes, Seth!" The doctor nodded. "Crick and Watson discovered the structure of human DNA, but *you* uncovered the fact that angels possess both XX and XY pairs of chromosomes. And it was *you* that eventually discovered how to make the two compatible."

"I thought you said I was working on an invincible army," Seth interrupted.

"You were," Dr Zahradnik agreed. "But we could hardly tell the Joint Chiefs of Staff that their trillion-dollar army was to be soldiered by hybrids. I convinced the Committee that *you* were the one who would raise the fallen ones up from the ashes of Armageddon. And we were almost there! Damn it, Seth!" The doctor trembled with frustration. "You worked day and night perfecting a human host that could accept the angel DNA…"

Dr Zahradnik pulled out an old black and white photograph of a man in a Nazi uniform standing in front of a pile of corpses. "This is your father. Do you remember him? Examine his face. Anything?"

Seth shook his head in the negative.

Dr Zahradnik opened another binder. He laid it before Seth to show him a photograph of a brawny, muscular man lying naked on a stainless-steel table. "Do you know what this is?" he asked while tapping his index finger on the photo.

"No."

"Inspect the face."

Seth studied the face.

"Now compare it with your father's face."

Seth assessed the face of the Nazi in the photo. "It's the same face. Is that my father as well?"

"No, Seth. That's not your father." Dr Zahradnik turned the page to reveal another photo of a burly man also with his father's face. Page after page, all of the men bore his father's face.

"The likeness is unmistakable—your ability is unsurpassed. Truly Seth, your work is far superior to anything I've ever seen." Dr Zahradnik closed the binders and placed them back.

"Who were those men?" Seth asked insecurely.

"They were supposed to be your army." The doctor eyed Seth disapprovingly but gently. "I didn't find the photos until after you were gone. In your progress reports, you indicated that the subjects were rejecting the celestial DNA and suffering from congenital organogenesis. You insisted that the problem was a simple blockage of the spatial distribution between the blastula and post-gastrulation stages, and you assured us that once you corrected the problem, we'd be ready to mass replicate."

With a groan of regret mixed with satisfaction, Dr Zahradnik sorely contested, "I believed you! When the Committee grew impatient, I recited chapter and verse all your accomplishments! And there were many, Seth! There were many indeed! They've been greater and more wondrous than anything I've ever seen." His voice crescendoed and fell with intensity, but the satisfaction left his eyes—leaving only a scowl that thinly veiled his sense of rancour, anger and betrayal.

He slapped his open palm down on the table. "Your subjects weren't dying because of congenital defects. Damn it, Seth! You were killing them! The memory of your father and the fear of your brother were slowly driving you mad."

The doctor's sudden outburst jolted Seth from his lethargic indifference. He sat up straight like a schoolboy in the principal's office.

"Don't get me wrong, Seth. I supported your work. Good God! I defended it and put my own life on the line to keep the Committee from discontinuing your funding the way it discontinued your father's. But I couldn't explain, much less defend, what you were doing. You genetically designed each one after the likeness of your father, then one by one you slew them. After each attempt 'failed', you engaged in another, and another and another. Each and every last one of them were destined to fail because you never intended to allow them to succeed."

Dr Zahradnik slammed his fist on the table, and Fiala quickly rounded the corner offering a pleasant yet concerned smile. "Is everything okay?"

Dr Zahradnik regained his composure. "Yes Fiala. Yes, of course, Dear. Everything's fine."

After Fiala left, Dr Zahradnik continued in a more subdued tone. "All of them were the spitting image your father. Every one of them represented your brother. It became apparent to me that your obsession with your brother was driven as much by competition over your father's legacy as it was by fear." He shook his head regretfully. "I knew nothing of what you were doing at the time. Otherwise, perhaps I could have intervened sooner. I found the photos and the many even more bizarre journal entries hidden in one of the morgues after you left."

Seth sat there watching and listening as though Dr Zahradnik were speaking about someone else. *This couldn't have been me,* Seth reasoned. *Still, who else could it have been? The very thought of it makes me ill. I've never hurt anyone—no one that I can remember anyway.* Yet, Seth failed to convince even himself. He couldn't discount any of it.

"And this is the work that you want me to come back to?" Seth interrupted. "No thanks!"

"Seth, you were so close!" Gesturing toward the notebook of his father's work, the doctor encouraged him, "You encountered the same problem that your father had. The human recipients rejected the angel DNA. The results were hideous beyond imagination." Dr Zahradnik shook his head in disgust. "This is why you became such an avid study of your father's work, and eventually you came to the very same conclusion."

"What? The need for a blood relative?" Seth sneered sardonically. "You can't be serious."

"Oh, but I'm deadly serious, Seth. You eventually gave up on perfecting a *human* host, and you became obsessed with cloning angels directly from the DNA sequence."

"That's insane!" Seth objected.

Just then the phone rang. "Yes?" Dr Zahradnik answered in a short but professional tone. "I see. Accompany him to the East Wing please—noon tomorrow. Thank you. That would be lovely." Putting the phone down, he casually mentioned, "I took the liberty of ordering you a drink. You look like you can use one."

No sooner did he finish his words when a slender female employee tapped on the open door. No words were spoken. She gave Dr Zahradnik a submissive glance, raised her eyebrows as if requesting permission to enter and he bid her entry with a flip of his hand. After she served the drinks, Dr Zahradnik dismissed her in the same fashion.

Seth sipped his rum and Coke. Feeling a bit less agitated, he opened up a little. "But I still don't understand how any of this concerns Graziella."

"Once you finally gave up on perfecting a human host, you threw yourself into successfully cloning a replica directly from the angel DNA. At the time, I believed you were inspired by brilliance. But the truth is, you were driven by madness."

Dr Zahradnik pulled up a picture on the computer.

"Graziella!" Seth's eyes lit up. "Why won't you let me go to her?"

"It's not me that's stopping you, Seth. The sooner you accept this truth, the sooner you'll be able to decide for yourself whether or not to go to her."

Seth watched while Dr Zahradnik typed something on the keyboard.

"I found your biological mother," he revealed. "Such a tantalising woman! It became clear what your obsession had been all along."

A picture of Seth's mother appeared on the screen. She could almost be Graziella's identical twin.

"That's my mother?" Seth stared at the picture with a hollow smile. "My mother," his lips moved but no sound came out.

Dr Zahradnik snapped his fingers. "Seth! I need you to stay with me."

Somewhat startled out of his stupor, Seth continued to stare at the photograph. "Why does she look exactly like Graziella?"

"I found your mother in Quebec," the doctor explained. "She said she hadn't seen you since you were eighteen years old." Next, he reached for a different binder. He opened it and showed it to Seth. "What do you see?"

"I see a naked woman," Seth replied.

"Does she favour either of these?" he asked—pointing to the pictures of Seth's mother and Graziella on the computer.

"No. Not really," Seth responded.

"How about this one?" the doctor questioned as he turned the page.

Seth studied the picture. Something distinctly recognisable about this woman caught Seth's eye. She didn't actually resemble Graziella, but there were similarities.

One after another, Dr Zahradnik turned the pages revealing photo after photo of women who shared similar features with Graziella. But none of them were identical to her.

"They all vaguely resemble Graziella, but none of them actually look like her," Seth surmised.

Dr Zahradnik opened Seth's lab journal. Pointing to the last entry dated January 10, 1990, he asked Seth to read it.

Somewhat hesitant, Seth read aloud, "I've attained my greatest success: I've achieved perfect adult replication. You read this already," Seth objected.

"Keep reading," the doctor insisted.

"Even my most stunning creatures cannot compare with the elegance, purity and innocence of my most precious creation—Graziella."

Seth snapped the journal shut. "This is a lie! You're telling me that Graziella is a clone?"

"Not just any clone. Don't you see, Seth? Graziella was your masterpiece. You finally managed to replicate your mother. Look at the photos."

Seth stared at the photos for a moment.

"You even named her after your mother."

"My mother's name is Graziella?" Then the realisation finally struck him. "Are you saying that my mother was one of those exotic angel-women I read about?"

"Yes Seth. That's exactly what I'm telling you. Isn't it obvious? Just look at her. Your mother is half angel and half human. I could hardly believe it myself. But there could be no other explanation. So, I went back and checked the identity of the woman the Committee artificially inseminated. It was your grandmother, Seth! Seventeen years later, your mother came to America. She met your father, and eventually you were born."

"But that would make me..."

"Yes..." The doctor stared at him. "You're one quarter angel."

"And Graziella?" Seth stammered in bewilderment.

"Graziella is pure. Her DNA is 100% celestial."

A single tear rolled down Seth's face. Dr Zahradnik reached out and gave his arm a consoling squeeze. "You were faced with a very difficult dilemma, Seth. You couldn't bring yourself to dispose of Graziella as you had with the others, but you knew that the Committee would want to breed her. So, you fled. One day, you simply disappeared with Graziella, and we never heard from Seth North again."

Brushing the lapel of his suitcoat, the doctor continued. "I safeguarded your secret, Seth. You and I are the only living souls who know the truth. When the Committee found out about Graziella, I made up the story that she was your daughter."

With a look of genuine intrigue, the doctor pondered, "You were attempting to clone an exact *adult* replica of your mother. I never understood why you cloned Graziella as an adolescent child. It was as if somehow you knew..." Then, changing the subject, he continued, "The Committee later discovered that you'd hidden Graziella in Italy with a couple and an old woman. But you were nowhere to be found, so it sent an agent to apprehend Graziella and find out what she knew regarding your whereabouts."

"Graziella has a family?" Seth could almost remember. It was as if he were looking at a photo of himself in a place he didn't remember ever being.

"A surrogate family," the doctor conceded. "Unfortunately, her new 'papa' got in the way. After killing him, the operative started posing as the dead man's brother. He waited for an opportunity to be alone with the girl and obtain any information he could about you. When the old woman suffered a stroke, the imbecile got his chance. But the stupid son-of-bitch blew it. He raped her repeatedly. The poor girl—the more she resisted, the worse he violated her. Our reports indicated that she didn't survive the trauma, and we never did find out where you were."

Chapter Forty-One
Faith

"I'm a man of science, Seth. But thanks to you, I've also become a man of great faith. When you disappeared from the program in 1990, the Committee hunted day and night for you. It planned to kill you, but you were right where you were supposed to be."

"What's that supposed to mean?"

With a twinkle in his eye, the doctor enthused, "Faith is a delicate cactus flower that blooms in adversity. You *married* Graziella, Seth! Somehow, the two of you found each other—after eight years! The Committee searched the entire globe for you without success, but this exquisite blossom sprung up right in your own back yard. Fascinating! Just fascinating! I'd love to hear *you* tell me that story someday."

"Graziella is my *wife*?" Exhilarated and exuberant, Seth could hardly sit still.

"Don't you see?" Dr Zahradnik elated. "We have a record of the structure of celestial DNA. It's surprisingly similar to the double-helix of our own genetic make-up although vastly superior, of course. If we can transcribe that data into a digital medium and map that sequence onto living flesh in the same way that you transferred the Pentagon data…"

"You can replicate angels," Seth finished the doctor's grandiose ideation for him. Shaking his head in disbelief, Seth washed his hands of it. "I don't want anything to do with it."

Dr Zahradnik found his bitter disappointment impossible to conceal. Sounding more like a flat tire thumping along the side of a road than the lightning speed of destiny, Dr Zahradnik changed the subject. "I remember the day before you disappeared from the program all those years ago. I asked you if you loved Graziella. The conversation stands out in my mind because when two men are surrounded by wealth, power and death such as we were, *love* is not often discussed. I assumed at the time that you did not love her. It's understandable that you might have thought you did—Graziella provided the perfect surrogate for your mother. I hoped that you'd work out your obsession and return to work."

"But what about all that talk about Graziella being 100% angel? She's sounding pretty disposable all of a sudden," Seth dinned snidely.

"Now you understand my dilemma, Seth. With the newly discovered knowledge that you were of the celestial lineage, I believed more than ever that you were the one that would lead the Committee into world domination."

"But what about Graziella? She's an angel for God's sake! Isn't that what you're after?"

"She's *one* angel, Seth. The Committee needs millions. You obviously play a key role in the fulfilment of the prophecy since you're the only one who knows how to replicate the celestial DNA. Graziella plays a role as well, but I didn't realise what it was at the time."

"So, what *is* Graziella's role?"

"Let's just say that if you were a gun, Graziella would be the trigger."

"I guess that sounds about right," Seth agreed.

"Once I saw the two of you together again, my faith grew stronger every day. I eventually came to believe that, whatever they were, both of your destinies would find you in due course. Mostly, I became convinced that the Committee needed to stay out of the way. Of course, that's the very last thing it planned to do. One can only imagine the Committee's zeal if it ever discovered who the three of you actually were. Reflecting on it now, I can see that letting you go represented the most prudent option available at the time. Unfortunately, the Committee didn't agree. After you escaped with Graziella, it decided to kill you. I found myself caught in a difficult dilemma, Seth. By not disclosing your true identity to the other members, I signed your death warrant. But my silence also kept Graziella and your mother out of the equation. I committed myself to a lifetime of protecting you as best I could and keeping your secret hidden at any cost."

"So, the Committee actually searched for me that entire time and still never found me? Don't get me wrong, Doc—I'm really grateful for all your help, but that's kind of pathetic, isn't it?"

"The Committee employed the very best of the best to find you, Seth. The truth of the matter is I found you in February of 2000. If it hadn't been for me foiling a few leads, you'd no doubt be dead by now."

Seth's blood ran cold and he felt weak—as though he'd just experienced a near-death encounter. "You knew where I was all along?"

"Yes, Seth. I couldn't bear to believe that you were dead, so I simply refused to accept it. It wasn't all that hard to locate you either. In fact, it was far *too* easy. Honestly Seth, applying for an American passport using your real name? It's so obvious it's brilliant! No one would have ever thought you'd be that stupid, so no one else even bothered to check. But voila, a cursory search through passport applications and there you were. That's how I tracked you from Cotonou to New Haven."

Chapter Forty-Two
Night Is Coming

"Before you left Prague that snowy January in 1990, I asked you if you loved Graziella. You insisted that you did love her. And you vowed to do anything to protect her—even kill and die for her. "Killing is easy," I remember saying to you. "Even dying is easy." The true question is whether you were willing to *live* for Graziella." Dr Zahradnik clutched Seth's hand. "That's still the question, Seth."

Seth contemplated all that the doctor had shared with him. He couldn't remember ever being so cruel. But there was one thing of which he was absolutely certain, Graziella—a woman he couldn't even remember—mattered more to him than life itself.

Letting go of Seth's hand, Dr Zahradnik recollected, "You were a visionary—a ruthless, heartless killer. You never submitted to your adversary. But on that day, your frozen heart thawed. The brother who'd haunted you all those years to avenge your father's death and take possession of his legacy—he finally claimed the victory. You now had your own legacy to preserve, and long at last it finally found you. Seth North, all that he represented and everything he'd accomplished, completely disappeared on that day. And he hasn't been seen or heard from since."

With a gasp of exasperation and a tap of his cane, the doctor paused and stared at the gleaming floor. Then his eyes brightened momentarily. "I thought I'd found the old Seth North again when I read Craig Ryan's dissertation. But I was mistaken."

Dr Zahradnik shook his head to accentuate the severity of the loss. Then returning to the evening that Seth disappeared from Prague he recollected, "You disappeared with Graziella that very night. Yet even in your altered state, something inside you knew that the Committee would scour the globe for you. You instinctively realised that the Committee would never stop hunting for you until you were either recovered or dead. So, you left Graziella in your mother's hometown of Taranto. The local doctor and his barren wife agreed to raise her as their own. To divert the Committee's attention away from Graziella, you left a very obvious trail leading to America. Fully expecting never to see Graziella again, you endangered your own life in order to save hers. You answered the question, Seth. Or should I call you Craig?"

Dr Zahradnik casually pulled his coat sleeve back to uncover his watch. The white Cosmograph Daytona indicated nearly three a.m. Noticing the hideous scar that jutted out from beneath the face of the watch, Seth glared with alarm. Catching Seth staring at the scar, the doctor quickly pulled his coat sleeve back down.

"Even though the operative allegedly killed Graziella in Taranto, the Committee didn't collect her remains because I never revealed her true identity. Had it known she was successfully cloned from angel DNA; the Committee would have hunted for her as diligently as it's been hunting you. Dead or alive, it would have left no stone unturned. But somehow, by some miracle, you both survived. And even more remarkably, you found each other! Even though neither one of you knew who the other was. Absolutely astounding!"

The warm smile returned to the doctor's face. It shone with a proud, almost grandfatherly, appeal. For just a brief moment, Seth sensed a sort of kinship with the man. Dr Zahradnik clutched Seth by the shoulders and shook him heartily. Seth soaked in the sentiment as though he were the prodigal son returning home from the pig farm.

"You can imagine my disillusionment when your plane crashed, Seth. Those were difficult days. But I've clung to my faith, and the years have rewarded me with constant surprises."

"What about Graziella?"

"The rescue team found Graziella on the beach near the wreckage. She appeared to be dead at first as well, but she'd gone into shock and slipped into a coma. I secretly brought her back here to Prague where she remained unconscious for six months. With such a serious abdominal wound so close to her uterus, we were really concerned she wouldn't make it."

"Wait a minute! Graziella suffered an abdominal wound? She had an abdominal wound in my dream. I saw her lying on the beach after the plane crash with a terrible injury to her stomach."

"That was no dream, Seth—you were there." The doctor respired in deep breaths. The stiff lapels of his tailored suit coat just barely accommodated his aging chest as it expanded and contracted with oxygen. Seth couldn't quite interpret the expression on Dr Zahradnik's face. Resembling a mixture of compassion and pride, his countenance also bore the hint of deep joy marred by regret. The type of regret that comes from great opportunities that one has forsaken.

"For the longest time, Graziella has suffered a reoccurring nightmare of her own. She once told me that it's so real that she struggles to discern the dream from reality. One afternoon, she described her incubus to me with such great detail that I actually started to believe it myself—it struck me as so compelling."

"Will you tell it to me?"

Settling back into his chair and crossing his legs, the doctor shared what he knew. "Graziella related that her dream always begins on the beach in Cotonou where the plane crashed. She's lying paralysed on the beach with the waves washing over her body, but her spirit is roaming the beach in search of Seth North the clone. Seth risked his own life to come and find her. He also saved her from the CIA agents at the safe house in D.C. Most importantly, Seth promised her that he would find Craig even if it was the last thing he did."

"I promised her that?"

"Yes, Seth, you did. You made that promise to her on the plane before it crashed. Graziella once confided in me that she's never really believed that Seth North and Craig Ryan were actually two different people. Graziella swears that when she looked into Seth's eyes, she saw Craig."

"How could she tell?"

"She's in love with you, and she insists that her intense love for Craig is not something that she could mistake with anyone else. Graziella believed that Craig somehow lost himself, and she was counting on you to help her find him again. She's absolutely refused to accept that Seth North is dead because she's hoping against hope that Craig Ryan is still alive. Graziella can't let go of Craig's promise to her. So, until she has certain confirmation of his death, she can't help but cling to the faith that he will always come for her."

Seth struggled to hold back his tears.

"After the plane crashes in Graziella's nightmare, she can't find Seth anywhere. She combs the beach with her eyes—sorting the bodies from the debris as best she can through all the smoke and chaos—but Seth North is gone. She's lost him, and she's overtaken by tremendous sadness. Then someone appears on the far side of the wreckage—a person as translucent as a ghost. Like an apparition, the individual appears but not fully. The spectre is standing perfectly still and staring in the opposite direction. It's a man. He's preoccupied with something, but Graziella can't tell what it is. There doesn't seem to be anything else there. Graziella hurries over to him and gently places her hand on his shoulder. When he turns around, she realises that it's Seth. He's so happy to see her, and Graziella feels so relieved and comforted to have found him. His eyes reveal that it's actually Craig, and they profess how deeply he loves her. Graziella wants more than anything to hold him and to tell him how much she loves him too. But Craig is still lost, and her sense of loyalty to him won't allow her to speak those words to anyone else—not even to Seth. So instead, all she can bring herself to say is, 'Did you find him yet?'"

A wave of chills travelled through Seth's body. As he listened to Dr Zahradnik recount Graziella's dream, he instantly relived his own dreams in which Graziella asks him that very question.

"She's never forgiven herself," the doctor lamented. "She's convinced the encounter is real. The fact that Graziella has the chance to tell you how much she loves you but can't has haunted her these past four years."

Seth swallowed hard. Tears were coming but he didn't want them to. Handing him the handkerchief from his breast pocket, the old man gripped Seth's shoulder firmly while he wept. "It's alright, Seth. Love is a cruel master, but it's a wonderful prison."

Seth wiped his eyes and clung to the handkerchief like a security blanket.

"After the tragedy, Graziella mourned for her husband for two full years. But Craig Ryan has never been found. She still wonders everyday what happened to him. Her heart won't let you go. You see, Seth, Graziella is deeply torn between her need for closure and her faith in your promise to her. She eventually finished school and threw herself into her work, but Graziella still clings to that promise."

Dr Zahradnik relished the possibilities with a consoling smile. "It's important that you understand, Seth. The Committee knows nothing about Graziella—her life, her location here in Prague—nor is it interested. Graziella has been forgotten—she's completely off the radar. It's Seth North that the Committee wants, and it will *never* stop hunting for you. As for me, I believe that Craig Ryan is still very much alive and well. Who knows? You may find him yet."

Then, as if this were the very point that he'd been leading up to since Seth arrived, the doctor added protectively, "The sun rose on Craig Ryan all those years ago. But night is coming, Seth! It always does."

In a token of patriarchal fondness, Dr Zahradnik shook Seth's hand firmly. He held it for just a moment longer than Seth expected him to, and then he let it go. Seth left him sitting by the fountain alone—staring at his crippled leg. Half way up the stairs, Seth indulged in one last vision of his former life. Below him, Dr Zahradnik's frail form figured insignificantly. The great expanse of the marvellous room with all its accoutrements reduced the megalomaniac to a lonely old man. Seth couldn't help but feel sorry for him. He headed up the stairs to the elevator and then retired to his suite.

By four a.m., Seth still couldn't sleep. He tossed and turned and paced the floors. Seth kept thinking about everything that Dr Zahradnik had told him. Zuzu offered to keep him company, but Seth told her that he preferred to be alone. Finally—just as the sun came up—he fell asleep.

Chaos and panic ensued at the crash site. Seth found himself lying in the sand near a clearing at the edge of some brush. He tried to get up but he couldn't—he'd broken his leg. Worse yet, he'd lost Graziella! Seth searched as far as he could see. Everywhere, the beach was covered in human limbs and tangled metal. On the other side of the wreckage near the water, he spotted a female survivor. The tide was nearly sweeping her away. Crawling toward the motionless form, Seth recognised Graziella.

"Graziella? Graziella!" Seth screamed as he dragged himself toward her.

Kneeling beside his heart's desire with her face next to hers, Seth could hear her breathing but only just barely. Graziella whispered something to him, but he couldn't make it out—she breathed as though she were in labour. That's when Seth noticed her bleeding abdomen.

Shaking and shivering, Graziella struggled to speak. In a faint whisper she managed to utter his name, "Seth…Seth."

"I'm here, Graziella. It's all right…I'm here now."

"Find Craig…" Graziella swallowed hard as her eyes began to close. "You have to find Craig."

"I promise…" The words barely passed Seth's lips when he felt Graziella's hand let go. Her breathing grew still. Her eyes were open, but she was gone.

"Not Yet! Wait!" Seth agonised inconsolably. "He'll be here for you soon! Graziella! Not yet! Please wait for him…Please! You have to wait…"

Seth's words emanated from somewhere so deep inside himself that he scarcely recognised them as his own. This was pain like he'd never known.

"You can't die now!" he screamed at Graziella's lifeless body. Digging his fists into the sand, he pounded them against his head. "You can't die now."

Chapter Forty-Three
Glass Doors

Seth woke up later that morning to the smell of coffee and Zuzu's cheerful "Good morning!"

"Thank you, Zuzu, but I won't be having my bath or my breakfast this morning." Seth kissed Zuzu on the forehead and quickly dressed himself. He rode the elevator down to the balcony and descended the great staircase. After crossing the fabulous room, Seth hurried back down the corridor. He passed through the wondrous hall and entered the East Wing. Once inside, he passed nurses, orderlies and happy new fathers brimming with joy. As Seth approached the set of glass doors, he heard the sounds of babies crying and the chimes of a colossal grandfather clock. He counted the peals as he hurried toward the doors. The clock rang twelve times. Seth stopped abruptly. *Noon,* he thought to himself. *Tomorrow at noon!*

Seth cautiously approached the glass doors, reached for the handle and opened one of the doors ever so slightly. Peeking inside, he saw a typical hospital lobby with employees going about their daily routines. A little boy not more than four or five years old sat on one of the chairs in the waiting area. An older man, who appeared to be a chauffeur, sat next to him. The boy was playing with a stethoscope.

A vivacious young doctor in her late twenties called out excitedly, "Craig!"

Seth instinctively reacted by hiding behind the door. His heart racing for fear that he'd be caught, Seth conceded to the truth. *Dr Zahradnik is right. I'm not ready to see her.* Once he marshalled the courage to crack the door open again, Seth peered through the slight opening and watched Graziella glide happily toward the little boy. Filled with a pride and wonder he'd never known, Seth's heart yearned for them both. Graziella summoned the boy with her arms extended, and the boy ran to her.

"Mommy!"

Seth looked on as the two embraced.

"Did Uncle Gabek bring you here?"

"Yes. He said that I should wait here for you because you were busy delivering babies."

"That's right, sweetie," his mother concurred as she kissed his cheeks and hugged him tighter. "Ready for lunch?"

As Seth watched this heart-warming scene, he simultaneously felt more fulfilment and emptiness than he'd ever thought imaginable. His heart brimmed and broke at the same time. Seth consoled himself with the affirmation that Graziella had moved on with her life. She had her career and little Craig—and they were happy.

Of all the things that Dr Zahradnik shared with Seth, he knew only one of them to be true for certain—he *had* come for Graziella. He'd come for Graziella and not for himself. Seth watched as the family he'd longed for as far back as he could remember disappeared in the other direction. He fought the urge to chase after them. Seth wanted Graziella to know that he'd never given up and that he would never stop loving her. But something in his soul reassured him that she already knew.

Seth had always known that one day he'd have to let Graziella go. That day finally arrived. After pausing for just a moment to remember Graziella—the *real* Graziella—Seth North turned and walked away.

Chapter Forty-Four
Alone in Novosibirsk

"That's a really sad ending to the story, Gabriel. What happened to Seth? Where did he go?"

"Oh, the story is far from over. In a sense, it's just beginning," Gabriel assured me. "Once he left Prague, Seth dared not return to the United States knowing that the Committee still pursued him. So, he defected to Russia."

"Russia?"

"It was a natural choice," Gabriel substantiated. "Because of his exceptional knowledge of the Pentagon, he received the full support of the Russian government. Officially, Seth North died in a Chechen terror attack on July 8, 2003, when two Chechen women blew themselves up at a music festival in Moscow. Seth assumed a new identity as Rostislav Efimov, and Seth North was now officially dead to the world."

"What was he going to do in Russia?"

"Rostislav was granted acceptance into Sigma Xi along with a research position at Novosibirsk State University."

"Sigma Xi?"

"Sigma Xi is a prestigious scientific community that claims more than one hundred and seventy-five Nobel Prize recipients as members."

"Impressive. Where's Novosibirsk?"

"It's in Siberia—quite a coincidence when you consider his family history."

"What history?"

"Remember? Dr Zahradnik told Rostislav about how his grandfather froze to death not far from Novosibirsk. He died while attempting to return home after serving in the Czech legion. The Trans-Siberian Railway crossed the river Ob at Novosibirsk."

"Poor Seth, I mean Rostislav, up there in Siberia all alone. So, what was this place, Gabriel—some Podunk little town or what?"

"Novosibirsk started out small, but over the years it grew into a bustling metropolis. By the time Rostislav moved there it was the third largest city in Russia. But Novosibirsk also harboured a dark secret, and few beside Rostislav still knew about it."

"What kind of secret?"

"On January 30, 1933, Hitler became the Chancellor of Germany. Less than a month later the Nazis set fire to the Reichstag, and Hitler seized power under the pretext of protecting the nation. By that March, the Nazis had already secretly begun many of their experiments on Jews, undesirables and political rivals. Hitler opened Oranienburg concentration camp outside Berlin, and the system soon expanded to include Dachau near Munich in the south, Buchenwald near Weimar in central Germany and Sachsenhausen near Berlin in the north. It was during this very time—just after Hitler first rose to power—that Rostislav's father set his mind on joining the Nazi party."

"What did the Nazi's have to do with Novosibirsk's dark secret?"

"The Great Soviet Famine of 1932-33 became unbearable. Because of its huge influx of refugees, Novosibirsk was hit the hardest of all. Mothers ate their own babies in a desperate attempt to both save themselves and spare their infants the pang of starvation. Stalin responded by initiating pogroms to exterminate Jews, kulaks, and other 'enemies of the people' whom he blamed for the famine. These pogroms largely began in Novosibirsk."

"Mothers *ate* their own babies? That's horrible, Gabriel! How could God stand by and watch as that happened? Why didn't he do anything?"

"It all comes down to free will," Gabriel expounded. "The King won't force his will on anyone. Unfortunately—like nearly every other famine—this one was also the result of human selfishness and greed. There was more than enough food to go around for everyone, but still, humans always want to blame the King for their own crimes. The questions you should be asking are, 'How could the rest of the world stand by and watch as that happened? Why didn't the rest of humanity do anything?'"

"I suppose you're right."

"Anyway," Gabriel resumed, "the famine and the pogroms led to an arrangement between Hitler and Stalin—a mutual exchange of goods, if you will, in which Novosibirsk was a central broker."

"Oh, no," I flinched, "I sense another story."

"I promise this one is short. After World War I, Russia and Germany shared a common bond—they both found themselves on the outside of the European political game looking in. By April, 1922, the two countries signed the Treaty of Rapallo. Agreeing to forgive one another's debts and reparations, Russia and Germany established a pact of mutual cooperation that lasted well into the 1930's. Moscow purchased so much from German corporations that when it couldn't pay, Berlin continued to export on credit. And with Hitler's rise to power, the two countries shared yet another tie to bind them tightly together: both Stalin and Hitler hated the Jews. So, the two arranged a deal that would settle the Soviet Union's growing debt to Germany while continuing the favourable economic relations between the two countries. Stalin agreed to ship Jews to German forced-labour camps in return for continued credit from Berlin."

"Didn't the Soviet Union have its own labour camps?"

"Oh, yes," Gabriel affirmed, "Stalin used forced labour to industrialise, but the Soviet economy could never produce the heavy industrial products that Germany provided. Besides, millions more Jews resided inside the Soviet Union than could be found in Germany. And because the Russian people faced such dire economic hardship at the time, most of them gladly handed over the Jews in their communities to be forcibly deported—then they quickly confiscated their property and wealth."

"And how exactly did Novosibirsk figure in?"

"Novosibirsk served as a deportation centre for Jews. Before long, the enterprise became so profitable that the city was transformed into a huge commercial centre."

"Okay Gabriel, so where's this all going? The story of the ages, Graziella and Craig, Rostislav moves to Siberia…"

Gabriel got the hint. "Moving right along," he segued. "Because of Rostislav's unique access to the Pentagon's data, the Russian government put him to work on a variety of assignments: from going over strategic plans and war game scenarios, to identifying areas of weakness or vulnerability that existed along Russia's borders. Primarily, however, Rostislav checked for missing WMD and fissile materials lost after the collapse of the Soviet Union. Rostislav essentially served as an in-house intelligence operative. Because of his high security clearance, he enjoyed complete access to the former Soviet archives and he often searched them diligently for any record of his father or his grandfather."

"Did Rostislav ever learn what his father's original last name was? I remember Dr Zahradnik said he changed it when he came to the United States."

"No, Rostislav never confirmed his father's last name. But he could be fairly certain that it wasn't north. Rostislav couldn't deny that he'd sensed a familial bond with the doctor—plus he had nothing else to go on—so he searched the archives for Krzegosz Zahradnik. And while he found nothing documenting his grandfather, he did find one interesting lead that might reveal information about his father. A certain Krzegosz Zahradnik appeared in the Soviet international trade archives. He processed incoming Jews at Buchenwald, and his signature appeared on several hundred invoices from the camp between 1937 and 1939."

"Was it his father?"

"At first, Rostislav could only speculate that this might be his father. After all, the last name had been purely conjecture. And even if Zahradnik turned out to be his father's last name, perhaps he'd merely stumbled upon this name by coincidence. Zahradnik is a very common east European name, and Krzegosz is also extremely common. It seemed very possible to Rostislav that this could be his father. But with so little information, how could he be certain?"

"A coincidence?"

"Rostislav strongly entertained the idea that it might just be a coincidence until the day he found a photo of his father taken at Buchenwald. The photo appeared on the cover of a primer entitled *Efficiency in Camp Processing* authored by none other than Krzegosz Zahradnik. Apparently, the Germans placed a vested interest in assisting the Soviets in more efficiently processing their Jews for deportation."

"Don't tell me," I interjected, "It was the same photo that Dr Zahradnik showed him back in Prague?"

Nodding his head in the affirmative, Gabriel confirmed, "Rostislav had found his father."

"Not that the title isn't self-explanatory enough, but what was this primer all about?"

"The primer was sickening in its content," Gabriel warned me. "Complete with step by step instructions on preparing the Jews for instant liquidation, it also listed strict criteria regarding which Jews to ship and which to terminate. Only those capable of working or those with gold in their mouth were to be shipped. 'Work' included heavy labour for men, light labour for women and medical experimentation for children."

"That *is* sickening," I squirmed. "I don't understand, Gabriel. Why was Rostislav so interested in finding his father? He certainly didn't seem very interested in learning about him back in Prague?"

"That's true. Rostislav didn't exactly understand his interest in finding out more about his father either—he didn't remember him, nor did he feel any sense of affection toward him at all. The truth is Rostislav shouldn't have had any reason to care one way or another. But the search for his father piqued his interest nonetheless. At the very least it took his mind off of Graziella, so he filled the empty hours, days and years of his life indulging in it. He lived alone in Novosibirsk. And given that no one else seemed to share Rostislav's interest in his father, very little became of his findings. That is, not until the day that *he* arrived."

Chapter Forty-Five
Krzegosz

"Who arrived, Gabriel?"

"Nearly eighteen years had passed since that spring morning when Rostislav left Prague. However, not one day had passed that he didn't think of Graziella and the young boy that he'd seen with her."

"I guess searching for his father didn't fill the void after all."

"Not so much," Gabriel reverberated. "Walking away from Graziella rivalled the one thing that proved even harder."

"What could be harder than walking away from your one true love?"

"Staying away."

"Ohhh…"

"But Rostislav believed that he'd made the right decision, so he fought the urge to go back every day. Still, he couldn't help himself from continually wondering what might have been if only he'd stayed. Rostislav lived a life imbued with regret: regret for things he couldn't remember, regret for things he may or may not have done and regret that he based on the words of an old man who was probably long since dead."

"How old would Dr Zahradnik have been by then?"

"Ninety-one," Gabriel apprised. "Rostislav sometimes wondered about Dr Zahradnik. And although he constantly thought about Graziella and the boy, he never attempted to make contact or to find out any more about his estranged family. He decided it would be safer for them if he just let them go. And yet, he found this impossible. Rostislav could change his identity, his citizenship and virtually everything about his existence—but he couldn't change his love for Graziella—that he could not do."

One January morning, Rostislav came into work on time as usual—which either made him really early or everyone else considerably late. Surprised to find a young man waiting outside the office in the hall, Rostislav timidly mumbled, "Good morning," and fumbled with his keys to open the door. His social skills had waned substantially since his days at Stanford—he rarely spoke to anyone anymore.

The young man appeared to be in his early twenties. "Are you the director?" he solicited respectfully as he followed Rostislav into the office.

"No," Rostislav grumbled with an added grimace for clarity.

"Do you know when he'll be in?"

Rostislav began to feel just a little annoyed at the boy. *He obviously just doesn't get it. Doesn't he know where he is? He shows up at eight o'clock in the morning in Siberia! Who does he expect to be here? Rasputin? Chernenko? Yeltsin? Maybe he's expecting Yul Brynner to make a dramatic come back! No one in their right mind would be here at eight a.m. The fact that I'm here on time every morning only attests to my pathetic and lonely existence. I can't bear to spend one minute more than I absolutely have to alone in my dreary apartment every day, so I come to work. Dividing my time between home and work has been the only way I've managed not to go completely insane in Novosibirsk.*

"I'm sorry?" the young man asked rather surprised by Rostislav's sudden rant.

"Why don't you come back at 10:00 am—he should be here by then."

Rostislav managed to answer the young man rather politely given he'd not yet enjoyed his morning libation: instant coffee. Getting out of his apartment and having his cup of coffee every morning was the only two things in Rostislav's entire day that he actually looked forward to. It all went downhill from there, and he didn't much appreciate the intrusion.

"But I don't have anywhere to go," the young man responded.

Rostislav didn't care, but he could also relate. "Hmm," he grumbled under his breath. "Why don't you have a seat then? Coffee?"

"No Thanks." The young man crunched his nose and shook his head.

"More for me," Rostislav chimed as he rinsed out his coffee mug.

While Rostislav boiled the water, he started to whistle a melody that the young man recognised. "I know that song!" he delighted. "My mother hums it all the time. It's the Italian national anthem."

Rostislav wasn't even aware that he'd been whistling much less able to identify the tune. He froze for a moment. "It is?" he asked—strangely baffled and yet unable to ignore the coincidence. While Rostislav couldn't remember ever learning the Italian national anthem, there could be no question as to who taught it to him.

"My wife was Italian," he nodded in an affirming manner as he spooned coffee into his cup.

"What happened to her?"

"You know…things didn't work out." Rostislav gestured with an expression both half knowing and half wondering. He wanted to ask the young man about his mother, but as it turned out he didn't have to.

"My mother always hums that song to the babies after she's delivered them," he beamed with pride.

"So, your mother's…"

"She's an obstetrician," the young man gloated—over-enunciating every syllable.

More than a little intrigued, Rostislav ruminated over the possibility. *She's Italian and an obstetrician…*

"I'm Krzegosz," the young man added. "Actually, my real name is Craig. My mother named me after my dad. He died in a plane crash. But my uncle

Gabek always called me Krzegosz. It's kind of stuck. Hey are you all right? You got really pale all of a sudden."

Rostislav was not all right. And yet, he'd not felt better in years! Could this really be his son? Of course! It had to be! Who would have imagined? After all these years, his son just walked into his life. Destiny certainly poses rare surprises. Dr Zahradnik's words regarding Graziella instantly came back to him: "The Committee searched the entire globe for you without success, but this exquisite blossom sprung up right in your back yard!"

Two miracles in one lifetime were more than anyone could hope for. Rostislav took stock of the young man. *His mother's eyes and her smile are unmistakable. How could I have missed that before? It's amazing what you don't see when you're not paying attention.*

Krzegosz smiled but he didn't reply.

"So, your accent," Rostislav observed, "it sounds Czech."

"Yes, I'm from Prague." Krzegosz seemed genuinely impressed. "How could you tell?" he asked curiously.

"Oh, I guess I'm just good with languages."

"I bet you wouldn't be able to guess where my mother is from," Krzegosz challenged confidently. "Her accent is *really* different."

The comment instantly propelled Rostislav back in time. *God, I miss her voice!* He had only heard it in his dreams, but he'd never forgotten how it made him feel. *How is your mother?* Rostislav was dying to ask but didn't dare.

"Why do you ask?" Krzegosz jibed with a smirk.

An awkward silence followed. Rostislav didn't have a clue what to do next. *Should I reveal myself to Krzegosz? Will Graziella and Krzegosz be safe if I do? Could the Committee hurt them even now? Would I?*

"I know who you are, Dad."

The jig is up! Krzegosz knows? But how? The thoughts raced through Rostislav's mind faster than he could keep up with them.

"Uncle Gabek told me everything before he died."

Dr Zahradnik is dead then. Rostislav imagined as much. "How did he die?" Rostislav didn't really even care how he died, but he needed an opportunity to say something intelligent rather than just stand there with his mouth hanging open.

"Old age, I guess. I'm not really sure."

Krzegosz held the upper hand. He'd known the truth all along. Why the pretence? Why didn't he reveal himself earlier? "So why are you here?" Rostislav asked. He couldn't think of anything fatherly to say. He thought about how he wanted to hug his son and tell him that he loved him, but the situation felt extremely awkward.

"I'm here to see you. I hope that's all right."

Krzegosz seemed sincere enough, but there was something about him that Rostislav didn't trust. He couldn't quite identify what it was exactly. Might it be the weirdness of seeing his son all grown up? Or could Krzegosz be hiding something?

"Does Grazi…Does your mother know you're here?" Rostislav hadn't said her name out loud in years. It seemed like lifetimes since he'd stood there watching the two of them in the hospital. And yet, it seemed only a moment ago.

"No, Dad. Mom doesn't know *you're* here. That's what you really want to know isn't it?"

Krzegosz really did have his mother's eyes, and right then, Rostislav felt like they were reading his soul. Krzegosz's stare felt like steel blades piercing his brain. He wanted to hide from those eyes. He'd been a horrible father. Worse, he hadn't been a father at all. Dr Zahradnik must have been the only real father Krzegosz ever knew. And yet, Gabek Zahradnik wasn't his father—Craig Ryan was. Overwhelmed with guilt and exhaustion, Rostislav suddenly realised that all his running had been completely in vain. Seth North, Craig Ryan, Rostislav Efimov…what did any of it matter? You can never really run from your past—it always catches up with you. Rostislav also realised that he harboured more desire to know his son than he'd ever realised.

"How did you know where to find me?"

"Uncle Gabek told me you were here."

Rostislav's eyes widened with surprise. "He knew?" Krzegosz seemed more like the father than Rostislav at that particular moment. Rostislav felt much like he did back in Prague when Dr Zahradnik knew all the answers while he was still searching for the right questions.

"Uncle Gabek knew you were here all along, Dad. He used to pull me aside from time to time and tell me all about you and grandpa. He made me promise never to tell Mom. He said it would break her heart and put us all in danger. Uncle Gabek assured me that one day he would arrange for me to meet you. And he told me that I shouldn't ever worry about you because he was keeping an eye on you."

"That old son of a bitch!" Rostislav chuckled to himself.

"Uncle Gabek arranged for me to come here to attend the university after college, so here I am. I just arrived this morning."

"Shouldn't you have started in the fall?" Rostislav ascertained.

"I took a semester off in my junior year, so I only just finished in December." Krzegosz turned away. He appeared to be counting the cracks in the plaster. Then he asked, "Can I stay with you?"

Chapter Forty-Six
Getting Acquainted

Slipping the key in the lock and opening the door, Rostislav gestured for Krzegosz to step inside. "There's so much I wish I could tell you, but I just don't remember anything."

"Hey Dad, I think you've been robbed!"

Looking around, Rostislav calmly reassured him, "No, everything's fine."

"Well, how long have you been here?" Krzegosz asked with some curiosity—taking inventory of the complete lack of personal possessions in the place.

"Eighteen years give or take a few months."

Rostislav resided in a small one-bedroom unit located within walking distance from the university. Had it not been furnished when he moved in, nothing would be there at all. Rostislav's only possessions were a few clothes and the now pathetically obsolete notebook computer he'd brought with him from Prague.

"I can't believe you live here like this," Krzegosz called out from the bedroom. He stuck his head out through the door and asked, "Where do I sleep?"

"Why don't you take the bedroom? I normally sleep on the couch anyway. I'll give you some time to get settled in while I get dinner, OK?"

Rostislav opened the kitchen cupboard and quickly realised that there wasn't any dinner to get. He usually ordered lunch at work. And other than his morning coffee, Rostislav rarely bothered himself with making anything.

He decided they could catch a cab to U Nikolaya—an Arabic restaurant that he'd heard good things about. A little over a year or so ago, Rostislav's co-worker, Olesya, suggested they go there sometime. She flirted with him pretty persistently for a while, and Rostislav felt really awkward because of it. He didn't want to be rude, but he couldn't have been less interested—he was still very much in love with Graziella. And even though Rostislav couldn't remember stating his wedding vows, he fully intended to honour them. Fortunately, Olesya moved to Moscow.

When Rostislav heard the shower go on and the bathroom door shut, he wandered over to Krzegosz's new bedroom. This room alone now contained more items than the rest of Rostislav's entire apartment. Krzegosz brought clothes, books, CDs, games, a computer and his cell phone. A photo of Graziella sat prominently on the nightstand.

She's still so lovely! A little older but it hardly shows. She'd be about forty-five now.

"She'll be forty-six next month," Krzegosz corrected as he dried his blonde hair with a towel.

"I thought we'd go out for dinner," Rostislav suggested. He put the picture back in its place and turned it slightly for aesthetic appeal.

"Sounds great. I'm starving! By the way, Mom wants to know where all her back-child support payments are."

Taken aback, Rostislav didn't realise that Krzegosz was joking. "I'm sorry. I know I…"

Krzegosz put his arm around him and gave him a sideways bear hug. "It's okay, Dad, I'm just kidding."

Krzegosz stood slightly taller than Rostislav and much more muscular. The years had not been kind to Rostislav—he definitely showed his age. There could be no getting around it, Rostislav looked like shit. At sixty-three, he'd aged every minute of it.

"How old are you, Son?" The word felt strange as it crossed his lips. He'd been building up the nerve to use it. And as awkward as it initially sounded, he liked it.

"I'm twenty-two."

Rostislav felt like a dead-beat father, but he didn't know so he needed to ask. "When's your birthday?"

"It's today, Dad. Being here is Uncle Gabek's gift to…well to both of us."

Rostislav gripped his son by the shoulders. "Look at you! Happy Birthday, Son."

As their eyes met, Rostislav started to cry. All the emptiness and loneliness he'd suffered could finally be over. Or could it? *If only Graziella could be here with us. We could finally be a family.*

"Thanks Dad," Krzegosz beamed back. Patting his father on the back, he suggested, "We should go."

The two hailed a cab. Once inside, Rostislav directed the driver, "*Ленина, сорок пожалуйста.*" As the cab pulled out, he fumbled a little and finally admitted, "I'm dying to ask you about your mom. Would you mind terribly?"

Krzegosz's youthful smile turned to one of mature understanding. He acted twenty-two most of the time, but Rostislav also noticed that at times Krzegosz exhibited the maturity of a man in his thirties. "I'd be happy to share anything you want to know, Dad. Just don't start crying again, OK?"

Krzegosz's light-heartedness attracted Rostislav. His son's fondness for laughing and cracking jokes made him smile. Rostislav hadn't smiled in a long time, and he liked Krzegosz very much. Seeing his intelligence and liveliness, Rostislav would have liked to think that Krzegosz reminded him of himself as a young man. But Rostislav couldn't remember ever being a young man.

"Did she remarry?"

"Nope! She never even dated as far as I know."

"Really?" A huge smile swept over Rostislav's face. He didn't expect that a woman like Graziella would stay single all these years. The two sat quietly in the back of the cab. Darkness surrounded them with only an occasional pair of headlights illuminating their faces.

Krzegosz broke the silence. "What do you remember about her?"

Rostislav closed his eyes and relished the one and only memory he possessed of his family. "I only have one memory. It's of the two of you at the hospital the day I left Prague. You were only three or four at the time. Your hair was red then just like your mother's."

Krzegosz clenched his jaw. "I guess I just grew out of it," he surmised. "Uncle Gabek used to say that I take after Grandpa more than I do either you or Mom."

Rostislav stared at Krzegosz and thought of the photo taken at Buchenwald. He could see a distinct resemblance, but it was difficult to compare Krzegosz's smiling, animated face to the stern snapshot of his father.

The cab stopped in front of a boarded-up store front.

"Is this the place?" Rostislav asked the driver. "It's all boarded up. Can you take us somewhere else? Anywhere is fine."

The driver pulled out impatiently. He executed three successive right turns, and then a left and brought the cab to an abrupt halt in front of a Georgian restaurant. "Four hundred and sixty-three rubbles," he insisted.

Rostislav pulled out his wallet and offered him the money through the slot in the bulletproof divider separating the front and back seats. "Спасบо." And with a nod to Krzegosz, they departed the cab.

The two stood in front of the restaurant. A long line extended all the way around the block. "Great!" Rostislav opined.

"After you," Krzegosz laughed.

The line moved rather quickly, though—more quickly than either of them expected anyway. While they waited, Krzegosz talked about his uncle Gabek. "You knew he was your half-brother, right?"

Rostislav always suspected that Dr Zahradnik was one of the twin brothers, but he never actually put all the pieces together. "What happened to the other twin?" Rostislav already more-or-less knew the answer. But he half wanted to know more details, and he half wanted to know what Krzegosz knew.

"He died at Auschwitz," Krzegosz responded casually. He wore the same transparent stare that Rostislav noticed in Dr Zahradnik's eyes. But with Krzegosz, it masked a certain zeal—almost a sort of pride. "Grandpa killed him," he added very matter-of-factly. "Uncle Gabek told me the entire story once when I was seven."

"Seven? Oh, you poor boy!" Rostislav didn't claim to be an expert on parenting, but even he understood that stories of the Holocaust didn't make for good bedtime stories. With his hands in his pockets and his shoulders huddled together, Rostislav did his best to keep warm. "I'll never get used to these Russian winters." Sniffing and clearing his throat, he asked, "So what did he tell you?"

"He told me that in 1939—on the very day that they turned fourteen-years-old—Grandpa returned from Buchenwald to visit. He'd been sending money home to support Great-Grandma and the twins, and he told her that finally he had an opportunity to be accepted into the Nazi party. This would no doubt mean a substantial increase in pay, but he needed to take the twins with him. Great-Grandma wouldn't hear of it—she hated the Nazis and everything they stood for. Uncle Gabek told me that he remembered the two of them fighting about it for hours. Great-Grandma absolutely refused to let him surrender the twins over to the Nazis, so Grandpa shot her in the head right in front of them."

Krzegosz gestured to Rostislav that the line was moving forward. The two advanced a few metres and Krzegosz continued. "Grandpa received a huge promotion, and he became the head medical examiner at Birkenau."

"I thought he worked at Auschwitz?"

"He did, Dad. Birkenau was the name of the main extermination camp at Auschwitz, but there were literally dozens of other camps. The twins were eventually sent to one of the camps there as well. Uncle Gabek once told me that he remembered being so frightened when they first got to Germany. Grandpa presented the two of them before a tribunal and denounced them as undesirables. The guards arrested them, and they didn't see Grandpa again for about a year."

"Why'd they go back to Germany? I thought he received a position at Auschwitz."

"He was promoted *after* he turned over the twins."

"Oh," Rostislav acknowledged.

The line moved forward a few more feet. "When Uncle Gabek and Uncle Milos saw Grandpa again, he acted like he didn't know them. He did horrible things to them. First, he measured every detail of their bodies. Then he started cutting. First, he cut off fingers and toes, and he sewed them back on again. Then he sawed off forearms and legs, and he sewed them back on again. Except he only sewed pieces back on to Uncle Gabek—he left Uncle Milos without one of his legs and neither of his arms. After several weeks of cutting and stitching, Grandpa froze Uncle Milos for some experiment to see if he could bring him back to life. But Uncle Milos had become far too weak by then. Uncle Gabek said that he never completely understood why Grandpa did it, but he never stopped looking up to him."

The line moved forward again, but by this time Rostislav had lost his appetite. As the two stepped through the door, the hostess approached with menus. "How many in your party, Sir?"

"Two," Rostislav responded gesturing with two fingers extended.

"May I recommend seating at the bar with no wait?"

"Yes, please. That would be fine."

They claimed two empty bar stools, and Krzegosz read over the menu while Rostislav fidgeted nervously with the salt shaker.

"Can I order the prime rib?" Krzegosz petitioned hungrily.

"Of course, order whatever you like—it's your birthday." Rostislav felt bad that he even asked. The distance between them suddenly became more apparent. "I want you to know, for what it's worth, that I'm really very proud of you."

Rostislav attempted to make eye contact, but a waitress who approached with a basket of warm bread captured Krzegosz's attention. Reminded of the boy's age, Rostislav watched with a strange male pride as his son demonstrated his adept skills in the predatory arts. While the waitress took their order, Krzegosz struck up a conversation with her. Before she left, she wrote her name and phone number down on their bill and outlined them with a heart. When the waitress left with a ruttish smile, Rostislav picked up the bill.

"Rozaliya hmmm? She seems like a nice girl." He sounded almost a little jealous as he slid the bill over to Krzegosz.

"I'm not interested in nice girls, Dad."

When the food came, the presentation and aroma brought Rostislav's appetite back. He didn't want to talk about the past tonight—there would be plenty of time for that. He wanted to learn more about his son and Graziella.

"So, what will you be studying?"

Krzegosz fired a nod at him while he lifted his glass. "Medicine, of course."

"I'm happy to hear it. However, given our family background, I guess I shouldn't be surprised. It might have been refreshing to have an architect or a mathematician in the family. But legacies are funny things, Son. Like destinies, they're hard to know and even harder to control."

Then, in an attempt to segue into another subject, Rostislav broached the question, "Is your mother still…"

"Delivering babies?" Once again Krzegosz finished his sentence. "Yeah. I don't think she'll ever give that up, but she has less time now since she accepted the administrator position. Uncle Gabek got too old."

"Hospital administrator—I'm impressed. Graziella's doing well for herself. Does she ever mention me?" Rostislav blushed a little when he asked.

"All the time, Dad. It's been really hard not to tell her you're alive and rotting up here in Siberia. I still don't get it. Why did you leave? Uncle Gabek knew where you were all along. The Committee knows as well…"

"The Committee?" Rostislav cut him short. "What do you know about the Committee?"

"Oh, just what Uncle Gabek told me…the Committee hired Grandpa back in the day after the war ended, Uncle Gabek has worked for the Committee since *forever* and it was trying to get you to come back to work with it for years until…" Krzegosz stopped. He buttered a thick slice of bread and wolfed down a bite.

"Until what?" Rostislav pressed. Something in Krzegosz' eyes didn't seem right. Rostislav felt the same distrust that gnawed at him earlier. "Until what, Krzegosz?"

The young man paused for a second. Then his soft smile broke the tension. "Calm down, Dad. You just got too old. The Committee lost interest in you."

Chapter Forty-Seven
A Bad Idea

Several weeks passed since Krzegosz first arrived, and Rostislav loved having his son in his life. Krzegosz was very popular with the ladies, and he often either brought one home or stayed out all night. But the two still spent quite a bit of time together talking and laughing.

Rostislav couldn't stop thinking about what Krzegosz said to him at the restaurant. *Has the Committee really lost interest in me? Perhaps it might be safe to see Graziella after all?* Rostislav's two main reasons for staying away all these years were his fear of what the Committee would do to his family, and his fear of what he might do himself.

"Night is coming, Seth. It always does." Rostislav recalled Dr Zahradnik's warning with perturbation. *But what if night isn't coming? What if Seth North is gone for good? It's been thirty-one years after all. Maybe Krzegosz is right. Perhaps I am too old for anyone to worry about anymore. What harm could I do to anyone now?*

Rostislav almost called Graziella. He leaned strongly in that direction, but he didn't want to do something that he would regret. *What if Graziella doesn't love me anymore? What if I only cause her more pain by re-entering her life? But on the other hand, Krzegosz doesn't appear to be scarred by the experience. Maybe it would be okay.* He decided to discuss the idea with Krzegosz. He knew Graziella better than Rostislav—Krzegosz would know what to do.

"Absolutely not, Dad! I just don't like it. We've been hiding this secret from Mom all these years and now you just want to call her up? It's a bad idea!"

Rostislav didn't argue with him. "Maybe it is a bad idea. I'm sorry, Krzegosz, I'm just being selfish. It's just that the thought of knowing your mother again…"

Rostislav sighed such a heavy and exasperated sigh that Krzegosz felt sorry for him. "It's OK, Dad. Mom's the love of your life. I understand. But think of what the shock would do to her. How would you explain staying away for so long?"

Rostislav put the idea behind him. He'd allowed himself to get carried away with the comfort of love and family. He'd dared to want more than he deserved. Thank God for giving Krzegosz the good sense to talk him out of it. Rostislav already lived with more guilt and regret than he could bear.

"You're right, Son. Thank you. I'm just a stupid old man. The last thing I want is to cause anyone any more pain—particularly Graziella." Rostislav put the idea behind him and slipped back into the personal hell that he'd created for himself.

Chapter Forty-Eight
Krzegosz's Secret

Rostislav woke up to the sound of muffled conversation. Half expecting it to be Krzegosz with one of his lady friends, Rostislav thought little of it. He rolled over on the unusually comfortable sofa and remembered his dream from so many years earlier. Soon, Rostislav drifted back to sleep and found himself on Mathieu's couch with the comforting breeze blowing in through the window. In his mind's eye, Rostislav wandered into the couple's bedroom. As he stood there watching Mathieu and Bangoura, he felt the long-awaited touch on his shoulder. But as he turned around, instead of Graziella, Krzegosz stood before him wearing a mask of his son.

Rostislav sat up in a panic. The whispering continued. The acoustics in the pitch-black room were like a vacuum. With almost no ambient noise in the room at all, the slightest sound carried clearly throughout the small apartment. Rostislav remained very still trying to listen. He could only hear one voice: Krzegosz's. No female whisper escaped through the thin walls. Rostislav closed his eyes and concentrated all his effort to decipher the words. He distinctly heard Krzegosz speaking in Russian. He made out the words, *"Новосибирск Академгородок."*

Novosibirsk Akademgorodok is the academic community where Rostislav lived and worked. The university is there along with some thirty-five other research institutions. The medical school is there as well, so Rostislav thought perhaps Krzegosz and Graziella were discussing his classes. The very thought of Graziella being on the other end of the call made Rostislav feel closer and more connected to her. He basked in the warmth of just imagining her presence. But Rostislav's warm moment turned to anguish when he made out the words "kill them".

Kill who? Rostislav tiptoed silently toward the bedroom. Just as he approached it, the door swung open and Krzegosz stepped out on his way to the bathroom.

"Geez, Dad! You scared the shit out of me!"

"Sorry. I'm just on my way to the bathroom."

"Me too. Go ahead."

"No, that's all right, Son. Why don't you go first? I can wait."

Rostislav noticed that Krzegosz didn't have his phone with him. When Krzegosz went into the bathroom, Rostislav froze. He wanted to sneak into the bedroom and scroll through the call log to identify the mysterious caller, but he felt certain he'd get caught if he did. He was right—within seconds, Krzegosz came out.

"Thanks, Dad. It's all yours."

Rostislav didn't actually have to urinate, so he showered instead. By the time he finished, Krzegosz had already fallen back to sleep. Rostislav determined that somehow, he needed to find out who Krzegosz was speaking with and who he intended to kill.

The next morning, Rostislav slept right through his alarm. He woke up to the sensation of Krzegosz shaking him.

"Dad! Dad! Wake up! You're going to be late for work!"

When Rostislav finally opened one eye, he peered out at Krzegosz standing over him and literally jumped off the sofa yelling incoherently.

"Take it easy, Dad! It's just me. It's Krzegosz!"

"Oh, Krzegosz! I'm not accustomed to waking up with someone standing over me like that," Rostislav apologised—feeling more than a little foolish once he realised what happened.

"Didn't you hear your alarm?"

"I guess not. That's strange." He yawned, stretching and wiping his eyes.

It *was* strange. In eighteen years, Rostislav never once overslept. In fact, he woke up before the sun rose on most mornings. He couldn't explain it. Nor did he remember his dream about Krzegosz's mysterious phone call.

That day at work, Rostislav received a new assignment. Up until then, his work had been rather routine. He searched the former Soviet archives for inconsistencies with the Pentagon data stored in his brain. When Soviet intelligence contradicted the Pentagon's intelligence, he made a note of the inconsistency and filed his report at the end of the day.

Rostislav didn't know who read his reports or for what reasons—and he didn't care. He just wanted to live out the rest of his pathetic life somewhere away from the Committee where he couldn't hurt anyone ever again. What better way than as a forgotten analyst in Siberia? Rostislav often contemplated his good fortune in falling off the face of the earth and still landing on his feet.

The new assignment required a lot of the same work that he'd been doing all along. Except, rather than checking for inconsistencies in the location of missile silos, stockpiles of WMD and fissile materials, Rostislav needed to identify inconsistencies in the locations of a number of camps. He deliberately made it a point to avoid any and all references to such camps other than the WWII-era camps that his father once worked at. Rostislav didn't want to think about what *he* might have done. He remembered Dr Zahradnik making mention of the many camps that were set up by the Committee to house his 'victims'.

His new instructions were very clear: conduct a thorough inventory of the location of all secret labour and extermination camps in the Soviet archives and match them against the Pentagon's data.

What possible use could information this old be to anyone? The Soviet Union disintegrated more than thirty years ago, and the Pentagon data in my brain is nearly twenty-two years old. At least with the WMD search my work served a purpose: preventing the proliferation of lost or mismanaged stockpiles of weapons and weapons-grade material. But this? What could possibly exist in these camps after all these years that would be of use to anyone?

Rostislav sipped his coffee and stared at the memo for a moment. He strategised in his head how he would begin his search. *I wonder why I was taken off my previous assignment to begin this new project?* The memo was marked 'urgent'. *What could be so urgent about some dusty old camps?* Rostislav finished his coffee while he powered up his computer.

Many of the Soviet archives were now digitised, and Rostislav liked to search those first before making the trip to the physical archives. He'd been to the Russian State Historic Archive in St. Petersburg and the Russian State Documentary Film and Photo Archive in Krasnogorsk on a variety of occasions, but he'd never gone out to search for camps. This would require a different archive altogether. Rostislav would have to make a trip to the People's Commissariat for Internal Affairs (NKVD).

The NKVD succeeded the Cheka which Lenin created in 1917. By 1934, the Gulag (the Chief Directorate for Corrective Labour Camps) passed to the NKVD and detained several million inmates. These included murderers and thieves, but most were political dissenters. The greater majority of the Gulag camps were located in remote regions of Siberia and the Far North.

During Stalin's reign, the Gulag prisoners completed a number of huge infrastructure projects such as the Baikal-Amur main railroad line, the White Sea-Baltic Canal, the Moscow-Volga Canal and numerous hydroelectric stations and roads. They also constructed several of the industrial complexes central to Stalin's five years plans. Stalin exploited the Gulag's slave labour force for cutting most of the Soviet Union's lumber and for toiling in its many vast coal, copper and gold mines. Stalin found no end to the projects he would dream up and assign to the NKVD. This in turn, created a larger and larger demand for forced labour.

Prisoners were treated like animals in the camps. They were abused by the guards and suffered under the harshest conditions. Most received insufficient food and clothing and many were often deprived of sleep. This maltreatment, coupled with the severity of the cold, the hard labour and the long working hours, led to an extremely low survival rate among prisoners. Death and disease were rampant in the camps.

After Stalin's death in 1953, the Gulag remained in operation. Forced labour continued well into the Gorbachev period and beyond. While the prison camp system supposedly passed into oblivion when democracy came to the Russian Republic, Rostislav soon discovered that the archives revealed a far different story.

The Committee had been covertly co-opting the camps from the Russians since the end of the Cold War. It held political dissidents from all over the world in these camps, and a number of them were very near Novosibirsk. The archives further revealed that the Committee had assumed nearly the entire network by the turn of the Millennium. The more Rostislav searched, the more he realised that the Russian archives possessed no current data on these camps whatsoever. The Pentagon data in his brain, however, proved to be extensive.

"That's odd," Rostislav considered, "why would the Russian government want me to track down a number of camps that it passed to the Committee decades ago?" That's when it occurred to him. "The Russians *don't* want it. The Committee does! Something must have happened to the Pentagon mainframe. Otherwise, why would they need me?"

Rostislav sat there and steamed. Then a truly disturbing thought surfaced in his brain. "I've probably been working for the Committee all along. That would certainly explain how Dr Zahradnik knew where I was all these years. In fact, I wouldn't be the slightest bit surprised if the Committee arranged for this position in the first place. Have I been helping the Committee locate and secure the former Soviet Union's lost nuclear arsenal all along?"

"Was the Committee behind it, Gabriel?"

"It was," Gabriel affirmed. "Rostislav was correct in suspecting that his new orders were written by the Committee. He was also correct in suspecting that he'd been working for the Committee all along."

"Did the Committee set up the position there?"

"Dr Zahradnik arranged for it personally. It was the only way that he could guarantee Rostislav's safety."

"The Committee still wanted him dead?"

"Unless it could be convinced that Rostislav was worth the risk of keeping him alive."

"So Dr Zahradnik arranged for Rostislav to secretly continue to work for the Committee in exchange for its agreement not to kill him?"

"That's about right. But Rostislav was mistaken in suspecting that the Committee was interested in the former Soviet Union's lost nuclear arsenal. The Committee enjoyed full access to the newest and most advanced weaponry on the planet."

"Well, what did it want?"

"The Committee wanted something much more sinister."

Feeling like a total chump, Rostislav decided not to be a patsy anymore. He thought about his conversation with Dr Zahradnik regarding his last attempt to bring the Committee down.

Once again, here I am in a hopeless situation: one man against the most powerful group of elites in the world. But this time I'm a little older and a little smarter. This time I'm not going to fail. And this time I'm going to keep my mouth shut!

Rostislav decided to submit an expense report detailing a trip to the NKVD archive in Moscow. But rather than actually going to Moscow, he planned to visit some of the camps near Novosibirsk instead. *What could they be hiding?*

Back at his apartment later that evening, Rostislav anxiously paced the floor. Krzegosz wasn't home yet. While he regularly stayed out with young women on the weekends, Krzegosz always came home after school on weekdays. The two shared their evening meal together, and Rostislav had grown quite fond of the tradition. Over the past three months, he'd even become fairly adept at cooking. So far, Rostislav mastered spaghetti, macaroni and cheese and bagels. He had frozen pizza down to a science, and his steady improvement on mashed potatoes, rice and scrambled eggs showed tremendous promise. But what Rostislav treasured most was the time that he got to spend with Krzegosz. He felt fortunate to be able to enjoy the pleasure of his son's company four or five evenings a week. Rostislav had learned enough of the hard lessons of life alone to know better than to take this gift for granted—and he didn't. When Krzegosz didn't come home, Rostislav nurtured a bad feeling.

He'd planned to share the news of his trip to Moscow with his son over dinner. He wouldn't tell him his true destination, of course, as it might endanger Krzegosz. As it was, he feared he might be putting the young man in danger and he hated the thought of it.

Why can't I have a normal life? Why do I always have to find myself in these types of situations? Why won't the Committee just leave me alone?

As he thought about it, he reminded himself how the Committee traced his every move the last time he dared to challenge it. Rostislav made a mental note to keep his thoughts to himself.

Krzegosz still wasn't home by one a.m. when Rostislav drifted off to sleep. He tossed and turned and finally got up at four. Restless and worried, Rostislav decided to go to work. He tried calling Krzegosz's cell phone from the office, but he kept getting his voicemail. He endeavoured to contact him several times throughout the morning, and he left numerous voice messages for Krzegosz to call him back:

"Krzegosz. It's Dad. Why haven't you called? I've been worried. I wanted to tell you that I'm leaving for Moscow for a couple of days, but you never came home. Call me at the office if you get this before ten a.m. I love you, Son."

"I love you too, Dad," Krzegosz snickered as he waited in a car outside Rostislav's office. He planned to follow him knowing full well it would not be to Moscow. Krzegosz worked for the Committee, and he'd heard every 'thought' that Rostislav uttered the day before about visiting the camps near Novosibirsk.

"Okay, I didn't see that coming! Krzegosz worked for the Committee? And he was spying on his own father?"

"Krzegosz wasn't who he pretended to be."

"He wasn't little Craig all grown up?"

"No," Gabriel revealed. "He told Rostislav the truth about nearly everything else, but he'd never once met Graziella in person. Krzegosz didn't actually lie about Graziella being his mother, however. His mother's name was Graziella, she just wasn't the Graziella that he implied. Krzegosz wasn't Rostislav's son— he was his half-brother."

"He was Dr Zahradnik's son?" I blurted in surprise.

"Yes. Seth's mother conceived him during Dr Zahradnik's first visit to Quebec."

"His first visit?" I queried. "How many trips did he make to Quebec?"

"Two. After Seth disappeared with Graziella, the doctor returned to Quebec and tried to convince Seth's mother to let him take her and the baby somewhere safe. With Seth and Graziella on the run, Dr Zahradnik knew that it was just a matter of time before the Committee paid her a visit. When she refused, he acquired the infant Krzegosz from his mother and brought him back to Prague. Dr Zahradnik hid him away from the Committee and the world. Krzegosz never saw or heard from his mother again."

"But Gabriel, that would have made Krzegosz…what? Thirty-something? How did he pass himself off as a twenty-two-year-old?"

"Krzegosz was a quarter angel—time was on his side. It really had been his birthday the day he arrived, but Krzegosz turned thirty-one that day, not twenty-two. Still, he exhibited a youthful charm that made him appear to be in his early twenties. It helped that Krzegosz really did favour his uncle Krzegosz in every way. He looked like him, thought like him and consisted of pure concentrated evil. Dr Zahradnik used to praise Krzegosz for being the son his uncle always *wanted* to have but never did. Instead, he'd been saddled with the pathetic Seth North—weak and prone to crack under pressure. Dr Zahradnik groomed Krzegosz to fulfil the legacy his uncle left behind."

"Groomed him? How?"

"After Krzegosz finished medical school, he studied under the guidance of Dr Zahradnik himself, who supplied Krzegosz with Craig Ryan's dissertation and all of Seth North's lab notes. Dr Zahradnik hoped that Krzegosz would be able to continue Seth's work and ultimately master the technique for transferring digital data onto a biological organism. But his hopes were dashed—Krzegosz couldn't compete with Rostislav's genius, and he hated him for it!"

"So Krzegosz aspired to be everything that Rostislav wanted to forget?"

"And more," Gabriel noted. "While Krzegosz waited in the car, he dangled a locket in his hand."

"Graziella's locket? How did Krzegosz get it?"

"Dr Zahradnik gave it to him after the plane crash. Inside the locket, Krzegosz kept two pictures: a wedding picture of Craig and Graziella on one side, and a photo of their son, Craig, on the other. Krzegosz used to stare at the photo of Graziella for hours. He'd become enamoured with her, and he wanted her madly. This made him all the more jealous of Craig. Krzegosz's infatuation devolved into a jaded obsession, and he eventually developed a deep hatred for all three of them. Dr Zahradnik use to tell him that he should aspire to one day take over Craig Ryan's work. 'The Committee needs you Krzegosz,' Dr Zahradnik used to say. 'Don't worry, you'll have your day. Be patient.' But Krzegosz ultimately failed in this endeavour. And he didn't want to be patient anymore. In his bitter hatred, he went to work for the Committee at age twenty-six and anxiously waited five years for his chance to kill the infamous Seth North: more recently known as Rostislav Efimov."

"Krzegosz really wanted to *kill* Rostislav?"

"He didn't just want to kill Rostislav, he wanted to kill all three of them. He *hated* them. But Dr Zahradnik protected them. Krzegosz considered him old and soft, and it made him sick. Dr Zahradnik exerted a great deal of influence with the Committee, and so Krzegosz bided his time. Early one morning not too long before Krzegosz arrived in Novosibirsk, he decided that he'd waited long enough. He went into his father's bedroom and snapped his neck. At the age of ninety-one, Dr Zahradnik died at the hands of his own son."

"Rostislav was right about Krzegosz after all. There *was* something about him he couldn't trust. What was that moment in the restaurant all about?"

"Krzegosz almost let it slip that the Committee was trying to get Rostislav to come back to work for it—until, in fact, it got what it wanted."

"When he moved to Siberia?"

"Exactly. While Krzegosz waited in the car, he savoured the thought that the day had finally arrived. With Dr Zahradnik out of the way, at last he would be able to kill them all. He'd cut a deal with the Committee. Once he located its property, he was free to terminate Rostislav—but not before. The Committee wanted this particular property back badly enough to have agreed to let Rostislav live. Krzegosz planned to follow Rostislav, learn the location of the camps, and then take him back to Prague where he would host the first and last ever Ryan family reunion."

Chapter Forty-Nine
Tolmachevo Airport

Hoping that Krzegosz would call him back, Rostislav pretended to be busy preparing for his trip to Moscow. He shuffled through papers, filed reports and generally tried to appear busy.

Where is Krzegosz? Why didn't he call back? I need to leave by ten a.m., and the thought of leaving without knowing where Krzegosz is bothers me considerably. Actually, Rostislav could have waited as long as he wanted since the rental lot didn't close until eight p.m. Nevertheless, he wanted to keep up the charade that he was going to Moscow. Since his plane departed at noon, he needed to go.

It was a beautiful spring morning, so Rostislav waited outside on the sidewalk for his cab. Krzegosz ducked down low so as not to be spotted. When the cab pulled up, Rostislav got in. "*Аэропорт Толмачёво,*" he stated flatly and closed the door.

Krzegosz followed the cab to its destination. Rostislav stepped out, and with the same suit bag in hand that he'd travelled to Prague with eighteen years earlier, he entered the airport. Finding the check-in counter for Aeroflot Airlines, Rostislav took his place in line. When he reached the counter, he gave the clerk his ticket.

"Where are *you* going?" a familiar voice queried insistently.

"Krzegosz! Where have you been? I've been trying to get a hold of you all morning…"

"To let me know you were flying to Moscow," Krzegosz finished his sentence. "Yes, I heard your voicemails. Well, the first seven or eight anyway."

"I'm so glad that you're alright. I've been worried."

"Worried about what? That the Committee got me? Don't be so paranoid, Dad." Krzegosz put a reassuring hand on Rostislav's shoulder. "I was getting laid," he whispered as he leaned in a little closer.

"OK. You're all set, Sir," the clerk announced impatiently as he threw Rostislav's garment bag onto the conveyor belt. "Flight number S7-182 to Moscow boards in thirty-five minutes. Next please."

"So how long is your flight?"

"It's about four hours or so," Rostislav crooned as he checked his itinerary while trying not to walk into anyone. "Four hours and fifteen minutes to be exact."

"Where are you staying?"

"I haven't decided yet." Rostislav felt rather proud of his answer. While he couldn't very well tell Krzegosz the truth, he'd given him a satisfactorily reply without lying. Rostislav wasn't the least bit aware that the Committee was on to him. But still, he felt like he needed to cover his tracks.

"Hey kiddo, shouldn't you be getting back to class?" Rostislav urged as they approached security.

"It's alright, Dad. I emailed my prof and told her I needed to be at the airport today. Besides, it's Friday."

"Really? How thoughtful." Krzegosz's feigned consideration touched Rostislav, and he smiled at the young man appreciatively as they walked slowly in pace with the line. Removing his shoes and emptying his pockets, Rostislav approached the security station.

"Well, I guess this is where we say good bye," Krzegosz suggested pretentiously as he hugged Rostislav.

"Bye, Son! I'll see you in a few days."

"I have a feeling it'll be a little sooner than that," Krzegosz retorted under his breath as he walked away.

After passing through security, Rostislav put his shoes back on. Retrieving his items from the basket, he headed toward the gate. With his boarding pass in hand and his suit bag checked, everything seemed in order. The only things left to do now were to wait until the plane departed, catch a cab to the car rental agency and be on his way. As he sat waiting for the plane to board, Rostislav thought about Graziella delivering babies. He remembered the kind expression on her face when he saw her in Prague.

"Now boarding Aeroflot flight S7-182 to Moscow. Passengers with disabilities and small children…"

Rostislav waited a few more minutes, then he loitered in the bathroom until the rest of the flight boarded. Hiding out in a stall, Rostislav expected the usual filth and graffiti one would find in an airport of this size. But Tolmachevo Airport turned out to be surprisingly clean—Rostislav could just barely make out some recently painted-over graffiti. While he waited, men wandered in and out chattering among themselves. The sounds of rushing footsteps, flushing toilets and water faucets occupied Rostislav's attention for the next twenty minutes. Once his flight fully boarded, he flushed the toilet he'd been crouching on and left the rest room. Back out in the airport, Rostislav meandered toward security. He walked past the incoming lines of shoeless travellers and out toward the main exit where he hailed a cab.

"Sapphire Car Rentals downtown please."

Embarking upon his quest to bring the Committee to its knees, Rostislav felt exhilarated. He felt free. As the cab pulled up to the rental lot, Rostislav saw a handful of midsized cars, sedans and minivans sprinkled here and there. But mostly, the tiny four-door minis were parked everywhere you looked. This is because the mini was Sapphire's most affordable rental.

Rostislav staked his place in line and careened from one leg to the other while he waited. Once he'd been served, he jingled his keys and wandered the lot until he found his car. Pulling out of the lot and heading north toward Pashino, Rostislav set out on his way. The first camp he wanted to see spread out on the west side of the Ob River to the northeast between Sosnovka and Kolyvan. It had been built during World War One and used primarily as a prison camp. To the best of Rostislav knowledge, it hadn't been used in over a decade.

But all that would have to wait for now. For the moment, Rostislav found himself preoccupied by the heavy city traffic. The fact that he never drove didn't help the situation. He'd obtained a Russian driver's license when he first defected, but that's about all he'd acquired. He certainly didn't have any driving experience—none that he could remember anyway. Rostislav never once drove a car the entire time he lived in Siberia. He never needed to. Other than to order his lunch every day, Rostislav never used his credit card for anything either. Today marked a great adventure—a day of firsts. Rostislav could only be thankful for the few automatics that were still available on the rental lot because he couldn't drive a stick. The traffic preoccupied Rostislav so completely that he didn't notice the dark blue sedan following him.

"Who taught you how to drive, Dad? Just pathetic!"

Krzegosz drove exceptionally, and he liked to drive fast. But Rostislav puttered along well below the speed limit.

"Come on! Move it, Dad! This isn't Kiddie Land." Krzegosz had grown accustomed to calling Rostislav 'Dad'. One would never know by watching the two what bitter enmity Krzegosz harboured toward the man.

Once outside the city limits, the traffic thinned out considerably. Rostislav sped up a bit as he headed north on M53. Feeling a little more comfortable behind the wheel, he freed one hand and opened the window. This was a new sensation and Rostislav enjoyed the fresh rush of change blowing over him. He'd been more-or-less numb for so long that the words 'adventure' and 'freedom' were not even in his vocabulary anymore. Rostislav struggled to define the experience. Then the right word finally came to him: Alive!

"I'm alive!" he screamed at the top of his lungs.

"Damn it, Dad!" Krzegosz grabbed the earplug and pulled it out of his ear. He'd placed a small microphone with a tracking device under Rostislav's collar at the airport. Krzegosz turned the volume up all the way as Rostislav often mumbled his thoughts out loud. Outbursts such as this one were rare.

Rostislav stepped on the gas and sped up. "Whooooooo!" he screamed with delight. Savouring the anticipation of kicking the Committee right in the crotch, Rostislav felt like he could take on the world. But after a short while, he also began to get a conscious sense of the fact that he would never be going back to Novosibirsk. In the adrenaline of the moment, he hadn't really considered it. But now he cognitively processed the reality, and it significantly dampened his exhilaration.

What about Krzegosz? I hadn't really thought that through either. The Committee would certainly retaliate against Krzegosz and...

Rostislav pulled the car over. He stopped so quickly that Krzegosz was unable to pull over as well without being noticed, so he drove right past him.

Rostislav lost his nerve. He honestly didn't care what happened to him anymore, but he most certainly did care about his family. He parked on the side of the road for about a half an hour and thought it through. The birds chirped a happy banter that really started to get on his nerves, so he rolled up the window. Rostislav's wonderful mood dissipated into thin air as he stared into the forest.

Meanwhile, Krzegosz pulled over about a mile ahead and waited. The sign ahead of him read 'Pashino ten kilometres'.

Chapter Fifty
Mochishche

Rostislav finally decided that no matter what he did, the Committee would hold its power over Graziella and Krzegosz. Fire blazed in his eyes as he put the car in drive and pulled out. Krzegosz waited for Rostislav to pass by in his car. After a few minutes, he began to track him again. As Rostislav neared Pashino, he turned left off of M53 and headed northwest on a dirt road.

"I really hate those bastards!" Rostislav fumed.

"Getting pretty bold old man!"

Rostislav resolved to find whatever the Committee wanted at these camps and destroy it. Little did he realise that in his zeal he was leading Krzegosz right to it. "He's heading north toward Katkovo," Krzegosz reported to his superior on the phone.

"Make sure you keep him alive until we have this one wrapped up! Do you hear me?"

"I copy." Krzegosz disconnected the call. "Copy, my ass," he mocked cynically.

The two cars continued northwest toward Katkovo. Large sections of the dirt road oozed with mud and puddles from the rain the day before. It was a wretched road. At times, Rostislav didn't think his little mini could negotiate the difficult terrain. But all things considered, it performed quite well. Krzegosz strived to stay far enough behind Rostislav so as not to be spotted, but close enough so as not to lose him. It was tricky business out there in the middle of nowhere with no traffic or buildings to lurk behind.

As Rostislav passed Katkovo, he approached a detour redirecting traffic to the northeast. However, the Pentagon's data indicated that the Committee strategically placed the detour there to deter traffic from continuing northwest to Mochishche.

"I'll be damned!" Rostislav manoeuvred around the detour and kept going northwest.

"You'll be damned *what*?" Krzegosz waited for Rostislav to say more. "Come on! Spit it out old man!"

But Rostislav didn't say a word. What's more, a heavy downpour started that nearly washed out the road. By the time Krzegosz came to the detour, he couldn't even see that the road continued beyond the bypass. So, he simply followed the detour which sent him northeast toward Zavodskaya.

Krzegosz lost the signal from the tracking device on Rostislav's shoulder. He figured that Rostislav discovered the device and *that* was why he'd said, "I'll be damned." But in reality, the lightening from the storm operated much like a GPS jammer and interfered with the signal. So Krzegosz continued to follow the detour imagining that Rostislav was just ahead. He even sped up considerably trying to catch up with him. Krzegosz didn't realise that he was actually speeding away from his target.

Rostislav continued past Mochishche to the Ob River. He parked his car in a grove to keep it out of sight. Then, he carried on by foot until he reached his destination. Walking along the riverbank, Rostislav followed it north about a half a mile. There on the far side of the river, he eyed a small complex of buildings well hidden from satellite by the trees. Rostislav approached it quickly—all the while keeping a watchful eye for any signs of life at all. Nothing stirred.

The rain steadily grew worse. Krzegosz was now almost an hour northeast of Katkovo. Seeing that the road ahead was nearly washed out, Krzegosz floored it to make it through the water. His vehicle hydroplaned off the road and into a tree. Knocked unconscious, Krzegosz collapsed in the front seat. His car sunk deeper and deeper into the mud.

Meanwhile, Rostislav entered one of the buildings of the compound. It clearly once served as some sort of housing unit. Old raggedy mattresses stretched out on rusted metal frames in long rows on either side of the building. Between the two rows of cots, a long narrow walkway extended down the middle of the barracks. With only the occasional flashes of lightening to illuminate his way through the dark, abandoned dormitory, Rostislav stubbed his foot on one of the metal skeletons.

"Shit!" he cursed as he floundered over to one of the cots and sat down to nurse his throbbing toe. As he sat there, a flash of lightening revealed a line in the floor running adjacent to the bed frame. Rostislav bent down, and grabbing a hold of the cot, he lifted it up. The mounting lifted up on one side to reveal a crude stairway that led down to a secret passage under the building. Rostislav descended the stairway and began to grope his way along the corridor. The pitch-black passage flowed ankle-deep in water. Rats scurried everywhere and several climbed on Rostislav as he stumbled through the dark sewer.

Meanwhile, the storm had passed. The sound of Rostislav's voice roused Krzegosz back to consciousness.

"My God it stinks down here. It smells like shit and death!"

"That's nothing compared to what's coming when I find you, Dad."

Rostislav tripped and landed face first in the septic and mud. He panicked and immediately lunged out of the water and back onto his feet. The impact of the water against his body jolted the tracking device loose, and it sunk down deep into the sludge.

"Agghh!" Rostislav bellowed, desperately scrambling to escape the liquid sewage. Leaches stuck all over his body and rats crawled on his face and neck. This was the thickest darkness he'd ever experienced. The rats, the leaches and the sewage all made it seem like he'd died and gone to hell.

Rostislav honestly believed that he deserved all of it and more. In a strange sort of fashion, his guilt provided him with the strength and determination to keep going. He owed it to so many people to stop the Committee. He wasn't even sure what the Committee planned to do, but he knew it couldn't be good. So, he pressed forward—contending with the darkness.

Meanwhile, realising that he'd lost the signal again, Krzegosz attempted to back his vehicle out of the swampy mess and get it out onto the road. But the more he accelerated, the more his tires simply spun in place. It was no use. He was stranded.

No cars passed Krzegosz the entire time. Not even one.

"Damn it! It'll take me hours to walk back the way I came, and Zavodskaya will take even longer in the other direction."

Krzegosz tried to call his contact, but he couldn't get any reception on his cell phone. He feared that he would foil the operation. This could jeopardise his opportunity to kill the Ryan family trio, and Krzegosz was determined not to let that happen.

"I need to get word to the Committee. One way or the other, Rostislav must be found."

Krzegosz grabbed his cell phone and his gun. Trudging through the muck to the road, he started hiking back toward Katkovo. The rain had left large puddles and thick mud everywhere, and Krzegosz's feet sunk down an inch or so with every step. They made a soggy suction sound as he strained to pull them back out of the mud. It would be a slow and arduous trek back to Katkovo in the dark.

Down in the underground passage, Rostislav heard what sounded like rushing water. He waded toward the sound, and soon he could see faint shadows up ahead. As Rostislav approached them, the sound of the water became very loud. It sent chills up Rostislav's spine.

"What am I walking into?"

He nearly found out the hard way. One more step and he would have walked right off the edge of a precipice. The passage opened up to a steep bank where the river raged about twenty feet below.

"Oh shit!"

Rostislav literally thought he had soiled his pants. Not that he would have noticed given the pervasive faecal stench in the tunnel. The river raged so strong that one step more would probably have been his last. Rostislav considered his good fortune. Carefully, he peered over the edge. The embankment dropped too steeply to even try to climb down.

"There's nowhere else to go, and I'm *not* going back." Then the thought occurred to him, *Maybe I can climb up.*

Slowly, Rostislav inched his way to the very edge of the muddy cliff. Carefully trying to avoid slipping off the edge, he leaned over as far as he dared and canvassed the stone wall above him.

"I guess it isn't my day to die after all."

Immediately above him, on the outside of the tunnel, a series of steel rungs climbed up the side of the rock. Rostislav reached up and grabbed the first rundle.

His feet slipped out from under him and he almost lost his grip. The steel was wet, he was wet and this was not the sort of thing that Rostislav did every day. He wrangled for the strength to pull himself up and grab the next crosspiece. He didn't have the strength, but he exerted the will. So Rostislav pulled himself up just far enough to reach the next rung, and then the next and then the next.

The river taunted him from below as he defied death out of sheer determination. By the fifth steel rod, Rostislav could actually get his feet onto the bottom bar and support his weight. Panting desperately, he wrapped his arms around the metal rung and tried to relieve his aching limbs. He'd nearly reached the top.

"Just a few more feet…Keep going! Come on, you pussy!"

When Rostislav reached the top, he crawled onto the wet grass and collapsed. Frantically trying to catch his breath, Rostislav rolled over and stared up at the night sky—there was no moon.

Chapter Fifty-One
The Stockpile

Rostislav woke up in a field outside the camp compound. Nearly blinded by the sun and covered in dew, he had no idea what he was after or what he planned to do once he found it. But Rostislav knew one thing for certain: he was really going to miss his coffee this morning.

His head already throbbed as though a jackhammer were pummelling his brain, and muscles he didn't even know he had ached miserably. Labouring to his feet, Rostislav limped toward a corrugated green and brown Quonset hut. Given the oxidation of the paint, it most certainly had to have been artificially camouflaged decades ago. But now, with vines and other foliage sprawling along its exterior, the semi-circular structure blended right in with the forest.

Rostislav circumnavigated the building in search of an entrance. The only visible access consisted of two cellar doors on the north end. The hinges were rusty, and the corroded handles appeared not to have been used in years. Rostislav wrapped his hands around one of the old-fashioned handgrips and gave it a tug. Heaving with all the strength he could muster, Rostilav forced the decaying door open. As chunks of termite-infested pulp and moist compost flung in all directions, a horrible malodorous stench smacked him in the face and flooded his nostrils with acridity.

"Oh my God! Not again."

The cellar appeared to be dry at least, so Rostislav covered his face with his sleeve and ventured down the stairs. No sooner did he descend into the cellar when his eyes were accosted by the paralyzing spectacle of hundreds of vials that lined the walls. As Rostislav traversed the south end of the cellar, he began to remember the place. He'd definitely been down there before.

"I know this place. I *know* this place!" A crest of energised horror swelled up inside of him. "I can remember!"

In his mind's eye, Rostislav could visualise the cellar as it used to be. He'd spent six months down there after he first arrived in Prague to work under Dr Zahradnik.

The Committee had assigned him to a very sensitive issue for which they needed someone of his calibre. It wanted to impregnate a human with the angel seed, but it had been unsuccessful, or so it thought. So, Seth was sent to study the samples and find a way to make the two DNA strands compatible.

The Committee abducted hundreds of women and transported them to this very camp in Mochishche. Rostislav remembered the horror in their eyes, and how their horror inevitably turned to screaming and begging. But their pleading fell to the floor in vain. Seth North had been sent to do a butcher's job. And that's what he was: a butcher. He was a human butcher.

Rostislav remembered that the Committee had stored more stockpiles of the vials in the huge storage facility on the western side of the compound. He darted back out of the cellar. As the warm sunlight bathed his face, Rostislav was submersed in the memory of running on the beach with Graziella in Italy just days after their wedding. They were so happy then…

"I remember you! I can remember you!" Rostislav dropped to his knees. "Oh, please God!" he begged. "Please forgive me, and allow me to see Graziella one more time. Just *one* more time!"

A deluge of memories flooded every nerve and synapse in his being, jolting him from his amnestic stupor. He remembered everything. Every wonderful, magical moment with Graziella. But also, every inhumane, barbarous cruelty he'd ever inflicted. His cerebral absence had been both a curse and a blessing.

Rostislav remembered his mother: so captivating and beautiful. Her perfect celestial visage enamoured him with childish admiration. Rostislav also conjured up memories of his father: the grim disciplinarian that he'd feared and hated suddenly enforced his iron will upon him yet again. He relived the heart-breaking day that he fled from his home in shame, and he now deeply regretted that fateful hour when he returned. Tears welled up in his eyes as his repentant heart broke with remorse over what he'd done.

Rostislav recalled medical school and the overwhelming fear he'd harboured of his half-brother. He reminisced with fondness his days at Stanford with Mathieu. He realised for the first time how far back their friendship extended and just how true a friend he'd been. But mostly, Rostislav indulged himself in the innocence and wonderment of Graziella. He no longer clung to just one precious memory. Now, a lifetime of memories welled up inside of him. They showered compassion upon him like sweet mercy from heaven. And that's exactly what they were.

As Rostislav petitioned God for one last chance to make things right, his mind wandered to the day when he first saw Graziella. So heavenly, he could scarcely believe she was human. Then his mind plunged into the contorted confusion he'd felt when Dr Zahradnik revealed to him that she was not.

Rostislav could see his life as though he were watching a movie. He marvelled over how even though he'd changed characters from one scene to the next, still he could never deviate from the script. He'd never maintained any coherent linearity in his life until now. But always, he belonged to something larger than himself—even though he could never remember who he was.

As Rostislav knelt on the grass beseeching God's forgiveness and thanking him for the love he clearly did not deserve, the promise he'd made to Graziella penetrated the veil of darkness in his mind like fireworks exploding in the night sky.

Gabriel ended the story and smiled with bittersweet joy. Tears gushed from my eyes as I recalled the face of my love. Looking deep within to bask in the vision, her memory descended upon me like a sun shower on a cloudless day.

"I remember her, Gabriel! I can see her perfectly now. Thank you!" I sobbed. "Thank you!"

With the love of a brother, Gabriel laid his comforting hand on my shoulder. "It's time to go back now."

Chapter Fifty-Two
A New Beginning

Immediately, I found myself kneeling in the grass. The old familiar aches and pains of my advancing age returned as I attempted to make sense of what had just happened. But I knew what I needed to do. Renewed in my sense of mission and revitalised in my clarity, I crawled back on my feet and ran to the building on the west end of the compound. I pried opened the large barn-like doors and scurried down the ladder to what amounted to a ten-acre root cellar. The subterranean tomb crouched in black, iniquitous obscurity. But I didn't need to see what baneful venom lay shrouded in the darkness—I already knew.

"This is what the Committee is after!" I resolved to destroy the stockpile one way or another.

Meanwhile, when Krzegosz didn't reply to his superior's calls for updates, the Committee dispatched a heavily armed search and recovery team to his last known location. Pouring over the area, the contingent found Krzegosz—still battling with the muddy road.

"I lost Rostislav, and I don't know which direction he went in," Krzegosz informed the team. He radioed for a unit in Prague to take Graziella and Craig into custody under the pretence of using the two as leverage to force me to reveal the location of the stockpile. But he really wanted to kill all three of us in cold blood.

Krzegosz often ritualistically indulged in his fantasy of revenge. First, he would kill Craig and Graziella—but only after I grovelled in the dirt on their behalf. Finally, he would eliminate the preeminent Seth North—the man he'd simultaneously hated and admired his entire life. But I had no intention of allowing him one iota of his sick satisfaction.

The search team split in two—half continued northeast on the road toward Zavodskaya—and the other half headed back toward Katkovo.

Managing to find a bucket and a water hose, I chopped the hose into a ten-inch section with a hatchet I found in the large barn-like building. I planned to siphon the gasoline out of the rental car and use it to ignite the combustibles I'd gathered. Together with the car battery and the abundant straw in the barn, I figured that I should have enough flammable material to destroy the entire stockpile.

As I hurried over the bridge back to the car, the raging river below reminded me of my life. Unmindful of its origin—and speeding toward its uncertain end—the murky water knew only turmoil. I had been that way my entire existence. My only moments of peace came from Graziella. But I'd received a precious gift—a second chance. And now, like the river below my feet, I also had a purpose. For once in my life, I understood what that purpose was.

I quickly siphoned the gas from the tank and retrieved the car battery and the jumper cables. Absconding back to the cellar with the items from the vehicle, I set it ablaze and dashed to the west end of the camp to the cellar with the main stockpile. Spreading the combustibles about, I worked hard and fast, and soon my sweat-drenched shirt clung to my emaciated frame.

The team in Prague seized Graziella and Craig in their home and ferried them to Siberia in a helicopter. The search team that headed south toward Katkovo joined up with the helicopter near the detour where Krzegosz originally lost me. Assessing the alternatives available, Krzegosz decided that I must have continued northwest toward Mochishche. Joining Graziella and Craig inside the helicopter, Krzegosz ordered the pilot to search for any sign of a camp along the river. Upon spotting the camp, they set their sights on finding me.

Graziella didn't have the slightest idea who Krzegosz was, nor was she aware of his consuming obsession with killing her and our son. For his part, Krzegosz never once betrayed his true intentions in any way. He remained totally silent while the helicopter made several passes over the compound.

"There he is!" the pilot reported into the mouthpiece on his headset. Having spotted me pushing a wheelbarrow into the large barn-like building, he circled the chopper around and landed about a hundred feet away from the cellar. I'd already set up the incendiaries so that when I touched the jumper cables to the battery they would spark and set fire to the bucket of gasoline.

Anticipating the sweet gratification of revenge, Krzegosz pulled out his gun. "Get out!" he commanded. After marching my family over to the cellar, he fully revealed his deep animosity. "Stop right there!" Approaching Craig, he spit in his face. "You redheaded bastard."

"Leave him alone!" Graziella defended.

"It'll be a shame to cut your throat," Krzegosz snickered. "You have such a lovely accent."

I was still in the cellar when I heard the helicopter land. I was fully prepared to burn the stockpile and myself with it when I heard the voice of my son.

"Dad?"

"Krzegosz?" I questioned in amazement as I came up out of the cellar. "What are you…" then I saw Graziella and Craig.

Graziella and I instantly recognised one another, and Graziella let out a cry of wonder and amazement. "Craig?"

I couldn't speak. I just stood there staring at Graziella.

"Don't stare too hard old man!" Krzegosz mocked cynically—Graziella's locket dangling from his fingers.

"My locket!" Graziella spied the heirloom with fascination. "Where did you get that?"

"Why, dear Uncle Gabek gave it to me." Krzegosz laughed with sinister delight as he read the look of betrayal and confusion on my beloved's face.

His laugh sent chills down my spine. Up until that moment, I never truly suspected that Krzegosz was an imposter. But with the real Craig standing before me, it was obvious that *he* was the young boy from the hospital—not Krzegosz. Whoever Krzegosz was, he certainly wasn't my son. And there could be no doubt that he worked for the Committee.

There had always been something about Krzegosz that I never fully trusted. I'd felt it in my bones all along. I guess I just wanted my family so badly, that I chose not to believe it. And to think that I'd been gullible enough to be worried about Krzegosz's safety! For the first time in my pathetic life, I saw with the utmost clarity what I needed to do.

I drank in my moment with Graziella. "Thank you," I whispered. "Thank you…" Then bolting toward the cellar, I plummeted down the ladder.

"Where you going, old man?" Krzegosz squeezed off a shot. But having missed, he ran after me—carelessly dropping the locket in the dirt. Just as Krzegosz reached the bottom of the ladder, I touched the jumper cables to the battery.

"No!" Krzegosz bellowed desperately as he riddled me with bullets.

But it was too late. I fell to the ground just as the gasoline ignited. The blast torched Krzegosz's flesh—nearly melting it on impact. Set ablaze in his own personal purgatory, somehow Krzegosz managed to drag his fiery soma back out of the cellar. Lurching about—his frantic suffering pierced the air until the flames took his life. He died horribly.

A few feet away, Graziella and Craig were still taking cover on the ground as best they could—their hands over their heads—petrified by the explosion. Graziella feared the worst. It would be a physical impossibility for anyone to survive that explosion. She was right. Rostislav didn't survive, but Craig Ryan did.

A few minutes later, a bloodied and blackened corpse of a man crawled out of the pit and managed to close the doors before collapsing to the ground. The entire cellar was ablaze, and I consoled myself with the satisfaction that for once I'd done something good. Finally, I kicked the Committee right in the balls.

The heat from the conflagration charred me badly. Nearly unrecognisable, it was truly a miracle that I made it out of the cellar at all. The only reason I survived the explosion was because Krzegosz shot me. As I fell to the ground in the belly of the beast, the flames passed right over me and enveloped my assailant. But now, ironically, it was the multiple gunshot wounds that were doing me in.

As I laboured on the edge of death, Graziella embraced my ravaged flesh. "Baby?"

"*Come stai?*" I smiled and reached for her hand despite my condition.

Tears of joy and despair broke forth from Graziella's eyes like heavy rains after a drought.

"I found him, Graziella. I finally found Craig." Clinging to life, I laboured to keep my eyes from closing—not wanting to miss a single, precious moment.

"Hang on, Craig! You have to hang on! Promise me you won't give up! Promise me!" Graziella pleaded and insisted as she held me closer.

With literally my last breath, I acquiesced, "I promise…"

The words barely passed my lips when Graziella felt my hand let go. She rocked me in her arms—wailing for me to come back while our son tried hopelessly to comfort her. Graziella's tears were like rain on a newly planted field—sprouting the kernel of life buried deep inside my soul.

As I felt my spirit leaving, just before everything went black, I spied the locket. The mysterious inscription that had once been so elusive, now relinquished its secret and I understood: "You must choose."

Suddenly I was back in the rebel encampment—my mangled arteries gushing my life force into the dust. I considered the message. It had been written since before eternity began. It was then that I realised we all have our own message. It's our great privilege in life, and sometimes in death, to discover it—and to cherish it always.

Once again, my thoughts travelled to the innocence of my youth—celebrating the new moons and feast days with my brothers—and the complete happiness I'd known serving my King. I wanted more than anything to have that back. But something had changed I had changed, and now something clung even closer to my heart.

"I choose to keep my promise."

"And so, you shall…" Gabriel's words echoed in my heart. "And so, you shall."

Sometime later in the far-distant future, a small group of children played in a meadow on the bank of a great river. Among the children, an adorable little red-headed girl laughed and ran with the delight and innocence of childhood. Somewhat set off from the others, another child picked flowers—an awkward little boy with reddish-orange hair. He carefully inspected each flower for its colour, scent and the presence of any broken petals. Once he'd gathered more than his tiny hands could hold, he lovingly presented them to the little girl.

God smiled.

CPSIA information can be obtained
at www.ICGtesting.com
Printed in the USA
BVHW051132070623
665543BV00008B/168